JUMPING IN—FEET FIRST . . .

"So convince me. Tell me why the man needs our help."

"Medwal." Chelsea stated, and waited for it to sink in. "He's learned, by using his own methods, that Medwal is a Syrian Arab. "

"So what!" John interjected. "We knew that already. *Using our methods!*"

"Harbin, in his younger days, was an undercover man for the Israelis."

"He admitted that?" Dave wanted to know. "You're talking Mossad?"

"He never mentioned Mossad. In fact, I'm surprised he confessed as much as he did. As I said, he was in a wistful mood."

"Okay, so what does he want from us?" Dave persisted. "The fact that Medwal is of Syrian ancestry is pretty suspicious considering Reuven's obvious connection to Syria." He looked at Josh. "So—is this a job for the 'Sunset Detectives'?"

"Humpf! We're more sunset than detectives." After a brief deliberation he then shrugged his shoulders. "Okay. Why not. We'll give it a whirl . . ."

MORE MYSTERIES FROM THE
BERKLEY PUBLISHING GROUP . . .

FORREST EVERS MYSTERIES: A former race-car driver solves the high-speed crimes of world-class racing . . . "A Dick Francis on wheels!"
—Jackie Stewart

by Bob Judd

BURN   SPIN
CURVE

THE REVEREND LUCAS HOLT MYSTERIES: They call him "The Rev," a name he earned as pastor of a Texas prison. Now he solves crimes with a group of reformed ex-cons . . .

by Charles Meyer

THE SAINTS OF GOD MURDERS   BLESSED ARE THE MERCILESS

FRED VICKERY MYSTERIES: Senior sleuth Fred Vickery has been around long enough to know where the bodies are buried in the small town of Cutler, Colorado . . .

by Sherry Lewis

NO PLACE FOR SECRETS   NO PLACE LIKE HOME
NO PLACE FOR DEATH   NO PLACE FOR TEARS
NO PLACE FOR SIN   NO PLACE FOR MEMORIES

INSPECTOR BANKS MYSTERIES: Award-winning British detective fiction at its finest . . . "Robinson's novels are habit-forming!"
—West Coast Review of Books

by Peter Robinson

THE HANGING VALLEY   PAST REASON HATED
WEDNESDAY'S CHILD   FINAL ACCOUNT
GALLOWS VIEW   INNOCENT GRAVES

JACK McMORROW MYSTERIES: The highly acclaimed series set in a Maine mill town and starring a newspaperman with a knack for crime solving . . . "Gerry Boyle is the genuine article."   —Robert B. Parker

by Gerry Boyle

DEADLINE   BLOODLINE
LIFELINE   POTSHOT

SCOTLAND YARD MYSTERIES: Featuring Detective Superintendent Duncan Kincaid and his partner, Sergeant Gemma James . . . "Charming!"
—New York Times Book Review

by Deborah Crombie

A SHARE IN DEATH   ALL SHALL BE WELL
LEAVE THE GRAVE GREEN   MOURN NOT YOUR DEAD

HOT WATER

HERMAN WEISS

BERKLEY PRIME CRIME, NEW YORK

For Viola Rubin
1913–1998

HOT WATER

A Berkley Prime Crime Book / published by arrangement with
the author

PRINTING HISTORY
Berkley Prime Crime edition / July 1999

The Penguin Putnam Inc. World Wide Web site address is
http://www.penguinputnam.com

ISBN: 0-425-16965-0

Berkley Prime Crime Books are published
by The Berkley Publishing Group,
a division of Penguin Putnam Inc.,
375 Hudson Street, New York, New York 10014.
The name BERKLEY PRIME CRIME and the BERKLEY PRIME CRIME
design are trademarks belonging to Penguin Putnam Inc.

PRINTED IN THE UNITED STATES OF AMERICA

10 9 8 7 6 5 4 3 2 1

PROLOGUE

Thíra, more popularly known as Santorini, was a huge volcanic island until B.C. 1450 when a devastating earthquake broke up the land. The historic event left the original crater buried beneath 1,800 feet of the Aegean Sea.

The hotel at Oia, the northernmost town of Santorini, is built into the steep slope of a cliff that towers over the Aegean approximately two thousand feet below. The spectacular view from the hotel's bar at sunset lures a large crowd each evening. This scene is indeed one of the most dramatic natural attractions in the world.

A dark-complexioned man stood alone on the balcony of his private suite. Nightfall would soon settle as the sun began to sink below the horizon—its final golden rays rippling across the disturbed sea. A determined breeze scaled the cliff to tug at the man's kaffiyeh, but he was oblivious to it and to the magnificent vista before him. His eyes stared into the distance but he remained focused only on his inner thoughts. Oblivious to the other hotel guests congregating at the railing adjacent to his own, he turned suddenly to retreat into his sitting room. He moved slowly, using a cane to favor his right leg, which suffered from a sciatic spasm. The room was merely one of many in a suite furnished with expensive antiques. There could be no doubt the suite was created for the wealthy.

The Arab man could not quite remember what had perplexed him. Then his mind returned to the yachting video he had left in the VCR in the private study, the one room in the suite that included modern contrivances. The video concerned recently sold megayachts, including his own 200-foot *Luxor Princess*.

A pained light appeared suddenly in the man's dark eyes. He quickly found the remote and fast-forwarded halfway through the tape. It took only seconds to find what he was seeking. It was a launching of the *Sea Temple III*, a 172-foot cruiser built for Reuven Harbin, an American millionaire and former Israeli.

The dark-complexioned man froze the videotape. The man who stood studying the *Temple* intrigued him. Beads of perspiration began to form on his forehead. He sighed heavily, settled back into a leather armchair and withdrew a silk handkerchief from his pocket, which he used to dab his face. *It was impossible,* he murmured. *It cannot be!* Abu—Colonel Abu, his former brother-in-law—had disappeared almost twenty years ago and had been presumed dead. His mind sought answers to imponderable questions.

Could Abu be this man, Reuven Harbin . . . or had Harbin assumed the identity of Colonel Abu, fooling everyone, including me? He winced, not knowing whether it was caused by physical pain or the illogical thoughts that rushed through his mind. What could be the truth behind this frustrating puzzle? It would require the talents of a genius for either man to assume the identity of the other. Who forged the duplicity? Abu or Harbin?

The old Arab had been blessed with a keen and intuitive sense for most of his life. And yet this video of a white-haired, lean-faced man with a military bearing confounded him and provided little to substantiate his vague suspicions.

Abu's MIG had developed an engine problem and had gone down in the Golan minefields. The explosion and total destruction of the plane were confirmed and yet no body was ever recovered. It was a miracle when the colonel reappeared four months later, with the explanation that he had survived the crash and had been a prisoner of the Israelis. But the incarceration had wrought a change in his brother-in-law that was apparent to all, friends and family alike. Previously outgoing, he was now morose. Except in appearance, he was a completely changed man. During his debriefing he spoke of torture. It took all of three months for him to return to some semblance of his former self.

Then the fates, guided by Allah, took him again. The second plane crash was almost identical to the first. The destruction of the plane was complete; the body was never found.

Twenty years might have altered the face, changed black hair to white. He took a deep breath, knowing that only Allah could ease his quandary. The promotional video included a brief interview with the owner in which he mentioned his plan to take a cruise in his new yacht through the Greek Isles in the summer. A smile almost appeared on the old man's face. *It is fated! Allah be willing, I will wait in Mykonos.*

The old Arab took a moment before forcing his aging, pained body to his feet. Reseated at a computer desk he worked out a coded message for the fax machine. The Arab consulted his gold Rolex: No problem, it was only minutes after the noon hour on America's East Coast. His nephew, with Allah's goodness, would ease his troubled mind.

Shafik shuffled to the balcony. The light on the horizon was sinking into the sea. He wondered whether his intellect was also fading with age.

1

Joe Chelsea and Josh Novick sat on the country club terrace overlooking a vast expanse of greenery. The canvas umbrellas protecting the tables stirred only slightly in the warm breeze. The sun that lingered over the stately palms would drop over the horizon within the hour. Reuven Harbin, their host, fingered his glass of Perrier and waited for either man to disagree with the latest terms offered.

Harbin, after an intense study of their backgrounds, knew both men were former policemen who now shared an equal partnership in what was originally Novick's Security. Chelsea, in his sixties, had joined reluctantly, the decision being made only after being forced to retire two years earlier from the New York City Police Department due to, among other things, a bureaucratic disagreement. Nepotism had passed him over for a commandership and, very likely, a deputy commission later. It took months for Chelsea's cynism to soften. As a captain in Homicide he had left behind a more than credible record and had deserved the promotion.

Novick's background was quite different. As an heir, along with his widowed sister, to a nationwide fast food chain, he had probably been the wealthiest policeman in the entire country. Novick had retired from the New York Police Department five years earlier than Chelsea. Two bullets in his thigh from a shootout caused a permanent limp. Harbin admired Novick's decision to donate his entire pension to the Police Benevolent Fund. Before selling the chain inherited from their father, he and his sister had diversified their assets with real estate holdings. The security firm simply allowed Josh to remain active.

Harbin's interest at the moment was directed at Joe Chelsea, who appeared to have doubts or suspicions that he had as yet left unstated. Harbin couldn't see him as a man who would remain doubtful for long. "Have I omitted anything?" he asked.

Chelsea, after a sip of his Scotch and water, ran his fingers through his tousled gray hair. What he had learned of Harbin was that he was tough but fair in his business dealings. At length he said, "I keep asking myself why you're offering us these new quarters with free rental until the mall is finished. You've already completed a deal for our property that is more than satisfying to all. Why the extra perks?"

Harbin deliberated over his explanation. Embracing both men with a pleasant smile he said, "Call it an overdue reward. I know of your roles in the Benefactor Alliance breakup." He noted the raised eyebrows, but waited for the expected response.

Chelsea didn't beat around the bush. "You're associated with the Mossad." It was more statement than question.

"Not really. I was merely a consultant for the event that occurred off Nassau."

A silence followed the blandly offered response.

Harbin smiled affably. "I suppose that does bear further explanation."

"You might say that," Josh murmured before taking a sip of his Dewar's.

"There really isn't much to add. I assume both of you have checked into my background and have learned I had been an officer in the Israeli military." He gestured carelessly. "It's all ancient history. Now I'm merely a consultant, occasionally called upon for my past experience. I assure you that is the extent of my extracurricular activities.

"Now returning to the business at hand . . . Are your attorneys ready to meet with mine?"

Chelsea looked at Josh. He thought Harbin's segue quite eager but decided not to push it. To Josh he said, "Will Meg be available to finalize the papers?"

Margaret Tolan, Josh Novick's widowed sister, was three years younger than Josh, and an attorney in her own law firm specializing in corporate law. She managed all of their affairs.

Josh nodded and addressed Harbin. "How about this Thursday or Friday? It can be resolved by the weekend."

Harbin fingered his lower lip. "All right. How about we meet with our attorneys aboard my yacht this Friday morning. We can have lunch aboard and if necessary, dinner."

Josh and Chelsea exchanged glances, then both nodded in agreement. Josh displayed more than idle interest at the mention of Harbin's yacht. His own fifty-four-foot *Novick's Ark* had been destroyed in the Alliance incident and Josh had been shopping for a new cruiser for some time.

"Where are you docked and how will we know your yacht?"

"You can't miss it. The 172-foot *Sea Temple III* is tied up at the far end pier in the Palm Beach Marina. It's brand-new and awaiting its shakedown cruise. I can't think of a more pleasant location to sign the final documents."

Chelsea pushed out his chair and rose, his 210-pound six-foot-three figure was appraised by Harbin in wonder. "A 172-foot yacht? Why would you want it?"

Harbin smiled. It was a question often asked of him. He gave his usual reply. "You mean the expense? Why not? I'm well into my sixties—would you suggest I save my money for my old age?"

Reuven Harbin was known as a well-to-do business tycoon. A very small number of people also knew him as *Moishe Shtyim*—Moses Two. Moishe Shtyim was a living legend, a superagent of the likes of James Bond. But his identity—except to a select few—had never been revealed. The code name was associated with a number of operations so involved it was rumored that Moishe Shtyim had to refer to more than one individual. Only on two occasions since retirement more than fifteen years before had he been called upon to exercise his former talents.

His features stolid, Harbin fingered his gray mustache and took another sip of his Perrier. "Don't think it a foolish whim. Many a tax break can be attributed to the fact that certain meetings were held aboard yachts just like this one."

Chelsea held his gaze for a brief moment, studying

Harbin. A full head of white hair framed the piercing, dark intelligent eyes set in a rugged, olive-complexioned face. The man's physique and movements belied his sixty-odd years. In the few short weeks they'd known each other, Chelsea had never seen him angered or even upset. He was a controlled man, the type to play devil's advocate, if need be, rather than take sides. He had decided that the man could be fully trusted.

Chelsea stuck out his hand. Josh followed, saying, "On Friday it will be a done deal."

Harbin's face retained its stolid composure. He sensed that he had gained more than just partners in a new venture, he had gained friends. He looked around the terrace and noted that there were only three other tables occupied, none of which were close to the table the three men had shared. It was early yet for dinner. Two men passed, heading for the bar, most likely their usual destination after a round of golf. The fading sun washed them with an orange glow.

"Gentlemen," he said, "until Friday, then."

2

Through the open door of the study Margaret Tolan could read the time on the grandfather clock in the corridor: 6:10 P.M. Her refined features displayed irritation. Her voice calm, she addressed herself to the speakerphone on her desk. "Dee, you have no idea of Josh's whereabouts?" Deanna Mara was the middle-aged widow of a Vietnam casualty. She was secretary to both Josh and Chelsea.

"At this moment, no," she said politely. "I'll be leaving in a few minutes. Can I do anything for you?"

"No, I wish that he had called. Other than the security firm he's been extremely lax in his duties."

Dee said nothing. She had reminded Josh but apparently it had slipped his mind.

Meg Tolan asked, "What were his appointments for today?"

"Today, none. He did have two, but he cancelled both. He called this morning to say he would be at the club this afternoon. I haven't heard from him since."

After a pause Mrs. Tolan then said, "Dee, is it possible Reuven Harbin has talked him into taking up golf?"

Meg had never met Reuven Harbin personally, all details of the security firm merger had been worked out with his attorneys. Although Josh and Joe appeared to be happy with it, she had yet to give it her own stamp of approval.

"He didn't say," Dee said.

Five minutes later Meg stood at a window overlooking the sand dunes that bordered their Palm Beach property. The twenty-room mansion had been purchased by her husband almost thirty years ago. It was now a hundred yards from the high tide line; it used to be almost one-hundred and fifty. In the twilight the sinking sun caused the drift fences to cast elongated shadows.

Meg—only relatives and close friends were privileged to address her as Meg—turned from the window, her eyes squinting in deep thought. Her two married sons, one living in California, the other in Chicago, both visited her in Florida only on rare occasions. Which meant she never saw them for more than a few days a year. With the death of her husband, the only family members living near to her were Josh and his wife, Cindy.

At this moment she resented him for going off somewhere without leaving word. She had spoken earlier with Cindy and had learned nothing of his whereabouts. Were Joe and Josh getting involved with something other than real estate? With Reuven Harbin? She tried to picture the man.

Meg Tolan's face and figure belied her fifty-seven years. At five-four and one hundred and ten pounds, she had virtually the same figure as she had had the day of her marriage almost thirty-five years before. Her hair was dark with traces of silver that she didn't attempt to hide. Her eyes were hazel, darker when in deep concentration as now. She was still wearing the beige suit she had worn to her Boca Raton office. She didn't feel the need to change as she would be dining alone.

It wasn't a novel situation for her. A widow for three years, and with no family at home, it had become a way of life for her. Although her law firm kept her daylight hours occupied, evenings had become a lonely existence. Despite numerous invitations, she rarely indulged in socializing. She was a member of a number of organizations but she almost never attended their functions.

As she walked through her study and entered the dining room, a random thought flashed in her mind. Once the security contract was complete, a vacation alone, anywhere, to break the daily routine would be in order.

The middle-aged house servant was standing by. "I'll be dining alone, Albert," she said wearily. His eyes sad, he merely nodded. It had become quite the custom for the mistress of the house.

3

The American-built *Sea Temple III* took up most of the dock space at the end of a long pier. The luxurious megayacht had completed its round trip maiden voyage from Harbin's Haven, Reuven's private island in the British Virgin Islands, and was now in the port of Palm Beach. Except for the country club meeting with Novick and Chelsea, Harbin's time had been taken up with studying the ship's manifest. Until he personally considered the yacht ready no kin or friend would be invited aboard.

Harbin was alone, seated in the upper salon. He had downed a Jack Daniel's and, on the verge of pouring himself a refill, decided against it. Ari, the ship's captain, had left him minutes ago after aiding in the ordering of supplies, and Harbin's mood had turned pensive. He leaned back against the white overstuffed chair and took time to survey his surroundings. The room's dark mahogany walls stood in contrast to its white and pastel blue furnishings. A circular cocktail table separated the crescent-shaped sofa—which could seat eight—from the four heavy chairs opposite.

Harbin grimaced, remembering Ari's observation early on. "The *Sea Temple III* is a magnificent ship, Reuven, but was it really necessary to replace the *Temple II?*"

His reply was simply, "Ari, I have so few vices left. Do not begrudge me my hobbies."

Ari's reply was almost contrite. "Far be it from me to begrudge you anything, Reuven. I'm certain you earned it."

Harbin sat quietly, thinking, "Thanks for the thought. I know some people wouldn't agree." Anya, for one, Harbin reflected.

A widower for more than fifteen years, he reflected that his late wife had never known such luxury. She would never have understood it—it was beyond her comprehension. She had abided his secret life, knowing he was working for Israel, and that all else came after. Their two daughters were the lone solace in the Spartan life she had endured.

Harbin sighed deeply, then pushed himself to his feet and left the main lounge. Standing at the port beam he noted that the marina was silent aside from the occasional burst of laughter or music from a variety of boats that were tied up near his own. It was Thursday night, party time for early weekend sailors. Breathing deeply of the somewhat salty night air, he gazed upward toward the heavens and noted the stars in the clear night sky. Unaccountably, he recalled the two occasions his talents were required after his official retirement. The first episode had brought him in contact with the original *Sea Temple*. The *Sea Temple II*, following, had played a major role, along with the acquisition of an island in the

British Virgin Islands, in protecting three elderly sisters from assassination.

Then, refusing to dwell upon the encounters, his mind began a catechism: Why did people seek him out in times of distress? Was it a penance for former deeds? Had he been appointed by a "Higher Authority" to earn the wealth he had accumulated since the retirement of Moishe Shtyim so that he might continue to be of some use? His illogical self-denigration brought on a deep frown as he recognized that no answers existed.

And then, his mood taking an abrupt turn, an imperceptible smile eased the rugged lines in a face that had seen so much. It was a lovely evening despite the clinging humidity; it boded well for the start of a new venture—not merely new business partners, but ones gifted with natural talents in other fields. And with a new yacht . . . Was the merger an omen?

"Will that be all, sir?" The steward broke into his ruminations.

Harbin turned to face him. "Eli, please tell Ari to join me on the rear deck."

With a sense of elation he went back inside, and strode throughout the capacious salon to the afterdeck. From the bar he removed a bottle of Jack Daniel's and two glasses. About to pour, he then changed his mind. Lifting a phone from the wall he called the galley and told the ship's cook to have Ari bring back a carafe of coffee.

The ship's manifest for a contemplated Mediterranean cruise had to be discussed with Ari, even though the number, not to mention the identity of the guests, was still in question.

•   •   •

Josh Novick looked up from sorting out papers on his desk and glanced at his partner, who seemed to be in a meditative state. "What's up, Joe? Something about the setup you don't like? Tell me now, before I call Meg."

Chelsea shrugged. "The setup, as you call it, is okay. You can call Meg."

"Okay. So, what's bothering you?"

Chelsea leaned back in the leather armchair facing the desk. "I was reminding myself that just months ago I hated the retirement forced upon me. Now, I'm more involved than ever. And getting rich at it."

"That's a crime?"

Chelsea laughed. Crinkles appeared in a face that was beginning to show his sixty-six years. It was Chelsea's eyes, gray, sometimes darker, that imparted a younger, inner strength. "I was also wondering what the old squad, including our former police commissioner, would say to it."

Josh heaved a sigh. "What's the difference? It's all old stuff. At this stage of our lives today is all that matters. Enjoy and make the most of it and maybe tomorrow will arrive on a happy note.

"And let's not get involved with anything like the Benefactor Alliance again."

"Amen to that."

Chelsea mulled it over: the Benefactor Alliance. It was not easy to forget. It had entered his life like a freight train ever gaining momentum until it had dominated the first months of his so-called retiring years.

It had started with the murder of a holocaust victim who was only one of many they later learned. The Benefactor Alliance had been an international, invisible cartel presided over by former Nazi biologist Dr. Emil

Seltzer and later his son, Jon Seltzmann. The organization had been preparing itself for years to achieve world domination through industrial merging. Dr. Seltzer's experiments for the past four decades had dealt with memory alteration. He referred to his subjects as Factors. False memories on any subject matter could be installed in his Factors' brains. Dr. Seltzer had developed microchips that when installed caused the Factor to utilize whatever knowledge was implanted in them. They were well on their way to success, having placed Factors in several governments when Chelsea and Novick, along with an old ex-FBI friend, Dave Ward, learned of their existence by chance. Through the combined talents of the Sunset Detectives, so-named in jest by Chelsea, the illegal, vicious combine was virtually wiped out. Although the individual industrialists continued to exist, the Alliance, as well as the doctor and his son, were dead.

Josh started to punch numbers on the phone when he caught Chelsea frowning once again. Sighing, he removed his hand from the phone. "All right, Joe. Let's have it. What's going on?"

Chelsea rubbed his cheek, his eyes narrowing in reflective thought. "After we left Harbin and drove through the parking lot of the country club, did you happen to notice the cable-television company van standing there?"

"Not especially. What are you getting at?"

"Its roof had a satellite dish attached and it was turning—very slowly but definitely turning."

Josh blew out air from between his teeth. "Jesus! Not again, Joe! You're not going paranoid on me? Didn't we already have enough extracurricular activity?"

"There was a blonde woman in the driver's seat. She

was wearing ear phones until she caught me observing her."

"And that makes you suspicious of what?" Josh looked disgusted. "You worried about the Alliance again?"

"The Alliance! Forget them. They no longer exist. I'm thinking Harbin's got a problem."

Josh leaned back in his chair and, as if seeking guidance from a Higher Authority, looked up for a second. "Joe," he said quietly, containing annoyance, "why would anyone be causing trouble for Harbin?"

"There were only three occupied tables on the terrace beside ours. They were all golfers discussing their scores. I'm almost certain that car was operating an electronic ear and it could only be tuned in on Harbin. In no way could it be for us."

"You're suggesting industrial espionage?"

Chelsea tapped his nose. "It bothers me and it's never been wrong." He pushed out of his chair. "I'm going to call Dave. He's the computer expert. Let's see what he can dig up on the cable company ownership."

Suddenly weary, Josh could only shake his head as he watched Chelsea walk away. He felt trouble brewing.

Spencer Medwal glanced at the desk clock; it was five minutes past the midnight hour in Palm Beach, Florida. With a key on his charm bracelet he unlocked the bottom drawer of his desk. He lifted out the ringing phone.

"My employees found nothing to warrant your suspicions that this man has led a double life. More information is needed than was given me." The voice was a woman's, her speech patterns over the phone very precise, although with a trace of accent. Carrie Willis continued. "At this moment Harbin is on his yacht—a megayacht by the way. The yacht, the *Sea Temple III*, is docked at the Palm Beach Marina. To all appearances, other than the ship's crew, he is alone. Do you wish the surveillance to continue?"

Medwal licked dry lips with some uncertainty. The entire mission was being performed as a favor for his uncle Shafik, who was as fatalistic as all the old Arabs. The idea of the late Colonel Abu becoming Reuven Harbin, an American millionaire, was total idiocy and as for Reuven Harbin having acted the life of a well-known Arab colonel for better than three months . . .

"Stay on it another day or two," he said finally. "But whatever method you use, I remind you I don't condone violence."

"Don't ever question my methods. They're my concern, not yours. As for additional information, for whatever its value, I can tell you Harbin is finalizing a merger with a local security firm, Novick Security, and the principals with their attorneys present will sign the contracts aboard his yacht this coming Friday. For Harbin it is only a small addition to his vast empire."

Medwal couldn't restrain a grin. Carrie Willis was good—good and expensive, but worth it. He had two stolen paintings—a Rembrandt and a Titian—in his possession to attest to it.

Before he could reply she said, "If you wish to continue with my services there will have to be a surcharge. This assignment calls for additional equipment."

Cold bitch! Medwal muttered to himself. He wondered, not for the first time, if, regardless of her talent, he had made an egregious error in hiring her. He took a deep breath, tempering his inner rage. When and if they should ever meet—it was his decision, totally—she would learn she was *his* employee. He spoke calmly. "Very well, but can you guarantee results? All I want is information."

The voice was cold in reply. "I've yet to fail a client. You can always hire someone else. Yes or no?"

"Yes. Yes," he replied through clenched teeth. "When will I hear from you?"

"When I have something to report."

The phone clicked off.

4

It was fifteen minutes of noon when Meg Tolan parked the silver Jaguar in the marina lot. She recognized her brother's white Porsche a couple of spots away; she had declined his offer of being picked up. The sun beat down upon the macadam, washing her in shimmering waves of heat as she got out of her air-conditioned car. Retrieving her briefcase from the trunk, she saw Josh coming toward her.

Smiling, he greeted her with a kiss on the cheek and said, "You've got a surprise coming."

"Surprise!" She lifted her eyes. "Just what I need." And then, "Where is this boat?"

Josh had opened a gate that led onto a floating dock. "There," he said, "at the end of the marina. It's called the *Sea Temple III*."

The yacht was tied to a concrete pier; its size prohibited the use of a stall. Meg stared and hesitated. "I see what you mean by surprise." Josh took her briefcase.

A waiting crewman helped her ascend the steps attached to the starboard beam. Meg was slightly annoyed that Josh hadn't warned her beforehand. The wooden walkway, with its spaced boards, had been trying. She should have been told to wear loafers. Becoming aware of her outfit she now wondered whether she was properly dressed.

Josh detected her discomfort. He gave Meg's beige Chanel suit an approving study. "I must say your outfit is quite fitting for the occasion. It's our first contract with someone of Harbin's stature." Meg rolled her eyes. She wasn't in the mood for flattery.

"Please follow me," the crewman said. Meg noticed the accent of the dark-skinned sailor, but couldn't place it. He led them through a corridor and up a staircase to an upper deck. There he nodded them toward the lounge where Harbin and Chelsea were waiting. Harbin's attorney, Albert Timmon, his son-in-law, sat at a table nearby.

Meg held back at the entrance, a bit awed. Until now, she had taken little notice of her surroundings. She'd been a guest on private yachts before, but this . . .

Chelsea came forward instantly to take her hand. "Meg, I want you to meet our host and new business partner." He turned to Harbin who was no more than five feet behind him.

"Reuven, this is our—"

Harbin was staring at Meg, his expression deep, his face a mask of . . .

Of what? Meg asked herself, feeling self-conscious in his steady gaze. Was her lipstick crooked? She licked her lower lip nervously.

"Reuven . . ." Chelsea repeated. "Are you all right?"

Harbin tapped his forehead, as if wiping out a daydream. He came forward, his hand outstretched. "Please forgive me, Mrs. Tolan. For a moment . . ." His lips compressed briefly, then softened into a smile. "Please do come in."

Josh glanced at Chelsea and noticed a frown creasing his forehead. He gave him a nudge and a look that asked: *What's happening here?* Chelsea merely shook his head and murmured, "Later."

Harbin ushered them to a sofa. To Meg he said, "I'm pleased you're here. It's amazing that in all the time I've spent with your brother we've never had the opportunity to meet."

Meg observed him without immediately responding. Tall, distinguished, and even charming. She couldn't guess his age; his full head of white hair was contradicted by the fact that he carried himself like a much younger man. His eyes, gray-blue—or was it steel-blue—seemed to be appraising her at the moment. "I do need an explanation," she said finally, finding it difficult to meet his gaze. Then, as an afterthought added, "Do I remind you of someone?" She noted his eyes narrowing in thought, as if he was attempting to make a difficult decision. He glanced at his son-in-law. The attorney wore a curious expression. "Albert, wait here. This will take only a few minutes." The man, tall, lanky, in his early thirties, nodded with understanding.

Harbin held out a hand for Meg. "You do deserve an explanation for my rude behavior. Please, if all of you will accompany me. . . ."

Chelsea and Josh exchanged inquisitive glances but remained silent.

Harbin ushered them out of the lounge and along a corridor that led to a door that opened into a sitting-room cum bedroom of the master suite, the lone suite occupy-

ing the forward upper deck. Harbin had omitted showing
his private suite to Chelsea and Novick during their
morning tour of the yacht.

His visitors were overwhelmed by its furnishings and
the massive murals on the walls. A pale blue curved
vanity, recessed in an arched alcove, was reflected in the
mirrors facing it. An immaculate writing desk contained
only a small lamp. A highboy seemed to be growing into
another wall. There was a lush sofa and two accompanying chairs, all in pale blue, set around an octagon-
shaped coffee table. All this on thick ecru carpeting. One
was almost tempted to take off his shoes and walk
barefoot upon it. The wall portside was a royal blue,
displaying the Old City of Jerusalem painted in shades of
gold and orange. The starboard wall contained a mural in
similar coloring to Masada as seen from the air.

There were a number of doors leading to a private
sauna, whirlpool bath, and a private office, which held
what looked to be state-of-the-art electronic equipment.
Harbin's guests were too mesmerized to question him as
to its uses.

Billowing drapes cut the room in two. Harbin touched
a wall switch and the drapes slid aside to reveal the
sleeping area. A king-size bed faced aft, its headboard a
curved wall of windowpanes overlooking the forward
open deck of the ship. Two oil paintings hung on
opposite walls.

Harbin took Meg's hand as though she needed aid to
ascend the single step. He indicated she look upon the
painting on the wall to the left of the bed.

Meg paled.

Except for the blue eyes she might have been looking
at herself in a younger time. After a sharp intake of

breath Meg was the first to break the stunned silence in the room.

"Who is she?" she whispered, almost reverently. She hunched her shoulders slightly, attempting to brush off the imaginary fingers that were traveling up her spine.

"Anya," Harbin replied, his voice subdued. "The painting is as she looked twenty years ago, five years before her death."

"Christ!" Josh muttered, shifting his gaze to his sister. "If I didn't know you weren't a twin . . ."

Meg regarded him a moment then turned her gaze to the painting opposite. It was Reuven Harbin, much younger, with darker hair and minus mustache. The eyes in each painting seemed to be studying the other in silent devotion.

"An Israeli artist did the portraits a few years ago," Harbin said. "Anya would never have posed for it. I had them copied from old photographs."

Meg was about to remark how beautiful his wife had been, then thought better of it. Instead, intrigued, she moved closer to Anya. Despite the high cheekbones and hollow cheeks, Anya's blue eyes were the dominant feature. On closer inspection a trace of sadness was present in those eyes. *An aberration by the artist—or a true perspective?* The angle of her features appeared a bit more drawn than Meg's had ever been, otherwise . . . It was a lovely face, but one that had suffered hardship, she thought.

Looking up, Meg noticed that the room's tiered ceiling hid an intricate lighting system that made the image appear almost three-dimensional.

"Your wife was a beautiful woman and the setting here is most complimentary for it." *For you and you alone to enjoy,* she mused silently. She took in the huge bed and added to herself: *No one would dare sleep here with Anya always present.*

Meg touched a finger to her lips in silent reprimand for her outlandish musings. Harbin was observing her, his smile kindly, almost understanding. She felt her cheeks begin to burn.

"I did promise you lunch," he said.

Josh Novick had significantly increased his family fortune by carefully following his sister's advice. In the beginning of Harbin's friendship with Josh he had found it curious that, in the province of high finance, Josh consistently followed her lead. He had long since decided that Meg was an extremely talented woman.

Josh was strangely quiet during the meal, as were the others. Everyone sensed Meg's determination that they not discuss business while dining. It was a holdover from her parents. Throughout the dinner, Meg was acutely aware of Harbin's silent observation of her. She decided that he was simply puzzled by her likeness to his late wife.

"Fillets of sole, California-style," Harbin had explained. "My chef spent some time there." She was somewhat surprised when he offered her the recipe: fillets dipped in eggs and then flour and fried in butter. The avocado slices atop the sole had been done in a like manner. It was served with a garnish of orange and grapefruit segments. Meg had not expected such a meal and, perhaps due as well to the excellent Robert Mondavi chardonnay, she was in a relaxed mood.

She took a sip of her wine and eyed Harbin over the rim of her glass. Her host was clad in a white suit and, despite the open-neck shirt, presented a dignified, yet imposing figure. His eyes, although kindly, held a look of command. She wondered whether she should be careful, on guard.

Guard? she thought. *On guard against what? Not the contract certainly.* She knew in advance every clause added. She looked away and set her glass down, feeling that her thoughts were not making very much sense.

Harbin stood and pushed back his chair. "Would you prefer coffee and dessert on an open or closed deck?"

"Does it matter?" Josh asked.

"It's quite warm today; the lower deck is enclosed and air-conditioned."

Meg decided she could use some fresh air, humid or not, and the decision was made. Harbin nodded to the waiting attendant, who immediately left to set the table on the afterdeck, just outside the lounge.

Although the deck was open on three sides, a roof overhang protected it from the sun. Meg observed the bar and refrigerator, the table set with linens, the padded bench curving around the deck. Quite luxurious, she thought, moving to a rail that overlooked the marina. Some slips were occupied but a greater number of boats were tied to buoys anchored in the protective basin. She idly watched the boat people meandering along the dock, many of whom stopped to admire the *Temple*. She was reminded how warmhearted and friendly these people were. A man on the dock had caught her arm when she had stumbled. "Those heels simply won't do, madam. Loafers or gumsoles are almost a requirement."

Uneasy suddenly, she turned around to find Harbin regarding her with hooded eyes. *Was he curious—or was he seeking something from her?* It was a look that made her self-conscious. She stared at him, feeling naked under his gaze. Always open-minded, and never one to back away, she asked, "Is there something wrong with my attire?"

A trace of a smile appeared. "It seems I'm forever apologizing. Please forgive me. You couldn't be more properly attired." He held a hand to his forehead, then gestured with an open palm. "Please believe me, you're a delightful surprise."

Meg's lips pursed. *Oh, no! Not another charmer!*

There had been a number of them since she had become a widow. It was the principle reason she didn't go out often—and then only with family.

Harbin was quick to read the expression. "Mrs. Tolan, what I said wasn't meant to be anything other than a compliment." He pulled out a padded chair from the table. "Please sit. It is time we discussed the purpose of today's meeting." He detected a quizzical smile playing on Joe Chelsea's lips. It was odd that he should see it in a man: the Mona Lisa, I-know-a-secret smile.

An astute man, Harbin was at a loss as to its meaning. Novick was silent, sipping a cup of coffee, having already placed Meg's briefcase upon a chair by the table. Chelsea stood by the bar, nursing a frosted stein of beer and observing all with a blank expression.

Harbin slid into a seat beside Timmon, who was removing papers from his briefcase. "You've got the floor, Mrs. Tolan," he said matter-of-factly. "I assume you've studied the documents and that they meet with your approval."

Meg spoke for fifteen minutes, going over the finer points without interruption. Occasionally Harbin would allow his gaze to rest upon her face. Her hair was shorter

and darker than Anya's had been and, of course, the hazel
color of her eyes was different, but the face itself was just
as he remembered Anya's. The likeness dredged up
memories long ago set aside. He idly wondered whether
she had the same warm perseverence. Harbin, not quite
comprehending the effect she had on him, dipped his
spoon into the Strawberry Cup Paola. The hint of Grand
Marnier in the whipped cream was palatable on his
tongue. Meg, still occupied with the contract papers,
hadn't touched hers.

"My brother and his partner have already explained
the rent-free period while the building of new quarters
continues. I still have to question the reason behind it."
She eyed Harbin for a moment. "I find it difficult to
understand. You know the expression 'Beware of Greeks
bearing gifts'?"

Harbin leaned back and smiled faintly. He was caught
in a dilemma of his own creation. Not since Anya had he
been overwhelmed by a woman. At length he said,
"Trojan Horse? Why would you think there's an ulterior
motive involved? Why not simply accept my offer as a
good deed between friends?"

"Mr. Harbin, previous to reading the original contract
drawn, I had my staff pursue extensive research into your
business ventures."

Timmon started to protest but Harbin held up a palm
forestalling him. To Meg he said, "And what did you
find?"

"Although I've learned that you've had no complaints
from other business affiliations, I have a strong sense that
you don't give or accept anything without purpose." She
paused a moment. "What will it cost Novick Security at
a later date?"

Harbin's gaze flew to Novick and then to Chelsea. The former police captain appeared amused, which was puzzling.

Timmon took advantage of the pause in conversation. "I thought the signing to be mere formality."

Again Harbin held up a hand. "Why should you suspect anything of me other than what was drawn up in the contract?"

Meg, wary, made eye contact with him. Although the man appeared genuinely sincere, she nevertheless had to continue the course she had staked out.

"Both my brother and Mr. Chelsea are men of honor. In their former line of work they had an expression, 'You owe me one.' It is an oral promise, never written up, but always fulfilled at some point in time.

"I ask you again. What will the favor eventually cost?"

Albert glanced at his father-in-law, unable to respond for him. Harbin leaned back in his seat, but his eyes remained fixed on Meg. She thought it odd that the rest of his face could appear so expressionless while his eyes seemed to be smiling.

Harbin turned to his attorney. "Put an addition to the clause in question: Never will there be expected any reciprocation or renumeration for the free rental previously offered verbally." To Meg he said, "State it in your own words. I'll accept it." Timmon nodded his consent and left the deck.

Josh leaned to Chelsea and whispered. "How about that sister of mine? Is she something or what? She questioned the very same clause you did."

"I suggested to her that there might be some part of the deal that had yet been unstated but the 'I owe you one' way of putting it was hers. I hope she will be capable of handling future business dealings as brilliantly as she did this."

"Are we on the same wavelength? What are you talking about?"

Chelsea touched his arm. "Later. Meg's about finished."

Meg got to her feet. "I need a computer with a CD ROM and then a notary to witness the signing. I expect you have both aboard."

Harbin stood up. "In the salon. Please follow me."

Chelsea delayed Josh. "Hold on. They don't need us for a few minutes."

Josh turned on Chelsea. "What's bothering you? Everything's all set. What more do you want?"

"I don't want anything—except for Meg not to get hurt."

Josh didn't bother to hide his exasperation. "Are you trying to make a point, or what?"

"Josh, have you become so old you can't see it? The two of them have eyes for each other and I'm not sure whether they're aware of it."

"What gives you this idea?"

Chelsea looked at Josh with a reflective smile. "It reminds me of the manner in which Ellie and I met."

"So now you've become the voice of experience in matters of the heart. C'mon, Joe. Really! Meg and Reuven Harbin? They never met before today."

Chelsea turned abruptly, put his beer glass on top of the bar and walked to the starboard side of the ship.

"New subject," he said. "Take a look." He tilted his head toward the parking lot of the marina.

Josh snorted. "So, it's a cable television van. It's the same company. This outfit is the largest one in Florida.

Ward already checked it out. It's legitimate. Don't read anything else into it."

"Why is the van parked at least a hundred yards from the closest building?"

Josh expelled a deep breath. *God help us if the retired captain of Homicide was bored with the security firm and was again becoming itchy for action.* He tossed his head defiantly. *Well, not this time!*

"Joe, this company is big. I mean big—as in huge. It has an AA rating on the stock exchange. Dave said the owner is an Arab in his eighties, semi-retired. His son, Spencer Medwal, runs it most of the time, but from a New York office." He touched Chelsea's arm. "What on earth can you make from that?"

Chelsea pulled out a pipe and tobacco pouch from his jacket pocket. While filling the bowl he pondered a reply. He was saved as both men were paged for the official signings in the salon.

Ari was introduced to them as the *Temple*'s captain. He was also a notary. Once the documents were completed Harbin said, "I had intended to serve champagne, but I would prefer reserving it for dinner this evening. We can all relax awhile on the deck and before dinner we can toast to our new business venture." His eyes lingered on Meg as the proposal was made.

"I don't think so." For a fleeting moment she detected a cloud surfacing in the gray eyes. "I'm sorry, but we cannot stay for dinner," she added, prepared to be persistent in her refusal.

She avoided eye contact with him. Something was happening—she felt out of control and could find no refuge from her emotions. *My body chemistry is amiss,* she told herself. A weakness in her legs forced her to sit down on the sofa. After a long minute she looked up to find Harbin observing her. A strange light flickered in sad eyes, as if he was reminded of something tragic in his past.

God! He's associating me with his late wife!

The weakness mingled with disappointment wasn't something she could comprehend. His dark good looks resembled no one else. The lines in his face were expressions of pure character. *What was this power he exuded?*

Josh stood over her, concerned. "Sis, are you all right?"

"Quite," she said, recovering, and forcing a tight smile. She prayed her fingers wouldn't tremble as she picked up a cup of coffee from the table in front of her. An effusive warmth followed the first sip. Disconcerted, she blamed it on the hot liquid.

Josh stood, not knowing what to make of her manner. It bothered him that he had most likely missed what had caused her distress. He glanced at Chelsea, seeking aid, but instead detected a trace of amusement in his eyes. It made the situation even more puzzling. He moved away from the sofa and positioned himself at the window overlooking the cove. It was strangely quiet; a light breeze barely rippled the still waters. Abstractly he watched a forty-footer coming in, its sails doused, its prow causing a negligible wake. He idly wondered whether Chelsea had hit the problem on the nose. Was there something going on between Harbin and his sister?

"Josh . . ." Chelsea was at his side, taking his elbow. "You're beginning to brood, pal," he said quietly.

"Brood?" He made a face. "Is that what I'm doing?" He stared at him but was unable to be indignant.

"You don't cotton to what I said about your sister and

our host?" Chelsea kept his voice low so the others wouldn't hear.

Josh couldn't mask his emotion. "Meg and Reuven? You can't be serious." He waited a beat, then said, "I can understand the attraction, widow and widower, both middle-aged, but . . . each seeking what? Solace?"

"Solace? Reuven Harbin? Never. You can't deny the man holds his age better than most. From what I've seen of him since we met, women regard him as quite a handsome and eligible figure. Frankly, with all his business commitments, I don't know when he'd find the time to indulge himself with the opposite sex. But it doesn't alter the fact that Harbin and Meg are drawn to each other. You can't deny Meg is quite an attractive woman in her own right. Wouldn't you agree?"

Josh gaped. Reuven and Meg? He tossed his head in disbelief. "You've been reading a romance into something that can't possibly happen. I can't vouch for Reuven, I don't know him that well, but I don't think Meg—even before marriage—ever went out with many men."

Chelsea snorted. "As Dave's Mae Warren would say, 'You're bloody naive.'" Before he could pursue it further, Harbin called them over.

"Next weekend is the Fourth of July. Whatever plans you had for the holiday, I ask you to cancel them." Harbin spoke confidently. "The ship will be ready to sail in a couple of days and I'd like nothing better than to have all of you, including your wives, be my guests on a personal shakedown cruise to Nassau."

Josh stared, dumbfounded. Meg said nothing, her attention far away, focused elsewhere.

"I wish you would consider it, Meg," Harbin continued. "I don't often find the opportunity to entertain such delightful guests."

"Meg?" Josh slipped Chelsea a sidelong glance. *So they were already on a first-name basis.*

Meg remained silent. For a number of reasons. It was many a month since she had spent any time with anyone outside the family.

"Meg . . ." Harbin almost whispered her name. She caught his eyes. Something silent, unnameable, passed between them.

"What would I wear?" she asked, her voice sounding alien to her.

"Casual. Ducks. Shorts, a bathing suit. The top deck aft opens onto a twenty-foot pool." He noted Josh's hesitation and Chelsea's frown. "Is it a yes or no?" he asked, glancing from one to the other.

"It's fine with me," Chelsea said. "I know it would be agreeable with Ellie if you could include another couple. We've worked too closely with Dave Ward and his friend Mae Warren to omit them on this holiday." He nudged Josh.

"Yes. Okay. I guess Cindy and I can make it," he said, eyeing his sister. Meg relaxed visibly. Relief? Longing?

As if reading his expression, Meg returned her attention to the coffee cup, but the maneuver didn't slow her heartbeat. She wasn't altogether certain she could pinpoint what was happening to her. Why had she succumbed so easily? Yes, succumbed—there was no other word for it—to Reuven's invitation to a holiday cruise. Her excuse, mentally at least, was that she needed a change of scene; it would be good for her instead of another lonely weekend on her estate. The man was so solicitous—how could she refuse? This tremendous, ex-

quisite—if one could describe a ship this size as exqui-
site— Well, anyway, Reuven did appear lonely. She
would be doing him a service.

Meg took a sip of the now cold coffee, knowing her
thoughts were rambling like an old fool's. She had to
stifle a feeling of rising panic. She *was* an old fool! The
man was charming her simply because of her likeness to
a woman he once loved. The occasional lugubrious mask
wasn't lost on her. Yet . . . she couldn't brush aside the
evanescent reasons for her acceptance. She gave him a
surreptitious glance. The man's face was now impassive,
unreadable. A man of many facets, she decided. It would
be an adventure learning of them.

Her face flushed with the thought and, for a few
seconds, there was a tinge of guilt attached to it. Her late
husband had monopolized her life for more than three
decades. Reuven Harbin's social invitation would be her
first indulgence since becoming a widow. She wasn't
sure whether she could cope with it. She looked up,
suddenly aware of the silence, and detected an almost
imperceptible smile on Harbin's face. He might have
been listening to her thoughts. His eyes looked out from
under graying, arched eyebrows.

"Meg," he said tentatively, "you're not changing your
mind?"

"No, I've accepted your invitation, Har—er, Mr.
Reuven."

An hour later, as everyone was leaving, Harbin accompanied Meg to her car. As she drove out of the lot she was
aware that he remained, watching her departure. Suddenly she recognized that he had a quiet elegance usually
associated with "old money." Technically speaking he

would be considered nouveau riche. And yet he had none of the so-called vulgarity attached to new money.

She drove mechanically for some minutes before realizing that an emotion of a distinctly sensual nature had overtaken her when he had taken her hand to help her into the car. Her face coloring, she tossed her head reprovingly to recover from the sensation. Her behavior was unreasonable and something she couldn't comprehend. Reuven Harbin was a complicated individual, a business tycoon who spent his off-hours insulated in his yacht. She shook her head, frowning. No, she was being unfair; it wasn't true. She idly wondered if he was alone for most of the time he spent on his glorious megayachts.

The thought prompted a reprimand. She was behaving childishly. Provoked, she pushed her foot down hard on the gas pedal.

5

Years of rigid training had tuned Reuven Harbin's senses to be hyper-aware of his environment. Despite his fifteen-year "sabbatical" he had never completely abandoned his former ways. As he turned to leave the yacht club's restricted area, a brief flash of light hit his eye. Without losing a beat in his stride, out of the corner of his eye he glimpsed a cable repair truck parked three slots to the right of the gate leading onto the pier. *Unusual,* he thought, alerted.

Then his eyes noticed the small parabolic dish atop its roof. It was the dish, turning and catching the bright sun that had caused the brief flash.

A parabolic microphone!

Harbin continued through the gate and along the dock, seemingly unperturbed had anyone been watching. He smiled and nodded pleasantly to passersby. It was a beautiful day despite the humidity, the early-summer sun bathing the marina. The slips were filling as boats were readied for the coming weekend. Harbin could see nothing that should arouse suspicion.

Having maneuvered past a number of electric cables and water hoses strung along the dock he stopped, seemingly to retie a loosened shoelace. In reality he was listening to the sounds pervading the area. He heard music coming from one boat, a thirty-five-foot sloop, the idling engine of another. These sounds were intermingled with idle conversation. He could hear a man and woman weighing the merit of heading north to Vero Beach on the morrow. Another two men were discussing sailing to Miami for the Independence Day fireworks. It all sounded quite normal.

Heat waves rose from the graying wooden planks and surrounded Harbin. He straightened and continued on his way toward the *Temple*. Once aboard, he headed for the captain's bridge to meet with Ari.

Ari was more an associate than an employee. He had also served as captain of Harbin's previous two yachts.

"Everything's shipshape," Ari said, greeting him pleasantly. The thirty-five-year-old former member of the Israeli Mossad was elated with the new *Temple*.

Harbin said, "Sight your binoculars on the cable repair truck in the marina parking lot. Give me an opinion on it."

His smile fading, Ari complied. Thirty seconds later he said, "We got a listener. Is it something we should fret about? Industrial spying?" He frowned. "How would anyone know we would be tied up in this marina? I received no instructions until late last evening."

Harbin nodded, satisfied with the observation. "Get the plate number and put a trace on it." He turned to leave. "I'll get back to you."

Ari lifted the phone from the wall. He hit a switch adjacent to the phone and punched in a number. Moments later he received a response from the Israeli office in the U.N. A code name was whispered, and within ten seconds someone else took over the phone. Ari delivered Harbin's orders and they were accepted without hesitationi. Ari replaced the phone and checked his wristwatch; he would have information on the cable truck within ten minutes. He then went to the navigator's desk and sat behind it, ruminating.

It was five years since Reuven Harbin had rescued him from the depths of despair. Three years earlier, while on assignment with the Mossad, he had lost his wife, killed in a terrorist bombing in Israel. Harbin had laid cause to his hiring by saying he needed an electronics expert, which just happened to be Ari's expertise. Ari knew nothing of Harbin's background beforehand—other than that he had been a colonel in Israel's Air Force. It was only later—and because of particular circumstances—that he learned the truth, that he was in the employ of a living legend. Only Ari and four other living men knew of Harbin's past identity as Moishe Shtyim.

Harbin was sitting alone in the bridge deck lounge when Ari returned to hand him a decoded fax message. It stated that the cable repair company was legitimate, servicing much of Palm Beach County. It also noted that none of their trucks had been reported stolen.

Harbin didn't doubt the contents of the fax, but something didn't gel. *Why the microphonic ear?* He returned the message to Ari, who didn't need to be told to shred it.

"Any further instructions?" Ari asked.

"Have two men tail the van. Once it's garaged, have them find out what is inside. If there is recording tape I want it confiscated." Harbin looked up. "Who's available on board?"

Ari concentrated briefly. "Dani and Egon. No one else qualified at the moment." He waited a beat. "How large a crew will we be taking on for the weekend sail?"

"A full complement—ten at least. Find out if Rebecca's returned from Israel and, if so, whether she's available for specified or unspecified duty aboard."

Rebecca was a former Mossad agent—and an especially fine chef. She had been in Harbin's employ on another occasion.

On that note Ari left to call the Israeli consulate. Harbin always conscripted his crew from the consulate, a perk granted him for his former service and excellent reputation as an Air Force commander.

Harbin stood up, contemplating his responsibilities to his family, his firm. He did not have the time, nor the inclination, to pursue any further clandestine adventures. He sighed.

Moments later he descended to the lower deck and strode the length of the lower lounge. He knew exactly where he was going. And why.

The master bedroom suite was dark, the drapes drawn. What little light there was in the room illuminated the portrait of Anya. Harbin only partially understood his emotions as he gazed upon the features of his long-deceased wife. The likeness to Meg was astounding. He settled into an overstuffed lounge chair and contemplated his long-dormant feelings.

Was it guilt for having forced Anya to live without him much of the time? Or was the guilt due to the fact that he had come upon another woman who moved him? He leaned forward, peering at the portrait as if it could provide answers.

His head bowed, he sat there another five minutes

without stirring. Unknown to him, a single tear made its way down his cheek. The phone on the table adjacent to him rang, interrupting his thoughts. It was Ari.

"We will have ten in the crew, including Rebecca. You wish to screen their backgrounds?"

Harbin quickly composed himself. Did Ari seem somewhat excited about the availability of Rebecca? Two years earlier, Rebecca, or Rivkah as she was called in Israel, had accompanied a less fortunate employee back to Israel for burial.

Harbin grimaced from the memory. He cleared his throat. "Ari, I'll leave the screening in your hands. But I don't believe it's really necessary. Our friends are always cautious. And, Ari, for the next two hours, unless you have additional information on that van, I don't wish to be disturbed."

He laid the phone down and sat back, suddenly feeling weary. An oppressive silence hung over the suite, but his thoughts were loud and insistent. He could not shake himself of Meg Tolan's face and her likeness to Anya.

An uncontrolled sigh escaped. Something had happened during the short time they had spent together. He cocked his head, a quizzical expression forming. Was it merely the likeness? In all other respects the two women were totally unalike.

A heaviness pressed on Harbin's chest; he knew lives couldn't be relived. Images of Anya and Meg flitted through his mind and he wondered if he was merely trying to erase Anya's troubled visage.

He turned his head to face a far corner of the suite. Although it was dark in the room, he could visualize the framed photos of his two married daughters and his five grandchildren. It was odd that neither his daughters nor any grandchild resembled Anya nearly as much as Meg Tolan did. It had been years since either of his two daughters reminded him of the past. Fifteen years in America had totally Americanized them, despite their occasional visits back to Israel to meet with old friends and some remaining family on Anya's side. Harbin had no living relatives on his side, other than one brother, his partner. His other brother was deceased—the brother who had talked him into a successful business venture here in the States. The Harbin Association assets had now passed beyond five billion, and were still growing.

Harbin frowned, deepening the ridges in a rugged face. *Enough,* he chided himself, *spending so much time on past regrets.* It was a true sign of age. He pushed himself to his feet.

He hit a button on the wall; the drapes started moving, exposing the forward windows, and allowing daylight to gradually flood the gloom. Before departing he couldn't resist a closer study of his Anya.

Yes, Anya, in looks she does resemble you—but in no other way. Meg is—or was, before widowhood—a woman in high society, a world unknown to you. She didn't stay home, tend to her family's needs, and wait for her husband to return from the private wars to which the Mossad had assigned him.

Meg Tolan was a woman with business acumen. Not only did she advise her brother in his holdings but she acted as a majority stockholder in her late husband's financial empire.

The frown again appeared. Other than the visual resemblance the two women were worlds apart. He stared at Anya's eyes and, for a split second, imagination or not, he thought he detected a slight alteration in her expression.

Feeling flustered—an unusual position for him—he waited long seconds before looking away. *What is it, Anya?* he asked silently. *Why am I attracted to her?*

The portrait had no answer—and neither did he.

6

The three couples sat at a table overlooking the Intracoastal Waterway. Dave Ward and Mae Warren had joined the Chelseas and Novicks for lunch.

Ward was ex-FBI, now running his own charter fishing boat out of the Palm Beach Marina. He had met Mae Warren on a cruise five years ago and she had become his girl Friday. The pair was quite open about the fact that they had soon become more than just business associates.

It had taken some coercion to get him to accept the loss of charters over the Fourth of July weekend. But in the end, Joe and Josh's description of the opulent *Sea Temple* had served as adequate temptation.

They enjoyed the meal in silence for a while, aware of the jovial conversation of other diners, until a humid gust swept across the Waterway to jingle the Oriental chimes strung beneath the underhang of the restaurant's rafters. Ellie's attention was drawn to an adjacent table where an elderly couple was having dinner. The woman seemed to be watching her companion carefully as he chewed his food. The white-haired man had sloping shoulders and he leaned forward to take a slice of white bread. The woman's eyes never left him as he spread butter over it. He then picked at his plate of sliced chicken mechanically. His eyes appeared vacant, as if his mind were elsewhere, in another time, in another place. She reached over and used a napkin to wipe his upper lip. He smiled a gentle thanks, without voicing it. The woman ate sparingly, her eyes sad, a forced smile never leaving him. She reminded him to chew carefully. He merely nodded.

Chelsea noted Ellie bringing a tissue to her eyes. When he started to question her she nodded to the adjacent table.

Chelsea took her hand, squeezed it, and said, "Let's just look ahead and pray we still have some good years left."

She sniffed, then smiled quickly. "That wasn't exactly the mode you were in last fall when you took to the high seas to combat evil." The remark was heard by all, and understood. Dave Ward decided to switch the subject by addressing Chelsea.

"Are you satisfied the cable repair company is clean?"

Chelsea made a face, he didn't want it discussed in the company of their wives.

Ellie read his expression. "Oh, no," she said. "The boys are at it again."

"It's nothing special," Josh offered before anyone could speak.

Mae Warren poked Ward. "Tell me it's nothing special. And, Dave, make it good. I don't want to hear about another invisible cartel."

Chelsea held up a hand before Cindy could voice her

piece. "It's just a van our security is investigating. Why read anything else into Dave's remark?"

The silence that followed lasted only seconds. Ellie broke it with, "Security indeed! Do I have your word that it doesn't resemble anything like your previous 'moonlighting'?"

Chelsea mocked looking aghast. "This so-called cable repair van has nothing to do with us. It's Reuven Harbin's problem—if one does exist." He turned to Josh, who sat opposite him. "Do we tell him about it or not?"

The klaxon horn of a late cruiser interrupted further discussion. Cindy glanced from the yacht to the twin towers of an oceanside condominium. "Considering the yacht this man owns and the wealth he must control, I wonder why he is still single."

Josh rolled his eyes. "Cindy, do me a favor. Promise you won't pry for the entire weekend."

Later, when they were leaving the restaurant, Chelsea got Ward aside. "Dave, it could be nothing, but keep a sharp eye. I saw that same van on two occasions. I don't believe in coincidence."

Katya Willeskava put her binoculars aside. She sat behind the wheel of a nondescript gray Honda parked in the marina lot. She was watching the *Sea Temple*. She should have given up the post thirty minutes ago but there was something about Reuven Harbin that intrigued her and she continued watching, hoping for another glimpse of the mysterious man.

Katya had started her formal training thirty years ago when she became an orphan at the age of five. The Committee had singled her out to be raised as a member and receive special training, and she had been relocated to a village 100 kilometers outside of Moscow, where she was adopted by a new "family." The village was a reconstruction of a typical New England community. Language, customs, food, shopping, and education were all typically American. She was being prepared for service in the United States and her schooling was flawless—she must appear in every way to be an average American woman. In her teen years she received additional training in the martial arts.

For the past ten years Katya had been living as Carrie Willis, an American manager of a successful Fifth Avenue boutique. She had awaited orders for special assignment from the Committee but none were forthcoming. With the advent of glasnost, she had eventually discarded her cover profession and, in place of the active duty for which she had been waiting, she went in search of her own secret assignments.

She placed ads in *Soldier of Fortune* and other mercenary magazines, stating that a female former KGB agent was available for private employment. A post office box was listed for replies.

Only one reply piqued her interest. It was from someone claiming to be an agent and offered a telephone number with instructions to ask for Operator 111. When she called and requested Operator 111, she discovered it was a reroute of the phone line and the brokerage house she thought she had called was merely a front. A man's voice, disguised through an echo box, eventually answered. His age was impossible to determine, and she assumed the indistinguishable accent was fake. The voice informed her that he had aleady invesitgated her background and verified her credentials. She immediately suspected that he was former CIA.

The man wasted no time, offering her a contract, unwritten but binding. He would supply her with assignments and take twenty-five percent off the top before crediting a Cayman Island account in her name for the remainder. Expenses would be shared. She had the option of refusing an assignment, but once she accepted she was committed until completion. Under no circumstances could she try to uncover his identity. The warning was stated simply, but with ominous overtones.

Willis returned the binoculars to the leather case and sighed deeply. She was growing tired of this solitary work and was starting to feel the need for a stable, personal relationship.

The boutique had provided opportunities to meet buyers and salesmen but she had felt no kinship with them. If she was honest with herself, she'd have to admit it was the voice of Control that kept her from entering into any serious personal relationships. The voice had cast a spell over her. He was a total enigma—his age, looks, perspective on life. He was all business, except for an occasional compliment on her performance.

She tried to shake off the mood. She twisted the ignition key and noticed that a cable repair van was pulling out of its spot. One of the few things she knew about Control was that this cable repair company was used for surveillance. She often used the vans herself. She had been aware in the past that Control had been following her, monitoring her work, and she wondered now if the person in the van could be *him*. The cable business permitted him entry into countless homes and offices where a variety of electronic surveillance equipment could be installed without anyone's knowledge. Maybe she'd look further into the company to see what she could find—but with extreme caution. His warning rang in her mind.

Carrie's green eyes contained a strange light at that moment. It had been ten years—time to do a little research *without* an assignment.

She put on her sunglasses before shifting into gear, her thoughts returning to Reuven Harbin. She sighed. The assignment at hand came first. The question of who really owned the cable company would have to be put on hold temporarily. With one final glance at the *Sea Temple*, she drove out of the marina parking lot.

Like Carrie Willis, Spencer Medwal was intrigued by Reuven Harbin, but for a different reason. The millionaire's background beyond the past fifteen years was too vague. He had been able to dig up very little beyond the fact that Harbin had been a colonel in the Israeli Air Force. *Why would Harbin have only former Israeli military personnel in employment aboard his yacht?*

Through his "associates" Medwal had learned of Harbin's ownership of a private island in the British Virgin Islands, and its fortresslike protection. *Did it have a purpose or was it a rich man's whimsy?* The man had turned sixty-five on his last birthday; what could he possibly be involved with other than his own giant corporation?

Harbin was truly a man of mystery. Medwal sat back, unable to contain a smile. *Just like myself.*

Spencer Medwal had just passed his fifty-first year. Five of those years had been spent with Special Forces in Vietnam followed by another five with the CIA. He had been working undercover for so long that at times he had to reassure himself of his true identity. His father, an arthritic eighty-three-year-old, allowed his son a free hand to run the cable company as he pleased but Spencer had progressed far beyond the firm's confines. His stable of twenty agents was divided in locale, twelve still active within the CIA and eight others on call, including Carrie Willis—the lone woman in his operation. Three, excluding Willis, were gifted in the art of termination.

He was fortunate that none of the twenty knew his true identity—although he never believed luck had any role in keeping a major portion of his life secret. No marriage, no entanglements, he remained businesslike in all his endeavors. There was the risk that they might trace him back through the cable company but he felt that his identity was sufficiently buried.

Medwal left the swivel chair to stand at the tenth-floor window and gaze toward the horizon. Biscayne Bay was dark but for some slow-moving lights. He turned away from the window and studied himself in the full-length mirror that hung on the door of his wardrobe closet. A smile came easily; he was satisfied with what he saw. He prided himself on his physical appearance. At six-foot-two, 180 pounds, he presented an imposing figure. His face was square, rugged and lined—the eyes a deep brown, lacking softness. His hair was thick but cut short, leaning to salt and pepper.

He turned away, wondering why his uncle Shafik should be concerned with Reuven Harbin. Leaving his office, he began making plans. Carrie Willis was to do double-duty on the Harbin assignment. The cryptic identity of Reuven Harbin was indeed intriguing.

At one a.m. Ari phoned Harbin in his suite to report on the cable company. The business still appeared to be clean. The company was owned by a Harrison Medwal, but an aging disability had his son, Spencer, running the operation.

"And, Reuven . . ." Ari said, "this is where it gets a bit spooky. The son is former CIA—and before that was a member of Special Forces in Vietnam."

"Put further investigation on hold," Harbin directed, thinking about the information. "Are we prepared for our guests tomorrow?"

Following assurances from Ari, Harbin said only, "Okay, but keep surveillance alive on board. I sense we're heading into something—and I don't know what."

7

As Harbin stepped out of the shower and began to towel himself off before the mirror, he noticed the scar that had been created to match Colonel Abu's scar from an appendectomy. Despite Harbin's sixty-odd years it was the sole blemish on his hard, muscular physique.

The sight of the scar dredged up almost forgotten incidents. By the time he was half-dressed he had to sit down and sort out his rambling thoughts. He turned to look at his wife's portrait.

Why now, Anya? After all the years? Why do I feel this emotion for this strange woman who resembles you?

The silence became oppressive and he turned from the painting. He knew the answer. It had been fifteen years since he had last bedded a woman—and it had not been his wife.

Harbin had returned to Syria perfectly disguised as Colonel Abu. Three months of studying the Syrian colonel who had suffered from a terminal disease had been necessary before making the attempt to assume the Arab's identity. Abu's friends and relatives did not know of his illness. They had assumed that he had perished when his plane had crashed over the Golan.

The memories flooded back: leaving Anya again for months at a time to live in a cell with Colonel Abu and learn of his inner beliefs and thoughts. The physical resemblance was the work of Israeli surgeons and technicians. Once he was prepared for his mission, he went to see his wife one last time.

His next meeting with his wife was at her graveside five months later. It had taken years for him to forgive the Mossad for not having notified him of her death in an Arab bus bombing. It was the principal cause for his leaving the Mossad, and Israel.

It had taken three months after "Abu's" return to Damascus for his "wife" Fatima to seduce him. His assertion that Israeli brutality had led to the loss of his virility did not convince her. But she was only able to lure him to her bed on two occasions. After these, Harbin became determined to end the masquerade. He planned another plane disaster.

Colonel Abu was now dead for all time.

Harbin sighed; his life had been altered by the meeting with Meg Tolan. He couldn't help wonder why fate had brought them together. His business ventures had been more than enough to keep him occupied, to keep him celibate, without trial or temptation until now.

Why now? Why did fate intrude to upset his life at such a late stage?

Suddenly, he was reminded of a bittersweet scene two weeks earlier while his family dined aboard the *Sea Temple* to celebrate the new yacht. His older daughter Carol's involvement in a charity organization led her to invite two elderly couples from a retirement community to join them. One couple, afflicted with arthritis, came aboard in wheelchairs. During the course of the evening Harbin had noticed they quite often had their chairs side by side so they could hold hands.

Recollection of the couple caused Harbin to contemplate his wedding vow: "Through sickness and health . . ." It was a statement he had never had the chance to fulfill.

Sighing heavily, he got to his feet. He had thought himself immune to such musings. After the failure of his first marriage, he wondered if he was truly capable of loving anyone again.

Harbin's experienced crew took no more than fifteen minutes to tie up at the concrete dock in Nassau's harbor. Among other yachts of varied lengths three cruise ships were in port. A festive holiday spirit prevailed along the busy docks. Ellen Chelsea, along with Cindy Novick and Mae Warren, stood on the rear deck of the *Temple* admiring the goings-on.

To no one in particular Ellie said, "Joe warned me beforehand of what's happening between our host and Meg. I didn't want to believe him, but . . ."

Cindy said, "I don't know. I find him charming, but as for Meg going overboard for him . . ."

"I don't believe you two," Mae Warren interjected. "You can't really believe love dies in one's later years."

Ellie held up a hand. "Whatever we believe will have to be put on hold. Meg's returning."

Meg joined them, wearing a half-smile. "Am I interrupting something?"

"Not at all," Ellie ventured. "We were merely wondering what you thought about Reuven Harbin's joint venture with Josh and Joe. I mean socially rather than in a business sense." She fluttered a hand. "You know— I'm not sure if I'm expressing it in the right way."

Meg gave her a sidelong glance. "Ellie, you're really asking me what I think of Reuven, aren't you?"

"Since you mention it . . ." Cindy said.

"Well . . . to be quite candid, I believe he has a brilliant mind. Anyone who could progress as far as he has in today's competitive world would have to be a genius." She paused for a second. "What makes him even more remarkable is that he's a Good Samaritan as well. I've never heard of anyone doing such good deeds while remaining extremely successful in business."

Mae Warren gave Ellie an unseen nudge and whispered softly, "She's got it bad. You can believe it."

Ellie said nothing. She looked over Cindy's shoulder, wondering what the men were discussing by the bar in the lounge.

At the bar Chelsea added a couple of ice cubes to his vodka. Although concentrating on his drink he said to Harbin, "If you have a pair of binoculars handy in your desk, I ask you to focus on the blonde woman at the far end of the pier. Use the starboard window." Josh shook his head. Ward merely smiled, sipping his bourbon. Joey was at it again.

"Any particular reason I should?" Harbin asked.

"She looks like the very same blonde I saw in the country club parking lot last week."

Harbin's face was seemingly unaffected by Chelsea's pronouncement.

He went to the wall and slid open a panel revealing among other items a pair of binoculars.

At the starboard window, he focused on the pier. After a few seconds he turned and faced Chelsea. "Why would you remember her? There's nothing all that distinctive about her from this distance."

"This one was wearing earphones when I last saw her. Which she promptly put away when she saw me watching."

"Why would that make you suspicious of anything? She could have been listening to stereo music—or anything."

"She was sitting in a cable repair van. I saw the same van in the marina parking lot a few days later."

Harbin realized Chelsea was trying to make a point, but was playing it out slowly. Ward and Novick didn't interrupt.

"Did the van have a parabolic mike atop its roof?"

Chelsea eyed him. "Then, you were aware of it. Why let me go on?"

"I had to know where you were going." He waved a hand of dismissal.

"Sorry, Joe. Really, I do find this interesting. I'm also interested in knowing what you do have—and why you took the trouble of investigating it. It's apparent your partners didn't like the idea of you doing so."

Josh intervened. "Reuven, this is a habit of Chelsea's we're trying to break. He's always reading something into nothing. On one particular occasion it brought us trouble we didn't need."

"The trouble existed nevertheless," Harbin said. "Whether you brought it up or not."

"No argument there," Ward interjected. "It's just that Josh and I think we should let sleeping dogs lie. Why get involved in other . . ." He shut his mouth.

"In other people's problems?" Harbin finished for him.
A tired smile appeared. "It's not just Joe Chelsea. It's also
been my problem.

"Now, to get back . . . I'm still interested. Just how
far did you get in your investigation?"

Chelsea eyed him again. He was engaging a sharp
cookie. "Do you know about the ownership of the cable
company?"

He got a nod, and, "Harrison Medwal, with his son,
Spencer, running the company because of his father's
handicap."

Chelsea nodded. Yes, sharp. "Did you know the
Medwals were Arabs originally from Syria?"

Syria!

"It appears your sources are quite good." Harbin
looked from Chelsea to Ward. "I gather you're the expert
in information-gathering. It seems I have been lax with
my sources." From the open panel he punched in a
number on an attached wall phone and got the ship's
captain.

"Ari, I want a complete biography on the Medwal
family. I've received news they're originally from Syria."
Silence. "Yes. ASAP."

He hung up the phone and turned back to Chelsea.
"You still haven't explained why you bothered getting
involved."

Dave Ward snickered. "The answer is only too simple.
Our friend Joey continues to struggle against boredom.
He *pretends* he's back on the Force working on a
caseload or, I should say, he continues to try to invent
one." To Chelsea he said, half-humorously, "You just
don't give up, do you?" In reply he received a shrug and
a pleasant smile.

Harbin said, "In this case, I'm grateful for his suspicious mind."

Josh decided to enter the conversation. "Is that why your crew looks like they can handle any unexpected situation?"

Harbin didn't blink an eye. "You never know what important dignitary might be aboard. I must be prepared against kidnapping."

Chelsea reached into his jacket pocket for his pipe and tobacco. "Why would the Medwals be interested in spying on you?"

"At this moment, it's for Ari to tell me."

"Will we be privy to the information he gathers? Or . . ." Chelsea stopped, catching himself. "I apologize. It's really none of our business."

Harbin laughed. "On the contrary, I welcome your questions — and your thoughts." He waved a hand. "For now, though, let's put it on hold. We've been neglecting the ladies. Do they have anything planned — casino gambling on Paradise Island perhaps? If not, I have card tables available or video cassettes of the latest films. Whatever they wish."

Chelsea smiled. "If it was my decision, I'd be taking a walk along the pier to meet with that blonde. That is, if she stayed put there."

Without delay Harbin lifted the binoculars again. He spotted the woman standing on the pier smoking, seemingly waiting for someone. He nodded to Chelsea before placing the binoculars down and lifting a phone.

"Ari? Is Dani handy? Good. There's a blonde woman at the northern end of the pier. She's wearing a two-piece green suit. She can't be missed. I want her tailed."

Chelsea glanced at Josh, whose lips were compressed.

Ward was shaking his head, mouthing silently, "Okay, Joey. You got your way. Here we go again."

Chelsea restrained a grin. He didn't know where they were headed but he sensed something big in the works—a new challenge. Harbin was no amateur. Certainly not with the crew he had working on board. They were definitely military. Their every movement shouted it: muscular and light on their feet, and eyes watching everything. And as for Harbin himself, who knew what he was capable of? What roles did Reuven Harbin play besides that of a well-known business tycoon?

Suddenly Chelsea turned to face Harbin. "Just who do you think is under surveillance? You—or us? If you would allow me an educated guess, I would say you."

"And why do you come to this conclusion? Is it because the Medwals are of Arab ancestry?" It was more statement than query. "You could be right," Harbin added.

"And if he is right," Novick interjected, "what then?"

Harbin waited a few seconds. "What would you suggest I do?"

"It's not for me to suggest anything. You're our host and as such . . ."

Harbin smiled. "Let's wait and see if we're justified in doing anything at all."

Secrets! The man has secrets! Chelsea felt it in his bones. Harbin wanted to tell them something, but it wasn't confession time yet. They were fencing verbally and everyone knew it. But to Chelsea it didn't matter. It was difficult for Chelsea to hide his elation. And it was a supreme effort to keep a half-smile from appearing on his face. The intimation and anticipation of something untoward breaking was definitely in the works. And the fact that he welcomed it was undeniable.

When Harbin excused himself to join the women on the rear deck, Ward turned to Chelsea and said, "Joey, I do believe you're trying to lead us astray again. And I'm not certain that I want to be a partner in this." Chelsea smiled. "Joey, I'm not kidding."

"Dave, stop with the horse crap. It's obvious Harbin trusts us—issuing orders in our presence and displaying a talent never advertised. We've already been dealt a hand . . . whatever it is."

"And wherever it goes?" Josh tossed in.

Chelsea held a lighter to his pipe. He looked over the pall of smoke. "Josh, don't fight it. Although you felt relief with the conclusion of the Alliance affair your appetite was whetted."

"Maybe so—but I'd be happier if I knew where we were heading. And while I'm having my say—whatever happens, the *women* do not get involved."

Ward started to light a cigarette. "I'm beginning to think we've lost our marbles, Joey. Why couldn't you have taken up shuffleboard?"

"Did I hear someone mention shuffleboard?" Ellie asked. She walked into the lounge, followed by Candy, and looked at her husband. "You? I'd have to see it to believe it."

Cindy said, "Forget shuffleboard. We've been aboard ship too long. We've decided we'd like to stroll into the square."

"And we'll join you," Chelsea quickly replied.

Dani stood five foot ten and carried about 160 pounds. His complexion was dark like that of an outdoorsman.

His hair was dark, with a crew cut. He wore cutoff denim shorts and a flowered sport shirt. A 35mm camera hung from his neck. He resembled any one of a number of tourists boarding and disembarking from the big cruisers. Lifting the camera, he focused his zoom lens on the blonde who had just discarded her cigarette by dropping it at her feet and then stamping on it. She looked up suddenly, as if hearing the camera shutter click, which would really be quite impossible amidst all the commotion.

She's got intuition, Dani thought. *Be careful, boychick!* This woman could be dangerous. He wondered why Harbin was interested in her. Perhaps he was doing a favor for the three retired policemen. It was Harbin's policy to have the ship's crew memorize a short biography of his guests no matter their identity. He, as well as the others, never questioned Harbin's authority on board or land. It was so instructed by the ambassador himself.

Dani didn't mind, it was rather nice working aboard a private yacht this size, and it was easy to get along with the captain and his employer. For the first two weeks he couldn't understand why his services were required but now he was beginning to feel in his element.

He got off two more quick shots of her before she started walking away. *She walked too quickly. Had he been made?* If so, she was good!

He waited, allowing her some distance. She was going into the market. Dani smiled. She'd never lose him, not even in a crowd. That blonde in a green suit couldn't be missed. He was thirty yards behind her when she stopped at a stall and sifted through the merchandise. He held up, casually examined his camera, and again permitted her another ten yards. He stopped to help two women make a decision on a rattan handbag. When he glanced up he saw the blonde pull out a mirrored compact from her purse and use it to look behind her. She wore no particular expression as she entered a ladies' apparel shop, but before she entered he saw her search the plateglass window for a reflection of what was behind her.

Dani sat at an outside table at a restaurant across the street, sipping iced tea, and getting nervous. Twenty minutes had passed. Four women had come and gone, but no blonde. Was she buying out the store? His eyes searched the street as he sipped his second glass of tea.

Another ten minutes and he would know if he had been outsmarted. He was certain she hadn't made him. He left a couple of bills on the table and started to cross the street in a hurry. And then was waved back by a black constable. "All must cross on the walks at the intersection," he stated authoritatively.

The shop had three customers, none of them blonde or young. He found a saleswoman. "Perhaps you can help me," he said, displaying annoyance. "I was supposed to meet my sister in this shop. I wonder if she was here already and left. A blonde woman wearing a two-piece green suit?"

The slender saleswoman smiled. "I believe you mean the woman who took off her blonde wig before purchasing a yellow dress and matching pumps."

Dani squinted, otherwise keeping a straight face. "Pulled that again. Always changing her appearance. Thinks it's a game. Our mother's not going to like it. My sister's expected for dinner. I hope she shows up."

Carrie Willis wasn't sure whether she was being followed or not until she saw the man enter the shop. He was from the *Temple*. She smiled. The man was good—but not good enough. She left the restaurant, the very same restaurant Dani had used for surveillance, her expression not altogether happy. She had been singled out. It should not have occurred.

She would have been shocked had she known she was still being observed.

But not by the yacht's crewman.

The man's flowered, print shirt hung over his tan trousers. Spencer Medwal's so-called disguise fit in perfectly with the tourists. He nodded, watching Willis leave the restaurant, wondering what her next move would be. He smiled, realizing she was now retracing her steps, tracking her original shadow. Medwal followed at a safe distance, intrigued by her method of working.

Harbin was on the bridge speaking with Ari when Dani appeared. After first explaining and then attempting an apology, he was cut short by Harbin.

"Forget it. We both underestimated her. The camera—what did you get on it?"

"I got her on film with whomever she spoke with on the way to the ladies' dress store. Also, to be safe, I got a shot of everyone who left the shop."

Harbin smiled. "Dani, your apology was unnecessary. Get the film down to the darkroom. Let's see what develops."

Minutes later Harbin had the photos spread out on a card table for the benefit of his male guests. The women were below in their staterooms, dressing to go out for the evening.

Chelsea pulled out a portrait shot of the blonde Carrie Willis in the market, then placed it beside a brunette in a loose-fitting yellow dress. "Quite a change artist," he remarked. "But there's no doubt of it. She couldn't change her face." He looked up. "What would be your next step?" he asked Harbin. "Or should I first ask if you have any idea why you are under surveillance? It can't be industrial espionage. The present merger doesn't rate it. It has to be something else—something of greater importance to have someone of her talent . . . This woman is a class act."

Their host nodded. "Well done, gentlemen. It seems we all agree. But, as for why I am under surveillance . . . I can only guess she's working for Spencer Medwal. But it's pure speculation."

"Which means we wait until we get more on Medwal," Chelsea said.

"Who is Medwal?" Meg asked, entering the lounge. Advancing, she added, I hope you gentlemen are not doing business without conferring with me."

Ellie, directly behind Meg, frowned at Chelsea. "Yes, Joe, who is Medwal? Why is it necessary to get something more on him? I thought this was to be a pleasure cruise."

Harbin held up his hand defensively. "Ladies, please. There is no subterfuge here. The Novick Security Firm is a business. All they're doing is checking into the background of this person—who is really of no great importance."

Mae Warren harrumpfed. "Where and when have I heard that before?"

Cindy said, "I believe it was when our Rover Boys decided to check on the Benefactor Alliance."

• • •

Spencer Medwal pulled the slot machine handle. He believed that seating himself behind a slot machine was the simplest way of being unnoticed. If Carrie Willis was present she had become invisible. Chelsea, Novick, and Ward were playing blackjack and their women were trying their luck at roulette. Harbin and the Tolan woman lingered by the blackjack table briefly, but soon appeared to lose interest. They walked away from the busy table, ambling aimlessly until deciding to push through a horde of people waiting impatiently for an available slot machine.

Although there were dozens of isles of slot machines in the casino, Harbin and Meg just happened to pick Medwal's to pass through. Medwal pulled at the handle of the quarter machine and turned his back on the approaching couple. He would have gone unnoticed but his machine started clicking off quarters as if it were stamping them out at the mint. Eight hundred quarters was the final count. Another four hundred would have been the jackpot for that particular machine. With neighboring players watching in envy he was temporarily thrust into an unwanted limelight.

In passing Harbin spoke to Medwal's back. "It's your lucky night. Take the money and run."

Medwal shrugged without turning around. "I suppose so. Some nights are better than others."

Seconds later, clear of the crowded isle, Meg said, "Maybe I got a wrong impression, but did you think that man was rude? It seemed he deliberately turned away from us." Meg touched Harbin's hand. "Reuven, did you hear me?"

He took her hand in his. "Yes, I heard you. I also agree with you, but for a moment my mind was elsewhere."

"And where was it?"

He held a finger to his lips, then took her arm to escort her toward the lobby, away from the clatter of mechanical devices. Harbin was about to break a lifetime custom—he was going to take a chance and trust Meg with details of his work life. He had never told Anya anything of his duties and how he performed them. She would usually only know when he was leaving and when he would return. He knew Meg was going to differ from Anya in this respect.

Lifting his arm he allowed her to see the miniature camera attached to the inside of his cuff. "My mind was on that man's face," he said.

Meg stepped back from him. "Reuven . . . who are you?"

He smiled. "You know who I am."

She waited, seeking more. "No, I don't. Not really." When he took her arm again, she held back. "There's something unreal about you that smacks of . . . I don't know what."

He touched his lower lip. *Yes, she was different from Anya.* "Not tonight, but when the opportunity arrives . . . I promise you will know all."

"Reuven, I won't accept a cryptic reply like that as an answer."

He looked at her searchingly. "Very well. Tonight I'll give you a book to read. Discussion and explanations will follow."

"You're not going to tell me the title beforehand?"

He deliberated before whispering, *"Modern Legends of Israel."*

• • •

Medwal stood at the cashier's window feeling extremely perturbed. He was guilty of ignoring a self-enforced cardinal rule: No matter the odds, never be in a position where you could possibly be exposed. *Murphy's Law*, he thought. *No use in fighting it.* Grimacing, as if in pain, he turned from the caged window.

And saw her!

She was watching him, her smile one of amusement. Or was it approval? He held her gaze, recognizing immediately that he had been made. But a single thought dominated his attention: She was stunning. A gold sheath fit her body as if it were molded to her. Her hair was jet black and long; he couldn't tell if it was her own.

Oh well, he thought. *After ten years there was bound to be a meeting at some point.* He walked over to her. "Would you like a drink?" he asked.

"Love to, boss!"

As he approached Harbin, Chelsea was aware that his attention was drawn to a couple at the bar. "Anyone we should know about?" he asked.

"You bet," Ward answered for him. "It's the woman we lost yesterday. The guy I don't know about. Maybe a pickup, maybe not." He adjusted his tie, unused to wearing one. "I think I need a drink," he said, leaving them. "See you later."

Harbin remained silent. Meg couldn't hide her astonishment. "Joe, Reuven—are you going to tell me what's going on?"

"Nope," Chelsea said. "This is Reuven's game." He touched Harbin's sleeve. "Just out of curiosity—what kind of camera is it?"

A small laugh followed. *I really am slipping.* "A Minox," he simply said.

Meg was not to be put off. "I'm still here, Reuven. Alive and well, not just part of the scenery. And as for you, Joe . . ."

Harbin took her arm. "Later, Meg. This isn't the place for this discussion."

"Or disclosure?"

He gazed at her. "My, you are persistent. I wish I had been warned."

Chelsea watched, smiling. "I suggest," he said, "we go out to the terrace."

Medwal ordered a straight rye for himself and a pink lady for Willis. Neither of them spoke until the drinks were served. Medwal broke the silence. "How did you make me?"

She took a sip of her drink and seemed satisfied. "The van. I checked. The owner, Harrison Medwal, was too old—and ill besides. It was easy from there on. Harrison had a son living in New York, running—imagine!—a brokerage house of all things."

"So? That still doesn't tell—"

"Oh, come off it, Spence. Or is it Spencer? Anyway, I was watching my target when you hit the machine. You were too obviously attempting to cover your face." She smiled disdainfully. "Do you mind if I call you Spence? It's so American and friendly. Not really the type of name you would expect for an American of Syrian background on the tail of a former Israeli turned American." She laughed quietly. "Spence—stick to administration—you've lost your touch for fieldwork."

Medwal took a deep swallow, almost finishing his drink. It did nothing to diminish his rising panic.

"By the way . . ." she continued, "why are you here? Checking on me or them?"

He smiled for the first time. "Be careful of what you're saying. The bearded man four seats to my left could be a lip-reader."

Her eyes turned without her moving her head. "Dave Ward," she whispered, "a sailor and computer expert, and possibly a silent partner in the Novick Security Firm."

"Very good. I was beginning to think you were dressed for play."

"Don't be snide. I'm always working. As you well know, the costume fits the assignment. And while we're at it, I'd like to know why an Americanized Syrian is interested in an Americanized Israeli."

His eyes darkened. "Be careful. Don't step on my heels." He lifted his gaze to her hair. "How many transformations do you own? I've seen you in a few."

She laughed. "I guessed as much. But back to the business at hand . . . Why is Harbin so important to you? I sense it's something personal."

He sighed. She was getting to him. "It's nothing but a favor for a favorite uncle. Family is important." He studied her face openly. "If you had one you'd understand."

She shook a finger at him. "Tsk, tsk. You're prying."

He downed the rest of his drink and, taking her arm, steered her toward the lobby. "Your outfit is attracting a lot of attention. What the hell are you thinking?"

"I was hoping to meet Reuven Harbin, but it seems he

only has eyes for his companion. Besides, I believe it is you who drew everyone's attention this evening."

He didn't seem to be listening. "Let's go out to the garden. We have some things to get straight."

By the time Ward finished his drink Chelsea had materialized at his side. "Get anything of use, Dave?"

"Nope, not much. But I could almost swear they knew I was a lip-reader."

"Well . . . ?"

"I think he's Spencer Medwal." He turned to face his friend. "What do you make of that?"

Chelsea ran a hand through his hair. "Maybe we should ask Reuven. I'm willing to bet he has ideas. Dealing with Arabs is—or was—more his territory than ours."

"You guys going to let me in on your little secrets?" Josh asked, emerging from a chattering group comparing their winnings and losses.

"Nothing really to do with us. But Reuven might have a problem."

"So then why is it your concern?"

Chelsea sighed. Ward rolled his eyes, and said, "Here we go again. Minding someone else's business."

"Not this time," Josh pleaded.

"Not even if he asks for our help?" Chelsea tossed at him.

Ward threw up his hands. "Why do I get the feeling we're sailing into hot water?"

Chelsea's lips twisted into a sly grin. "What made you come up with that, Dave?" He didn't allow a response. "As a matter of fact, I had a private session with Reuven on the way across. He invited all of us to cruise the Greek Islands for a week later this summer." Ward snorted his disbelief, but Novick cocked his head questioningly. "And, O great leader, what was your reply to this magnificent offer?"

"I said I would speak with you." He held up a hand. "He said it would be strictly for pleasure. Although, I have to admit it looks like there are a few people hovering around the scene that would make me think we might run into a little trouble along the way."

"You want my answer now, or do you want it in writing?" Josh quipped.

Chelsea touched his lip, as if reminded of something. "Oh, yes, I forgot to mention that the ladies are welcome as well."

Josh looked like he was about to explode.

"Relax," Chelsea continued. "I turned him down, told him we couldn't possibly get away from our office."

Ward gave him a studied look. "You really want to go, Joe, don't you? Regardless of what you told him."

"And what we think of the idea," Josh interjected.

"Well . . ."

Josh snapped his fingers. "It's Meg. Because of Meg. He has asked her, but she'd never go as his lone guest on that cruise."

"I don't think so," Chelsea was quick to reply. "Not entirely, anyway. I believe Reuven has a problem—and needs us."

"Joey, you're out of your mind. Did you take a good look at his crew?"

Ward shook his head. "If I took off a week from my charters, do you have any idea of what Mae would say?"

Josh put a hand on his arm. "Dave, you asked the wrong question. Don't you know the women would grab at the chance of cruising the Greek Islands?" He made a sudden turn to Chelsea. "Don't tell me, Joe. Please. You didn't just happen to mention this to anyone but us? Have you?"

"Only Ellie."

"Jesus," Josh sputtered. "You're not going to give it up, Joe. Are you? You're still seeking action beyond our firm."

"What action are we discussing?"

"Don't play it cute, Joe."

"Okay. I admit you're right. Don't you guys feel our lifestyle is a little boring? Unproductive? Granted our firm is doing well, but it's nothing more than a watchdog operation. Every once in a while a challenge is called for." He paused for a beat. "The time to retire is when we're too old and unable to do anything more than exist." He glanced from Josh to Dave. "Have you lost all sense of adventure?"

"Adventure!" Dave snapped. "Have you ever had a five-hundred-pound shark on your line?"

"Touché. You're right. No argument. But don't you still need a change from the daily routine of dropping a line in the ocean?"

Josh gave him a sidelong glance. "Joe, what adventure are you talking about? Taking a cruise through the Greek Islands? Do you know something we don't?"

"Yes, a bit." He hesitated, observing both his friends. Their efforts at protest, no matter their posturing, didn't ring true. "I had a private conversation with Reuven late into the night—before our morning departure. We sat on the afterdeck; he was smoking a cigar and I had my pipe. It was soon apparent I had caught him in a wistful mood. You made an astute observation, Josh. Meg wouldn't go if she were the lone guest." Josh almost smirked, but didn't interrupt.

Continuing, Chelsea said, "However, he did invite our little group along for another purpose. That of protection, he stated in all seriousness. When I mentioned his crew, he tossed it aside with the explanation that he was talking about when we went ashore."

Dave couldn't hold back. "Protection from what? Isn't he aware of our ages? Have you forgotten our previous escapade? You coined us the 'Sunset Detectives.' What are we now? The Sunset Brigade?"

Chelsea didn't instantly reply. The area had become crowded and noisy. He took their arms and herded them through the lobby toward French doors leading to an outdoor garden. Spying a bench surrounded by effusively growing hibiscus bushes he stopped. Dave contained his annoyance. "Joey, I don't want to repeat my question."

"Our ages are irrelevant. Reuven considers us, rightly or wrongly, his equals."

"Then he's a fool!" Josh stated imperiously. "I can't vouch for his physical capabilities, but I do know mine."

Dave scratched at his beard. "Joey, the man is flattering us. Forget Harbin's age. Have you seen him move? Like a forty-year-old. The man's been around, he's been trained and—what's more—he's in top condition now. I know. Early this morning one of his crew was hosing down the foredeck with Harbin watching. The man slipped and started to slide into a forgotten open hatch behind him. I watched Harbin zip across the deck, grab the man by his shirt collar, and with one hand pull him out of the open hatch. I saw the way he braced his legs for a foothold and I'm telling you that Reuven Harbin has had training in the martial arts." He looked up at Chelsea. "So, convince me. Tell me why the man needs our help."

"Medwal." Chelsea waited for it to sink in. "He's learned—by using his own methods—that Medwal is a Syrian Arab."

"So what!" Josh interjected. "We knew that already. *Using our methods!*"

"Yes, but we didn't know that Harbin used to be an undercover man for the Israelis," Chelsea added.

"He admitted that?" Dave wanted to know. "You're talking Mossad?"

"He never mentioned the Mossad. In fact, I'm surprised he confessed as much as he did. As I said, he was in a wistful mood."

Dave looked at Josh. "So, is this a job for the 'Sunset Detectives?'"

"Humpf! We're more sunset than detectives." After a brief deliberation he then shrugged his shoulders. "Okay. Why not? We'll give it a whirl." He turned on Dave. "But don't ever mention Sunset Brigade to anyone."

Grinning, the ex-FBI man held a hand over his heart. "I promise." Addressing Chelsea, he said, "So what's our agenda?"

"Three weeks from this coming Monday we fly to Athens. Reuven's footing the bill. Ari will be waiting for us there with the *Temple.*"

Josh said, "Has Reuven mentioned what we should be looking for?"

"Harbin promised a private meeting with us. A full

discussion." He checked his wristwatch: It was running toward midnight. "Let's call it a night. Any further discussion right now is pointless without consulting the ladies."

Josh shook his head. "I would think Cindy would be glad to break away from her mahjong group for a few days."

Dave said, "Just do me a favor. Don't mention anything with the word sunset to Mae. That said, I have an important question for you, Joey.

"Can either you or Harbin guarantee there won't be a repetition of our previous confrontation when our entire families became involved?"

"Guarantee? It so happens I brought up the very same subject with Reuven. He assured me that if he was expecting trouble, he wouldn't be scheduling a Greek Island cruise. With or without guests."

"And you're satisfied with that? Why Greece? Why there, especially? In my computer search I discovered he owns an entire island—Harbin's Haven—in the British Virgins. Why not cruise there?"

Chelsea sighed. "What more can I tell you? I have a suspicion he owns property—or some business—in one of the islands and he wants to check on it."

Dave blew out a deep breath. "Yeah, a restaurant on Mykonos. I got that out of the computer also. And, curiously, an Arab runs it for him."

Josh stared at him. "How come you never mentioned it before?"

A shrug. "I didn't think it was important. Anyway, it doesn't change anything."

Chelsea chewed on the stem of an unfilled pipe—his thinking crutch—which he had drawn from his jacket pocket. A light breeze touched his cheek. He looked around, almost expectantly, but no one was in the immediate vicinity. He shook off an odd feeling and shoved his briar back into his jacket. "Let's call it a night here and get back to the *Temple* where we can continue the discussion with everyone."

8

It was midmorning when they landed in Athens. Ellinikon Airport was bustling with tourists arriving from all parts of the world. Informational signs directed all in Greek, Aramaic, German, and English. Dimitrios, the driver of an oversized van, helped them with their luggage.

The city was partially covered with a haze that caused the eyes to burn. Dimitrios apologized for their discomfort, explaining that the cause was a noxious cloud called the *nefus*, which, because of the surrounding mountains, sometimes hovered over the city.

"Not an auspicious start," Cindy remarked. No one responded. Everyone was trying to get a glimpse of Athens as the van headed for Piraeus. They travelled along a road that followed the waterfront most of the way. The traffic was heavy and slow, the scenery not much to enjoy for first-time visitors.

Mae Warren was the first to offer any information. "I've been here before, Cindy. All of Athens is not like this."

Chelsea said, "It doesn't matter. This is about all you're going to see of Athens. In a few minutes we'll all be aboard the *Temple*."

"And as Gleason used to say," Josh added, "'And away we go.'"

Dave Ward said nothing. He merely crossed his fingers unseen.

Chelsea noted that Meg looked wistful. "You okay, Meg?"

She sighed heavily. "Brad and I spent three days in Athens many years ago." She rubbed an eyelid. "It brings back memories long forgotten."

Ellie took her hand. "We all have our memories, some good, some not worth remembering."

Cindy threw in a comment. "Enough of the gloomy past. As Joe always says, 'Work on today and tomorrow so as to create a better past.'"

Dave snickered. "Explain how it's done, Joey. I'm all ears."

"Cynic" was Chelsea's ready comeback.

Except for Meg all were in a jovial mood by the time the van reached the marina. Boats and ships of all sizes, including megayachts, were at anchor or tied up along a thriving waterfront. A line of tourists was waiting to board a gray, freshly painted retired naval destroyer. The *Sea Temple III* was waiting opposite, on a concrete pier.

Reuven Harbin was aware of Meg's mood as soon as she ascended the ramp at the starboard beam. Her manner puzzled him. As with the other female members of the party, she held her cheek to be kissed, but with an aloofness he didn't recognize.

In the past three weeks they had met at least seven times—for a show, luncheons and dinners—and had enjoyed each other's company to the point where a tacit sense of belonging was shared. A holding of hands and a goodnight kiss was as far as it went, but there was always the promise of a more intimate relationship.

He raised a hand and four crewmen standing by carried his guests' luggage to their assigned staterooms. He then addressed them.

"You must all be tired after your long trip. I suggest you go to your rooms and freshen up. Leave unpacking until later. In one hour luncheon will be served on the upper afterdeck." His eyes followed Meg as she trailed after the crewman carrying her luggage. In minutes they would be leaving the harbor.

The *Temple* slid past two commercial vessels anchored in the harbor, both waiting for an empty dock. In no time they would be in the Aegean, heading southeast for Mykonos. Harbin expected they would arrive before nightfall.

Josh and Chelsea, both wearing ducks and gumsoles, were the first to appear for lunch. After a moment's hesitation Harbin decided to question Josh on Meg's moroseness. "I wouldn't want this cruise to start on a wrong note. If somehow I've offended Meg . . ."

Josh said, "It's nothing you've done, Reuven. Meg was only just reminded that she had spent some vacation time here with her husband." He studied Harbin briefly. A frown had disturbed the rugged face. "Reuven, I must make you aware of Meg's relationship with her late husband, Brad. Unlike other married couples they shared a special bonding for all their thirty-plus years of marriage. Losing Brad was an extremely traumatic experience and she grieved for quite a while." He avoided

Harbin's pained expression before continuing. "Starting a new relationship has to be extremely difficult for her, although, with your help, it was obvious that she had made some headway. If it's any consolation, you are the first to have made her forget the past." He pointed a finger, stressing an added observation.

"That is—for a while, anyway. Until she landed in Athens, where particular memories caught up with her."

Harbin chewed on his lip. For a man who was always in control of any situation, he now felt at a loss as to what he could do. At length he placed a hand on Josh's shoulder. "Thanks, Josh. I'll do my utmost to make this a pleasant cruise for all."

Josh lifted a hand, wanting to change the subject. "You just mentioned a pleasant cruise." He caught Chelsea's disquieted look. "As you assured Joe, can you assure me it won't be *too* eventful for the women aboard?"

Harbin's eyes lifted. He glanced from Josh to Chelsea, and was aware of their wariness. "Why would you think there will be trouble ahead?"

Chelsea moved in. "Reuven, you've got Medwal and the blonde woman from the pier. Separately or together, they're working for someone. There's a reason behind it. I can't imagine why it doesn't bother you. It sure bothers me. And . . ." he added, as an afterthought, "I wouldn't think Greece a safe place for you, an Israeli citizen."

A smile came slowly to Harbin's face. "Israel recognizes dual citizenship with America."

Chelsea frowned. *Why was he being evasive?* "Reuven . . ." he began, but was interrrupted by Harbin holding a palm out.

"We're anchoring at Mykonos tonight for only a two-evening stay—unless my guests wish to stay longer.

As to why Greece was chosen, it's simply to check in on a restaurant I own there. I consider it an annual duty. But this time I wanted to make the trip with friends, and with a new ship."

Chelsea sought a response, finally coming up with, "You have no fears?"

"You believe the man—Medwal—or the woman would follow us here?"

Chelsea heaved a sigh. "On occasion I've learned to trust my intuition."

"And it now tells you . . ." The women were emerging from the staterooms below and crossing the salon. "We'll finish this later, Joe. In private. I promise." The four women were in slacks, for protection against a breezy open deck. The wind was strengthening as the *Temple* glided effortlessly through the harbor at Piraeus for the open Aegean. Harbin turned to the wall to switch on the stereo. The soundtrack from *Zorba* filled the deck.

"How appropriate," Ellie gushed. She was studying the table on the open deck, which offered the choice of boiled lobsters and a variety of other seafood. Harbin was aware of Meg's hunched shoulders as she sought a chair. Dave, wearing cutoff shorts, emerged from the salon with a wide smile. To no one in particular, he said, "Rich or poor, this is the way to live." For the first time Meg smiled, her tension easing noticeably.

All were in an enjoyable mood as they began the brunch with salad. A steady breeze tugged at the table-cloth. Josh remarked, "The Aegean appears to be bluer than the Caribbean, but not as clear."

"Acute observation," said Cindy.

Meg looked at Harbin. "What's our agenda for today—and tonight? What do we have to look forward to?"

Harbin was pleased with her change in mood. "To begin with, we'll be cruising the Cyclades. Right now we're doing about twenty-five knots and should reach Mykonos before dark. Some of you may know that I own a restaurant on the island. Weather permitting, we'll be dining there tonight beneath a bower of trees."

"Should we assume its specialty is Greek food?" Mae asked.

"Greek and Middle Eastern. They usually go together."

"Who runs it for you?" Meg asked.

Harbin smiled. "An Arab family. The patriarch of the family is a longtime friend, dating back many years."

Chelsea chewed on a piece of meat torn from a lobster claw, thinking, *A strange man, Reuven Harbin, truly an enigma.*

"Any special dress code for tonight?" Cindy asked.

"Casual. As you are. No need to change again. Except perhaps for Dave's cutoff shorts."

Ward stood up. "I don't know if anyone cares to join me, but I'm going to try the upper deck for a catnap. The long flight was tiring and I want to be refreshed for whatever tonight promises." There were some nods of agreement. Harbin added, "There's a canvas canopy for protection against the sun."

Athens was far behind them by the time brunch was finished. Islands were appearing, many seemingly unoccupied. The only sound to be heard other than the slap of water against the *Temple*'s hull was the occasional bird winging across the stern.

All but Meg and Harbin followed Dave through the salon to the top deck forward. Harbin glanced at Meg, watching for a sign of the friendship that had developed

before the trip. She sipped at her coffee, seeming unin-
terested in anything but the blue horizon. Neither spoke
until Meg broke the silence. "It's very pleasant out here,"
she said.

Harbin delayed a moment before replying. "It could
be," he said. "Life can be as pleasant as you make it."

She looked up. "Sorry." She made a face. "I guess I
have been playing the martyr."

He leaned across the table to take her hand. "You have
a perfect right to do so. It's been what? Three years?" He
grimaced. "It took me much longer to forget—and then
never entirely." He was quiet for a second. "Perhaps I
should remove the past from my sight, if not from my
heart."

Meg studied his face as if seeing it for the first time.
"You can do that without guilt?"

"I can't know—until trying."

She waited again, mulling it over. Finally she said, "It
must be easier for a man. You must have had many
opportunities to . . ."

He smiled. "Don't you believe it. I've never had much
time for romance."

Meg cocked her head. "And your yachts are confined
to business at all times?"

"The majority of the time. I confess I'm a man of
many moods but, in all truth, I have sailed on many an
occasion without guests aboard. I've mentioned ownership of Harbin's Haven, an island in the British Virgins.
Ninety-five percent of the time there is spent in board
meetings with different corporations. My family uses it
no more than two weeks a year."

Meg appeared thoughtful. "Why do you find the
solitude necessary?"

He seemed to be turning over the question in his mind. "I believe it's time I gave you that book to read."

In the lower salon, a wall of books formed the ship's library. But when Harbin pressed a hidden spring an end shelf split and opened outward. Another shelf was revealed, containing no more than ten books. Harbin selected one, then closed the hidden shelf.

"This volume is no more than eighty pages. It should take you very little time to read." In a sober mood he said, "Meg, I ask only one promise from you. This book is from a limited edition and is to be read only in private and never to be discussed with anyone but me. Is that understood?"

She could only nod as she read the title: *Modern Legends of Israel.* The author, Anonymous.

Harbin added, "I ask you to take it to your stateroom and read it in comfort. When finished, bring it to me so I can return it to its proper place. Once you return I'll answer any questions you may have. It will open a door into my private world—a world I hope you will understand."

Meg could only stare from the black leather cover of the book to his face, and wonder where all of this was leading.

Meg returned a short time later. Harbin immediately returned the book to its original location and then offered her a seat in an overstuffed lounge chair. He glanced at his Rolex and judged that they would not be interrupted for at least another hour. "Any questions to begin with?" he asked quietly.

"Yes. I found the reading fascinating but what am I to understand from it? The history related in it is extremely interesting but it is all legend, fiction, not fact. What was the point in having me read it?

"Really, Reuven . . . A character such as *Moishe Shtyim*—this translates as Moses Two, am I right?—is an impossible character. Totally unbelievable. There never could have been such an individual."

Harbin smiled. "Why did you choose to comment upon Moses Two above the other characters?"

"Because the feats credited to this man are beyond belief. I'm not surprised the identities of these so-called factual legends were never revealed. They couldn't be. They had to have been figments of the author's wild imagination. Why did you ask me to read this?"

Harbin leaned forward, his expression sober. "Meg, listen to me. It's necessary that you understand—and keep an open mind. I have reached a moment in my life I never expected to encounter. You're the first woman in more than fifteen years who I've attempted to become close to. And I know—no matter the denial—that you share a similar feeling for me."

Meg bit into her lip. How could she admit feelings that had lain dormant so long? She fought back tears. "What does this book have to do with me? Us?"

Harbin took a deep breath. "I am—I was—Moses Two." He noted the frown, the utter look of disbelief. "He was real—I was real. I had to tell you. No more secrets, like those I kept from Anya. She knew I was involved with the Mossad, but never to what extent. She never knew my code name. Moses Two was but a living legend, except to a handful of people in high government.

"I confess this to you now. The past is finished, but I

wish to hold no secrets again from anyone to whom I feel so close."

Meg was stunned, she could summon no response other than to let him take her hands in his own. She couldn't yet voice her feelings.

A former spy! A secret agent! How can I go on with the knowledge?

Harbin brought her hand to his lips. For the first time, he felt he could take her in his arms without a trace of guilt.

A pained expression followed her unexpected reluctance. "Meg—"

"Reuven . . . I can't . . . I couldn't . . ." She spoke haltingly before suddenly blurting out, "You shouldn't have told me."

"Would you rather have discovered by chance at some point in the future?"

Her lips trembled. She had always suspected him to be a man of extraordinary . . . *What? Gifts? Talents?* But to learn of this . . .

Harbin feared he was losing her—even before he had won her. He spoke with caution. "Meg, it's because of my feelings for you that I wanted you to know. I can't have secrets between us." He gently pulled her to her feet. He felt no resistance as he took her in his arms and kissed her. It was a kiss more of promise than of passion.

9

Carrie Willis sifted through a heavy crowd to return to Spencer Medwal, who stood waiting for her at a taxi stand at the head of the wharf. She had learned from the harbormaster that the *Sea Temple* had left the harbor two hours earlier. Willis spoke Greek fluently.

"Did he give a destination?" Medwal asked.

Willis's frown marred a smooth forehead. She was not accustomed to working with others unless she herself was in charge. She pushed a strand of hair away from her eye. "Mykonos. Arrival most likely tonight. For obvious reasons I didn't press harder."

He studied a schedule of flights to Mykonos. "Back to the airport. We have two hours to make a flight to Mykonos. My uncle will have accommodations for us."

"And then what?" Willis openly displayed her annoyance.

He stared at her. "You have not been hired to contradict me."

"I've always worked solo. Why should I pair up now? And who else do you have in mind?"

"That depends on my uncle. He gives the orders here—and we jump. I caution you to treat him with respect. He may be elderly, but he is a most imposing and powerful figure." He took her arm and guided her to the cab. She did not resist but he was aware of her distrust. He knew that she had worked alone since leaving Russia more than a decade before. For a brief moment he felt sympathy toward her. But it wouldn't do for her to think he had any feelings for her.

Two hours before his expected arrival Reuven Harbin learned of the *Luxor Princess*'s presence in the Mykonos harbor. He gave Ari instructions to move the *Sea Temple* to a private cove owned by a large modern hotel on an eastern shore. They would anchor fifty yards off shore to accommodate the yacht's draft. The yacht's davit would lower a Boston Whaler to transport passengers from ship to shore.

Anticipating Ari's question from the look on his face, Harbin said, "The *Luxor Princess* is owned by a Syrian known as Shafik. Although I spent some time with him many years ago, I doubt he would recognize me. On the other hand, why tempt fate?"

Ari nodded. "Should we be prepared for any particular type of emergency?"

Harbin looked at him. "We should be prepared for anything at all times."

At that moment Joe Chelsea entered the captain's bridge and was immediately aware of the abrupt shift in direction. "A change of port, Reuven?" he asked.

"No. Just harbor" was the ready answer. "It's less crowded."

Chelsea didn't prod further, but suspected other reasons. *Something's up! Something significant? Harbin doesn't react without cause. Crowded? Why would that bother him?* Chelsea was acquainted with Ari, but not with the helmsman who stood beside him. He could read nothing in their faces.

Harbin said, "The ladies . . . Have they a preference for dinner tonight? The weather prediction is good. Should we stick with the plan for dinner at Oasis Aziz, my lone investment in Greece?"

"For safety's sake?"

Harbin smiled. "You're an astute man, Joe Chelsea."

Chelsea said, "Which reminds me. There's no Customs in Mykonos?"

"The *Temple* went through Customs in Piraeus before your arrival. You passed through in the airport. Hopefully there will be no need for additional checks."

Chelsea laughed. "In the airport only our passports were looked at. Their security here takes for granted our luggage was scanned at JFK."

"This isn't Israel, Joe," Harbin remarked, taking his elbow and ushering him from the bridge. "And on that note, I will confess that Ari is now digging for information on a particular Arab, who is simply called Shafik."

Chelsea studied Harbin carefully. "You did tell me there would be no danger on this cruise."

"Yes, and I don't expect there will be. But, of course, there's always the unexpected." Chelsea gave him a questioning look, but waited. Harbin continued. "Only minutes ago I discovered Shafik's *Luxor Princess* was in port."

"And he's an old nemesis. Or is he?"

Harbin mulled over a reply. "Yes—and no. The odds

are against him recognizing me. I was in total disguise at the time, working undercover."

"You admit much to me, Reuven, but what else is there? I'd already assumed you were former Mossad— but this . . ." He fell silent a moment. "Does Meg know this?"

"Some," he said, knowing he could not reveal all.

Chelsea sighed deeply. "Reuven, I have to give fair warning. If there's any danger involving our women, we take off immediately for the States."

Harbin gazed beyond the blue sea, toward the white-washed buildings that stood on a rocky landmass in the distance. He said finally, "There will be no need for you to react. We will stay here just two nights. I do have to see Aziz on a business matter. Then we'll head toward Santorini."

Relieved, Chelsea nodded. "I'm sorry, Reuven—but you do understand?"

Harbin shrugged off the somber mood. "Of course I understand. Besides, I am too old to resume past adventures. Enough is enough."

Chelsea shook his head, weighing a reply. He wished he could stay and pursue whatever ghosts Harbin was chasing.

At length he said, "Not you, Reuven. You'll never be too old. I know you, as I know myself. We both have ghosts to contend with. Although I doubt mine compare with yours. Mine, I fear, could be only illusory."

Harbin placed a hand upon Chelsea's shoulder. "I knew upon meeting you and Josh that we were to become close friends, not merely business partners."

Chelsea laughed softly. "Reuven, in your own way you can be very persuasive." He waved a pointed finger.

"Tell you what. I'll go along with your original schedule, if anything untoward happens we take off."

Chelsea looked at Harbin, unable to define his ambivalent feelings about his host. The man had confessed former connections to the Mossad. *Were they really all confined to his past? And why would a man of his present stature be involved?*

Whatever his thoughts, hearing voices approaching he quickly said, "Time for a subject change. The others are arriving."

Cindy entered, holding a local map. The rest of the guests were right behind her. Cindy pointed a finger at what looked to be the principal harbor of Mykonos. "Why are we bypassing it. Are we shifting course?"

Meg looked at Harbin briefly then went to a port window. The shoreline appeared bleak and rocky. The ship suddenly rounded a corner of the island and a large modern hotel with references to Greco-Roman architecture emerged into view. Built on the slope of a hillside it rose three stories with a lighted pathway separating each level. A swimming pool was visible on the central level and to the right of it a crystal-chandeliered dining room where waitresses could be seen preparing tables for dinner.

Meg glanced from the building to Harbin. "You're not going to surprise us further by telling us you're the owner of this property?"

"Not at all. As I stated earlier, my sole interest here rests with my restaurant, Oasis Aziz.

"Which by the way, Cindy, you can find in the Little Venice section of your guide map."

Chelsea studied the darkening sky. A restless feeling

was overtaking him. "When will we be taking off for the town?"

"Yes, and how will we get there?" Mae asked.

"Cabs," Harbin replied. "Two will get us there in less than ten minutes.

It will give the ladies time to get in some shopping before dining if they so wish. If nothing else I'm certain you'll find the so-called shopping area interesting."

"That's for me," Cindy and Ellie said in unison.

"You okay, Joe?" Josh whispered. He was quick to sense the anxiety in his friend and business partner.

"Sure. Just anxious to get my land legs back."

Josh said nothing further. He knew Joe too well. Whatever was giving him the shivers he hoped it was not as earthshaking as their previous encounter. The Benefactor Alliance caper had almost killed them all. He shrugged off a sinking feeling. This was Greece—and it was their first holiday in some time. It was a rare occasion, a time to enjoy. To all he announced, "I'm ready. How about the rest of you?"

10

The drive to Little Venice was a roller-coaster ride through a labyrinth of tiny alleys. Heading north, they ascended a twisting cobblestone street where storefronts displayed green, red, and blue neon signs advertising beer or cigarettes. They pulled up to a tall limestone building.

Once inside the restaurant, a man rushed up to greet them. His hazel eyes shined brightly and a wide grin stretched across his face. "Reuven, Reuven—so long between visits."

"Aziz, later we talk. Now, do you have a table for us? My guests are famished. They have come all the way from America to sample your food."

Meg watched the Arab with warm feelings. It was obvious Aziz held Reuven in high esteem. The Arab rolled his eyes. "I have your table waiting for days. You did not let me know the exact date of your arrival. I trust all is well." The last was said with disguised concern. Without waiting for a reply he addressed Harbin's guests, "Come, all of you. Your table is waiting."

The table was set with fine linen and dinnerware. Once all were seated Harbin introduced each of them to Aziz. "I trust Adriana and your children are in good health."

"Well, my fifteen-year-old boy will be serving you this evening. He goes to the university in another year." His wife, Adriana, and their son, Ahmal, took that moment to appear. Adriana was tall and thin with short dark hair and gray eyes. Ahmal was dark and a good deal taller than his father.

Adriana kissed Harbin on both cheeks and greeted all like they were long-lost friends. She immediately offered a variety of starters. Tzatziki—a yogurt, garlic, and cucumber dip, and then okhtapodhi—octopus with black-eyed peas. Aziz's famed lamb souvlaki followed. At the end of the meal Harbin took the opportunity to excuse himself to speak with Aziz in private. "Business," he explained.

In a small office overlooking the restaurant, Aziz spoke to Harbin with a hushed seriousness. "Reuven, how can I help you?"

"The *Luxor Princess* is anchored in the marina. What of its owner, Shafik?"

Aziz stared for a moment. "Reuven—he is indeed here on the island. You did not know? Should we be alarmed?"

Harbin shook his head and smiled. "No, but I do need to know the address of his home."

Aziz took a pencil and pad from his desk and wrote down the information. With a frown he asked, "Will he be trouble for us after all of these years?"

As the two descended the stairs to the dining room they spotted the very man of whom they'd spoken entering the restaurant with an entourage of people. Harbin noted that the man had aged a great deal since he had last seen him. *But,* he thought to himself, *that doesn't mean he is any less cunning.*

"He comes here on occasion for my shashlik. I have the best on this island," Aziz whispered to Harbin.

"He has never questioned you about your country of origin? How it was that you came to open a business here?"

"Never! Why would he?"

Harbin said nothing more. He did not believe in coincidence. Shafik was on the lookout for Harbin.

"Reuven, it has been many years since he has seen you. Besides, your disguise was excellent."

"It is in my nature to be careful, Aziz. Come, I do not wish my guests to be concerned with my absence."

Harbin addressed everyone before seating himself again. "Now, if you wish, we can stay and watch the Greek dancers. Or, if you are tired, we can return to the ship."

The women decided that it had been a long day and that they had better forgo the show. As they gathered their belongings, Harbin said quietly to Josh and Chelsea, "As we are leaving we will be passing a large party in the front of the restaurant. Please watch them without making your interest known."

"What should we be looking for?" asked Chelsea. He squinted his eyes to make out the group, noting in particular that one of the dark-skinned men seemed to stand out as the "godfather" of the group.

"Just be alert for any unexpected movement," Harbin told them quietly. Meg's sudden appearance halted any further conversation. She seemed instantly aware that something sinister might be happening.

"Is there a problem, Reuven?" she asked, her eyes seeking his.

"Possibly. There's a Syrian Arab here. Shafik by name." He paused for a second, probing her eyes, trying to send her a message.

"Why should his presence . . ." She halted abruptly, comprehending what he had told her. *A Syrian Arab! From Reuven's legendary past?*

Harbin took her arm. "Let's go. It's time to return to the ship."

Chelsea quietly insisted Reuven and Meg be in the center of their group as they walked toward the front of the restaurant. Chelsea brought up the rear.

Midway to the door, a voice abruptly called out, "Abu! Colonel Abu!"

All chatter in the restaurant halted abruptly as heads spun to find the source of the loud disturbance. Harbin's step was hesitant, but he continued without pausing. The old Arab smiled triumphantly. Leaning back in his seat he said nothing further.

Walking past the shops on the street, Harbin was lost in desperate thought. *It's not possible! He couldn't have recognized me!*

Chelsea strode to catch up with him and whispered in his ear, "The old man didn't miss a trick; he saw your hesitation. He just smiled like the proverbial cat swallowing the canary."

Shafik stood in the doorway of the restaurant watching the party move down the narrow street. He pulled a cellular phone out of his pocket and punched an automatic dial button.

"You were correct," said the old Arab. "He is not only here in Mykonos, he was at the very same restaurant as I this evening. Have you discovered where the *Sea Temple* is anchored?"

"Uncle . . ." Spencer Medwal began hesitantly at the other end of the line, "I have discovered some other disturbing news."

"Yes. Please continue."

"Harbin's three male guests were the catalysts behind the breakup of the Benefactor Alliance. Should I notify Suliman?"

Shafik felt a dizzying ache sweep across his forehead for a few seconds. "Wait a moment," he whispered. Tears appeared in his eyes, not of pain but of grateful thanks to Allah. To his nephew he managed, "Allah is being kind to me in my final years. I must never forget this blessing."

"Any immediate instructions, Uncle?"

"No. Wait until my return." Then, as an afterthought, "Why is this information coming so late?"

"I wasn't looking for it. It was just pure chance. Or, as you might express it, kismet."

Shafik emitted a small laugh. "Kismet! Yes, of course. Allah always directs the path. But now I want you to go through with something I mentioned to you yesterday. I want you to go ahead and buy up shares in Harbin Enterprises. But under several names. Can you do that?"

"Yes, but I don't understand. You can't ever gain control. The Harbin clan owns or controls more than sixty percent. This I know for fact."

Shafik sighed. "If I can own more than five percent of

outstanding shares I can apply for board membership. Now, don't question my judgment. Do as I say, and also find out the location of the *Sea Temple*."

Back at the yacht, the men managed to sneak away from the ladies, who were contentedly sipping tea on the top deck. Harbin escorted them to a suite he had not yet shown them. Once they were all safely inside with the door closed, Harbin returned to the others. He pressed a button underneath a desk and wood-paneled walls slid open to reveal control panels and computer screens. Chelsea noticed that several of the screens seemed to be some sort of tracking devices.

"Oh my!" exclaimed Dave Ward. "May I use one of these computers?" Harbin watched him briefly and then sat down at a desk and lifted a phone. Within seconds he had Ari on the other end.

"Ari, I am going to put you on speakerphone and I want you to repeat what you have just told me." He hit the speaker switch and turned to his guests.

"I've just received a reply from an earlier inquiry. It regards a name I know you will all recognize. Arar Ib'n Suliman." Gasps escaped from the trio. They immediately recognized the name of a board member of the Benefactor Alliance.

"Our source is impeccable. Apparently, Suliman is Shafik's brother-in-law." Josh filled Dave in on the mysterious Arab's presence at the restaurant, though he himself was still in the dark as to the man's significance. As was Chelsea, who was looking at Harbin with a decidedly irritated expression.

Suddenly he spun on Harbin. "Reuven, when are you

going to come clean with us? What's all this with 'sources'? Who—and what—are you?"

For the next ten minutes Reuven explained to the group his final undercover assignment for the Mossad, stressing that it had occurred fifteen years ago. He also told them that he had discovered that Spencer Medwal was Shafik's American nephew. Once he was finished there were several minutes of silence.

Dave got to his feet. "So, what do we do?" He gave a long look to Chelsea. "Don't expect me to call in the Feds this time, Joey."

Harbin took up the reins. "Wait until I receive more data from my sources. Their information will most likely determine a course of action."

"In the meantime, what do we do to protect ourselves?" asked Josh.

Harbin smiled. "Joe, I also know how to play games. Meanwhile, let's just wait. Trust me. We'll hear from Shafik, and I'm almost certain it will start with a friendly gesture."

"How can you be so certain?" asked Dave with a measure of annoyance in his voice.

"I know Shafik."

Chelsea nodded. "But I have to comment that, for a man retired from clandestine work, you sure keep enough toys to stay occupied."

Harbin's expression remained bland, but he was greatly relieved that the subject had shifted away from the Arabs. "Toys? Hardly Joe. Harbin Enterprises owns or controls a variety of hotels and real estate ventures throughout the world. I can contact any one of them at a moment's notice—or simply tap into vital information on how the businesses are doing down to the minutest detail. This technology is needed to maintain business operations. I'm sure Dave can vouch for that."

Dave nodded to Chelsea. Josh stood up. "On that note, I think we should close up shop. Our ladies will be reading much into our absence."

Trailing behind his guests as they returned to the women, Harbin was suffering real doubt about his capabilities. If truth be known, it was rare that he felt such insecurity. He fingered his mustache. He wondered whether his age was finally catching up to him.

Chelsea turned to see Harbin hanging back. "You okay, Reuven? Did we leave something out of our discussion?"

Harbin caught up to him. "No. Let's just say I'm slowing down with age."

This drew a laugh from Chelsea. He shook his head. "Uh-uh, not you. You're in better condition than I was a decade ago. And I'm flattering myself."

Harbin didn't smile. "Joe, you had a problem retiring. How did you manage it?"

"Manage it? It was a traumatic experience, mainly because it was forced upon me." Chelsea paused. "Reuven, you amaze me. From the beginning of our association I saw you as a man who, despite your age, was capable of overcoming any adversity. Don't talk yourself into believing your talents will fail you."

Reuven took heart from his new friend's words of advice.

Carrie Willis was positioned on the crest of a hilltop overlooking the cove where the *Sea Temple* rested. There was simply too much interference for her to single out any one conversation aboard the enormous yacht. She was only able to pick out single words here and there. Shopping was mentioned a number of times by the ladies on board. Nothing earthshaking. And then, she heard conversation between two men about Delos—a suggestion of a morning sightseeing excursion. Well, she thought, maybe that was something the old Arab could use.

Her eyes strayed to the lovely hotel. She could see the guests dancing, dressed in colorful finery. She sighed wistfully. Was she tiring of the game?

She could not complain about her accommodations in Shafik's opulent residence. A suite no less. It was something to be admired, if shared, she thought, with someone of your own choosing. She had cringed at Shafik's suggestion that she share it with Spencer Medwal; the old Arab had clearly assumed she was his nephew's concubine.

Carrie Willis knew Medwal's uncle had voiced a private displeasure with her behavior. Medwal had explained to her that Arab women knew their place and were therefore controllable. At least to a point.

Harbin and his gentlemen guests sat on a deck of the megayacht contemplating the fact that they were being monitored by the female spy on a distant hilltop. Harbin's crew had notified him two hours earlier that she was indeed attempting to listen to conversation aboard the yacht. They had assured him that she wouldn't be able to pick up much. Suddenly, the portable phone that Harbin kept in his jacket pocket rang.

"Reuven, Sheikh Shafik is on the ship-to-shore and wishes to speak with you. I have him on hold," Ari announced breathlessly.

"Put him through, Ari." He eyed Chelsea seated across from him. "Salaam, Sheikh Shafik. To what do I owe this call? Have we met before?"

"Shalom, Colonel Harbin. A thousand pardons for the late hour. I have just discovered that we share something in common and, being that we are both anchored here in Mykonos, I thought we might meet to discuss it."

"Really, and what might that be?"

There was a pause and the Arab began, "By chance I received the latest video tape of newly launched private yachts of fifty meters or more in length. To my surprise, I recognized your *Sea Temple III* from the video."

"Really. That's very interesting. And was your vessel also featured in the video?"

"Yes, it certainly was. The *Luxor Princess*—all seventy meters of it. I would like to extend to you an invitation to come aboard for a tour of my fair vessel."

"I'm sorry, but I must decline. I have guests aboard. Perhaps another time."

"My dear Colonel, now I must confess to you that there's a need for us to talk other than just our shared interest in yachts."

"You intrigue me. Again I ask, have we ever met?"

There was another brief silence on the other end of the phone line. "I leave that for you to judge when we meet? I will tell you that it is specifically in relation to my nephew that I would like to speak to you. His father, Colonel Abu, perished in a plane crash fifteen years ago. And only two years ago my sister joined him with Allah's blessing.

"I assure you that it is of great importance to indulge an old man such as myself. Tomorrow, can you honor me with your presence for lunch aboard the *Princess*?"

Suddenly it dawned on Harbin. *Colonel Abu had no children!* He quickly tried to mask his alarm from his guests. "If two o'clock tomorrow is agreeable, I will manage it. With your permission, one of my guests shall accompany me."

"Of course, of course, bring whomever you like. I am moored in the bay of Agioe Stefanos. Shall I have a power launch pick you up?"

"No, it's quite all right. I have my own."

"Quite right. Thank you for accepting. Until tomorrow . . ."

Harbin replaced the phone in his pocket and turned to Chelsea. "I'm asking you to accompany me to this meeting."

"What should I expect?"

"Most of it you already know. My undercover masquerade as Abu may have been discovered by Shafik after all of these years."

"And you don't need backup tomorrow?" asked Dave

"No. No, I don't think so. You see, I know Shafik to be a very honest man. If he says he has something he would like to discuss with me then I believe that talk is his only plan for tomorrow."

The four men rose. "The tour of Delos for tomorrow morning is still on?" asked Josh. Harbin nodded. After they said their good-nights, Harbin lingered by the railing. His eyes swept over the bay. The shimmering water reflected colorful splashes of light from the hotel.

A boy, a son! Why hadn't the Mossad warned him of the result of his undercover existence in Syria?

He turned on his heel. The past is the past.

11

All that remains of the ancient city of Delos are remnants of its cobblestone streets and a few stray stone walls. For centuries Delos was considered a holy site and so it was decreed that no births or deaths could take place on the island.

The guests of the *Sea Temple* and their host walked leisurely through the ancient ruins. The morning sun was pleasant and there was a wonderful stillness to the history-steeped place. Unlike his guests, who seemed mesmerized by the beauty of this sight, Harbin was quite aware that two kaffiyeh-clad men had been trailing them for the last hour. He glanced over at Chelsea and caught his eye. The other man too had spotted the men. Chelsea pointed at his watch to indicate that it was time to go to the meeting with Shafik.

Chelsea—aware of Josh's and Dave's unspoken objection to Chelsea accompanying Harbin to the meeting—attempted to lighten the mood. "Well, Dave, what do you make of ancient Greek civilization?"

Ward snorted. He gave the landscape and the tide of

tourists a casual study. "I remember a movie many years ago. There were two Americans being led through an ancient Turkish city. When their guide extolled the ruins of a great civilization that died centuries ago, one of the Americans couldn't resist remarking, 'What have they done lately?'"

"We're supposed to learn from the past," Chelsea answered, in all seriousness.

"So we can repeat it more efficiently?"

"My, aren't we cynical today."

"Why are you surprised?" Josh interjected. "You're the one walking into the lion's lair."

"With his eyes wide open, yet," Dave added.

Chelsea held up his hands defensively. "Okay, okay. What's with you guys! Why did you agree to accept Reuven's invitation?"

Dave held out a hand, palm side up, as if giving Josh the floor, who instantly accepted. "To cement a new partnership, not a new case." He paused for a second. "Besides, from what I've seen of Reuven—and his crew—he doesn't need any assistance from us."

Chelsea bit on the stem of his pipe. He silently agreed. Before retiring the previous evening Harbin had invited Chelsea to join him at 6:30 in the morning in his private exercise room. Chelsea had suspected Harbin wanted to take measure of his physical condition. Chelsea's pride wouldn't allow him to turn down the challenge. It took only a few short moments for him to recognize Harbin's superior physique. It was obvious the man had spent a lifetime in training.

Chelsea had said, "Reuven, I'm not in your class. Why did you ask me to join you here?" He remained on the exercise bike he had been pedaling. "Certainly not for the competition."

Harbin wiped his face with a towel. "I assure you that was not my intention. It's just that I had to know if I was expecting too much from you and the others."

Chelsea appeared amused. "Josh and I would be collecting Social Security if we gave up the security firm. Just what should you expect from us?" He waved a hand and shook off a reply. "You haven't made any real demands for us to consider. As yet, anyway."

Harbin sighed, then sat down in a director's chair. "Joe, believe me, if I'd known of Shafik's presence here beforehand the trip would have been cancelled. With or without guests."

"I have to be honest with you, Reuven. I am starting to wonder if you intentionally ignored the fact that you might be putting all of us in danger. Maybe you are denying this even to yourself."

Harbin studied Chelsea for a few heartbeats. "Joe, if the outcome of the meeting with Shafik is negative, I will cut our cruise short. Fair enough?"

Chelsea was caught in a dilemma. He had never run from a problem. But to have family and friends . . . It would be the Benefactor Alliance all over again.

He weighed a reply. *Why had Reuven invited him along to meet Shafik?* It dawned on him suddenly that Harbin was again testing him. Chelsea grunted and his speech was measured as he said, "Reuven, don't do this to me. You're throwing the gauntlet, expecting . . ."

"Please, Joe, let us just wait until we know the outcome of this meeting. Perhaps all of our problems will be clearer then. In the meantime, we should prepare for our visit to Santorini. I would rather not disappoint the ladies."

Before leaving for their meeting, Harbin went to Meg's suite to say good-bye. The two embraced for several moments before Meg broke the silence. "Reuven, I want you to know that I will not leave with the other women if it looks like there is a problem with these men."

"My darling, if there is a problem, the services of an attorney will probably not be what is needed."

Meg laughed. "Not even for a paternity suit?"

He gave her a sidelong glance and pursed his lips. "The boy is not mine. Abu's wife was very aggressive with me and . . . I'm afraid I succumbed to her. But I know that the boy is not mine."

"But the real Abu had no children when he left Syria . . . ?"

"Coincidence, nothing more."

"Would it be improper if I attended the meeting also?"

Harbin lifted his eyes. "Very much so. Even if I needed an attorney, I certainly would not bring you to the sheikh's residence."

"If not for the boy, why are you really going? The visit serves no purpose. Shafik can only mean to do you harm."

A slight smile removed a frown. "Well, I would like to see the *Luxor Princess*."

The white hull of the *Luxor Princess* reflected a proud image in the rippling waters of the bay. Chelsea could not escape a feeling of awe as he climbed the ladder onto the glorious yacht.

Two kaffiyeh-clad Arabs escorted the men into a forty-foot salon that was an Arabian fantasy. Lush woven carpets covered the entire expanse of the room. Several low tables intersperced throughout the room were surrounded by colorful pillows designed with an Egyptian motif. The walls were decorated with murals of ancient Egypt: images of great pyramids and interiors alive with hieroglyphics. The lone concession to contemporary design was a huge curving sofa at the forward end. Another conspicuous absence was the lack of a wet bar. Chelsea reminded himself that Muslims did not drink alcohol.

"Why the Egyptian motif?" asked Chelsea, whispering. "I thought the sheikh was Syrian." Harbin replied that the man was of Egyptian ancestry. Nothing more was said until they were led into a more private salon, which did have a bar.

Sheikh Shafik, seated behind a desk, stood up with great effort to greet his guests. "Shalom, gentlemen," he said, his voice much stronger than one would have guessed from his bent physique. "Thank you for honoring my invitation.

"Salaam." Harbin responded politely. Wasting no time he added, "You left me no choice; your speech was too cryptic."

The sheikh's eyes narrowed. He waited out a pause, then seated himself in a high-backed leather chair, easing himself into a comfortable position. He then waved them to armchairs. "To be candid, gentlemen, I'm now not quite certain of my earlier presumptions." He rubbed his gray beard.

"And those presumptions were . . ." Harbin prodded.

"I believed you were someone else. I can see now that I was harboring false hope." And then, shaking his head, he said, "Forgive my manners. Can I offer you refreshment?" He shook his head again. "I truly am getting old." He hit a button on a console at one side of the desk.

In seconds a servant appeared with fresh figs, olives, and a bowl of fruit. Chelsea observed everything with an impassive eye, wondering if the old Arab was putting on an act. Why all the to-do about meeting only to admit he might have been wrong to do so. The Arab appeared genuinely ill-at-ease. *Disappointment? Or an act worthy of an Oscar?*

Harbin allowed a few quiet moments to pass. "In your phone call you seemed to attach some importance to a Colonel Abu. Why would you believe I should be concerned with this man? Not to mention his son."

Shafik waved a hand, almost too casually. Chelsea thought it a practiced gesture. He couldn't read Harbin. "At the time I did think so. Now, meeting you, I realize my senses are failing me. I can only apologize for the inconvenience I caused both of you."

Harbin stood up, and Chelsea followed suit. *The Arab was beating around the bush,* he thought. *An explanation would come. This Arab didn't work without a game plan.*

Harbin nodded. "No apology necessary, but I would appreciate knowing why you did contact me. You promised a tour of your very elegant ship yet have done nothing in that respect." Chelsea held back a smile, observing the two men.

Shafik clasped his hands together as if in prayer. "It truly proves senility will become my downfall. It was your resemblance—however farfetched it may be—to my brother-in-law." He struggled to his feet and reached for his cane. "Come, I must show you something. It will explain far better than I can."

Harbin met Chelsea's eyes and pointed to his watch. Behind Shafik's back he held up five fingers—he would allow five minutes more. Chelsea nodded.

The private study was an eclectic mixture of contemporary and ancient design. The flooring was constructed to resemble stone blocks. A bleached wood desk and a high-backed beige leather chair were the sole furnishings. But they simply didn't go with the painted walls. Painted on all four walls, including the entry door and ceiling, were ancient Egyptian figures with jackal heads. The heads were all in profile with a single eye staring directly at the viewer. It struck Chelsea that the ancient artists might have been Picasso's mentors.

Shafik picked up a remote control that made a wall panel slide open to display a set of electronic equipment. At a click of a button a five-foot movie screen descended from the ceiling.

With more emotion than he intended, Shafik addressed his guests. "I will be greatly interested to know what conclusions you draw from this."

Harbin watched the screen carefully. The tape had caught him inspecting the *Sea Temple III* during its construction in a Dutch shipyard. Reuven found nothing significant in this footage. "I apologize but I don't know what I am supposed to be seeing."

Shafik rewound the tape for a few seconds to display Harbin walking across the yard to speak with the yacht's architect and engineer. "You don't see it?" he exclaimed questioningly. Harbin merely shrugged and looked at

Chelsea, who was also mystified. What was there to look for?

"Your stride, Mr. Harbin! Your unique stride!" he said emotionally. "You could have been Colonel Abu—or vice versa. I have seen no other man match that walk." He was leaning forward on his cane, as if expecting a confession.

Chelsea watched Harbin for a reaction but none was forthcoming. *The man was good! Damn good!*

Harbin suddenly smiled. "For this—Sheikh Shafik— you invited me here? To accuse me of . . . what?"

This brought a sigh from the old man. "Forgive me— please, forgive me. I have been observing you ever since you boarded. And all for naught. I had thought . . ." He waved his hand, a dismissal of his own thoughts.

Harbin got to his feet and checked his watch again. "I have another appointment. You must excuse me Sheikh Shafik, but before departing I would like to know what you were implying over the phone earlier. What would be my connection to this man? Why would you believe it would be of interest to me?"

"Someone other than Abu fathered my nephew. Quite candidly I was testing you. You were a colonel in the Israeli Air Force at the time and had disappeared during the time frame of Abu's reentry to his country." He stroked his beard. "And reappeared after my brother-in-law's second crash. It took considerable investigation to discover this, but I'm afraid it means nothing. Nothing was proved." He held out his hands, palms up. "I can only apologize for this egregious assumption. Nevertheless, I'm pleased we have met."

•   •   •

After the two men had left, Shafik returned to the lounge to phone his nephew, Spencer Medwal. The old Arab's iron will returned. "Listen to me carefully, my dear nephew. I have new instructions for you—and they are to be followed without question."

12

Following another splendid dinner at the Oasis Aziz the party decided to take a leisurely stroll through the serpentine alleyways of Little Venice. Harbin and Meg led the way. As they descended a winding alley they suddenly heard people shouting just around the bend. Harbin quickly ushered them into a side alley as a surge of people came running down the street.

The alley was a deadend and the wave of people rushed into it, pushing the group apart. Dave fought panic as he searched through the faces to find another member of his party. Suddenly, he spotted a man racing toward Chelsea with a long curved knife. Dave, his hands crushed to his sides by the rushing mob, couldn't reach out to warn him. Out of nowhere a woman emerged holding a strange object in her hand. In seconds she had disarmed the assailant. The man, though clearly in pain, uttered no more than a grunt. The crowd, now shoving in all directions, shouted at one another in a number of languages.

No matter how he tried Dave couldn't catch the

attention of any in his group. Frustrated, he watched as
the woman again pushed the object into the man. He
screamed and, with sudden superhuman strength, shoved
Chelsea aside and burst through the crowd. The woman
quickly moved away from Chelsea, using the strange
weapon on anyone who blocked her path. Whatever
the tool was it was extremely effective. Whoever she
touched screamed and jumped aside with a strange lack
of direction. "Jesus!" Dave muttered, realizing that no
one was aware of what had almost occurred.

Just as mysteriously as the wave of people had
appeared they began to disassemble. The group managed
to reconvene in a narrow corner of the alley. One look at
Dave's face and Mae knew something was dreadfully
wrong. In response to her look of concern he said only,
"I'm ready to call it a night."

"Agreed," said Harbin. "Back to the ship. This has
been enough excitement for one night. What on earth
could have stirred these people up?"

Chelsea wasn't fooled. It was obvious that both Harbin
and Dave knew something. *Was the disturbance a
diversion? If so, what did it accomplish?*

"Everything okay, Joe?" Ellie asked with concern.

He squeezed her hand but otherwise kept silent.

Once aboard ship, the ladies announced that they were
ready for bed. The gentlemen decided to have drinks on
the open afterdeck. For what seemed like a long while
the four men sat in silence.

Chelsea could tell that something was bugging Dave.
The man was just too fidgety. He caught his surreptitious
glances toward Reuven. Suddenly, Dave lit into Harbin.

"Reuven, we're in serious trouble and I appear to be

the only one aware of it." He stared at Chelsea. "I'm telling all of you that Joey is lucky to be alive."

Chelsea straightened. "What are you talking about?"

"Is this a gag?" Josh asked with a half-smile.

In a serious tone, Harbin said, "Let him speak."

Dave described the entire incident, finishing with, "If it weren't for that woman who came out of nowhere to protect you, you would be dead right now. It was the woman from the pier. She stopped a man from stabbing you in the back and then disappeared into the crowd."

Chelsea turned to Harbin. "Truthfully now, is she one of yours?"

Josh preempted his reply with a look of disbelief. "Dave, how could she have disrupted that crushing mob? I couldn't even move my arms from my side."

"A cattle prod," Harbin said quietly, and to Chelsea added, "She's not one of mine."

"How about Shafik?" Chelsea asked. "You think it possible that . . ."

Harbin took his phone from his jacket and immediately had Ari on the line. "I want to be on the move without delay. We've had an incident."

Chelsea stood at Harbin's side. "Santorini or homeward bound?"

The *Temple*'s engines flew into action and the ship began to move out of the harbor.

"In the lounge . . ." Harbin said, "where we can discuss it calmly. It will be your decision. For now, we're heading south to Santorini."

Only moments after the ship began to move, the women came running onto the deck dressed in their bathrobes. Meg went rushing up to Harbin. "Where are we going so late in the evening?"

When no one responded she said, "Okay, gentlemen, so we are in danger. We ladies have expected as much. Why don't you all just come clean now." And so the men finally explained the whole business to the ladies.

In conclusion, Harbin said quietly, "Santorini for one day, then we sail for Venice." His eyes searched Meg's. *They had made such a good start. Would he now lose any chance of having her?*

Meg stared at him, barely containing her anger. "Was this your original plan? Did you know what could happen here in Greece?" She didn't allow a reply. "To put us all in danger—and you, Joe . . . it doesn't bother you a damn! You remain composed in spite of everything!"

Chelsea waved aside Ellie's attempted intervention. "Meg, nobody planned this bizarre event. You can't believe for one moment that Reuven would have invited us to Greece knowing beforehand . . ."

Meg interrupted. "If you must know—yes, I do believe he would do so. I know his background, his history. I don't believe he has divorced himself entirely from his prior associations. Or commitments. Whatever they are! Whatever you others may decide, I wish to leave at the first opportunity."

Meg refused Harbin's hands when he reached for hers. Instead she stepped back and opened her handbag for a cigarette, which she didn't seem to have.

Suddenly Ellie spoke up. "Meg, we don't know who exactly it is that is in direct danger. It seems tonight that it is Joe that someone wanted to harm. I don't think it takes a genius to figure out that this must be connected to Suliman just as much as it is to Shafik."

Harbin turned to gauge Meg's reaction. She looked as if she were about to speak. "Yes?" he said softly.

She shook her head, changing her mind.

There was an air of morbidity as all left for their staterooms.

Meg sat alone on one of the waterproof lounges located on the top deck of the ship. She was sipping black coffee and picking at a hot croissant that had been brought to her by a ship's steward. She was watching Santorini's port as it awakened.

"Entrancing, isn't it?" Harbin said. She spun around, unaware that he had been standing behind her.

"Please, Meg, please speak to me," he said when she didn't reply.

She waited another few beats, then, sighing, said, "I'm sorry, Reuven. My behavior last evening was inexcusable. To blame you for what happened—or rather what almost happened—was not fair. Josh's and Joe's involvement in toppling the Benefactor Alliance may just now be having its repercussions."

Harbin took her hand. "We are safe now."

"How about you, Reuven? I wish I could read your mind. I simply can't see how you can continue the cruise under these circumstances. You don't even know exactly who your enemy is." She removed her hand from his.

Dismissing the subject, he said, "I'd like you to go ashore with me later. After breakfast, before the tourists crowd the streets."

"I personally don't understand it, but it seems everyone is happy to continue this cruise as if nothing has happened. Even the women. I suppose the fact that they are married to former men of the law may have something to do with it."

Still he wouldn't be engaged about the previous

evening's events. "So, we go ashore then. After breakfast."

By nine a.m. they were greeted by a stiff but warm breeze. A few feet away from where they stood a street led to a restaurant built on three levels; two of the lower ones seeming to cling precariously to the cliff wall. Canvas awnings fluttered in the breeze. Unable to contain themselves the women insisted on walking down into the restaurant just to catch the scenic water view spread out before them. The *Temple* appeared as a small boat from this vantage point. In the distance, green outer islands were visible.

The streets of Santorini—really no more than alleys— were black cobblestoned meandering walkways, accommodating visitors of all nations. Although neon-signed jewelry stores were in the majority, restaurants abounded in some sections.

As on Mykonos, Harbin and Meg led the way. He had suggested to the others that they stay close behind him, although he didn't believe they could get lost. He also warned against the pickpockets that thrived in crowds, no matter the country. The Greeks had a reputation for being a friendly people, he explained, but there were always bad apples.

When Harbin ushered Meg into a jewelry shop Josh pulled Chelsea aside. "What are we going to do about the Mykonos incident? Just forget it? Don't expect the mystery woman to be constantly at your side."

"And we don't have eyes in the backs of our heads," Dave added

"Jesus, I'm lost," Josh said. "Don't you have any ideas, Joe?"

Chelsea wiped a bead of sweat from his forehead. "The key has to be Medwal. We have no other connection. The woman has to be working for him. It can't be the Arab."

Dave made a face. "Didn't we discover Medwal was related to Shafik?"

"Okay, so why would she be friendly to us? Or me, in particular? Why would she risk her life for me?"

"Not to mention how she knew where we would be at all times," Josh interjected.

Dave shook his head, totally dismayed. "All we're doing is asking questions. We haven't yet guessed who wants you dead."

Chelsea said, "I sense Reuven knows something."

"Which means he definitely knows more than we do."

"Which also means it's about time we spoke to him without beating around the bush." Dave displayed a bit of anger. "ASAP, Joey. I'm beginning to suspect he believes we're too old to take care of ourselves."

Chelsea grinned. "No way, Dave. You're climbing the wrong tree. I believe he needs us as much as we need him. He is smart; and experienced in ways that we can't even imagine. I repeat, he needs us. Not only as collaborators, but as trusted friends."

"I hope so, Joe," Josh muttered quietly. "I'm beginning to feel my age and lose confidence."

Chelsea's arm went around his friend's shoulder. "Not yet, Josh. That's only true if you believe it. And I don't. I'm still breathing, which means I'm alive. And until the Man Upstairs . . ."

Dave applauded facetiously. "Joey, my boy, you're dreaming. You're no longer a rookie starting out on your first patrol. There's gonna come a time when you no longer can respond when you want to . . ."

"When and if my physical being can't react properly to my brain's demands, that's when I'll literally hang up my badge."

"Oh, brother!" Josh exclaimed, rolling his eyes. "Joe, stop with the rah-rah language and get us out of this mess."

Chelsea threw his hands up in surrender. "Okay, when we're back on the ship I'll ask Reuven for a confab." He stole a glance at the shop, then tapped Dave on the arm. "Do you realize Reuven is five years older than you and Josh?"

It drew a snicker. "So the old boy has discovered the Fountain of Youth. What do you want me to say? Like Josh, I know I'm getting older—and the games we're playing are drawing on my reserves. I don't know that there's much left. When I saw that blade come up in the Arab's hand, I almost wet my pants."

"But you didn't."

"Joey, I don't care to have my bladder put to the test again." He smiled suddenly, without reason, and all three laughed.

Chelsea broke the good mood with, "I remind you, we watch each other's backs from this point on."

"Don't you mean yours?" Dave said. "Whoever it is wants *you*."

"And I doubt there will be another woman sentinel in the area," Josh added.

All looked around, their eyes searching for any sign that would signal anything out of the ordinary. They saw nothing.

• • •

From behind a shop window advertising gold and silver at fair prices, a man stood, waiting, his eyes hidden behind dark glasses. He was a big man, broad-shouldered, seemingly very fit. He turned his head slightly without taking his eyes from the street. He whispered to a smaller man not quite behind him, whose eyes darted from one end of the alley to the other. Both men were dressed in denims and casual shirts. Both had a bulge at their backs beneath the shirts.

"How much longer?" the smaller man asked. "We were told they were on this route."

"Patience, Mustafa," the big man stated imperiously. "If you had been trained properly, it would have been finished earlier." He took a moment to glance at the smaller man. "You should have been better prepared."

Mustafa groaned and muttered something about not being informed of a female bodyguard.

The big man seemed uncomfortable smiling. "Yes, I heard all about the she-devil, with the strength of the biblical Samson." The remark wrought a scowl, but nothing further was said.

They waited.

"How much longer?" Josh asked Cindy. "The shops are becoming repetitious. Every other store is selling jewelry. How about stopping for a cold drink or something?" He pointed out a bustling restaurant in a nearby alley. The Aegean could be seen spread out before them, awash in the noonday sun. A stiff breeze swept the cliffside, washing away the malodorous air manufactured by the donkey trail that stood fifty yards to their left and below them.

"I'm with you, if no one else is," Mae Warren offered. She looked for Dave, who was lagging behind everyone.

Harbin looked behind them. At the top of an incline, at the intersection of the alleys, he could see two of his men. Sighing with relief he followed the women.

Chelsea hung back, waiting for Dave. He had noted Harbin's concern and had caught him spotting the two members of the ship's crew. It should have relieved Chelsea, but he felt his nerves tingling. Along with Josh and Dave he had been on alert for the entire stroll and had caught nothing. To Dave he said, "I see nothing, but sense . . ."

Dave stared at him. "You, too?"

"Did you catch the two men from Reuven's crew?"

"Christ! You're better than I am. I expected there would be, but I saw nothing of any consequence." He touched Chelsea's sleeve. "Which means I could have missed something more." He waved a hand in dismissal. "Anyway, how are you taking this excursion? To be truthful, Joey, I think I've finally found my limit." He reached into his shirt pocket and pulled out a small tin of antacid. "Occasionally I suffer from reflux. Could be an early sign of an ulcer. What do you think?"

"Why are you asking me? See a doctor."

Dave looked at him searchingly. Why was Chelsea so disgruntled? "Something bothering you, friend?"

Chelsea rubbed his face, then grabbed Dave's shoulder. "Sorry, Dave. I just don't like to discuss illnesses, mine or anyone else's."

Dave backed away. "Shit, Joey! You're not going to bring up the subject again of not growing old?"

"Hold on, Dave. In all fairness—you've never heard

me say I feared aging. What angered me was my forced retirement."

"Okay, for whatever difference it makes—what now? Why does it bother you when I mention I might have a health problem?"

For want of a reason Chelsea couldn't immediately reply.

"Okay," Dave began again. "Let's save it for another discussion—at another time, when we can sit down with Josh and catalogue all our handicaps arising with—like it or not—our age."

Chelsea's smile was forced. "You sure do know how to cheer up a fella. Where you been lately?"

"Right here, keeping an eye on your back. Don't forget it. I'm still good for something." He caught Chelsea's eye. "I'm not decrepit yet. Neither are you or Josh. So why worry before it's time? And if this is the way for us to enjoy life let's continue with the way we're going. Now, let's take a lesson from Harbin and join the others before they fear we're deserting them."

Chelsea nudged Dave's arm and prodded him down the incline. He spoke in a whisper. "There's two men on the spot where Harbin's men were minutes ago. I saw them earlier. Keep an eye open. It may be nothing, but . . ."

The women had ordered ice cream, the men soft drinks. They were seated at tables beneath a flapping awning. The view could only be described as awesome as they sat overlooking the vast sea in bright sunlight.

Chelsea and Dave divided their attention between studying the beautiful landscape and searching for the two men they had seen earlier. Neither could find anyone resembling either of them.

"I could have guessed wrong," Chelsea whispered to Dave.

"What are you looking for?" Ellie asked him. After thirty-five years of marriage his body language was no secret to her.

"Nothing in particular. Just being careful. To be honest, I'd be happier being on board the yacht."

From his other side Josh, having overheard him, whispered, "Joe, are we in danger?"

Chelsea shrugged. "I just like being careful, Josh. I say let's call it a day and get back. The women are probably tired anyway. We all must have walked at least three miles." Ellie lifted her chin with the remark, but remained silent.

As they got to their feet, Chelsea moved to pull Harbin aside. "I caught your two men, but they disappeared and then there were two others," he said.

"Describe them."

Harbin nodded with the description of the first two, but frowned at the other. "Recognize them?" Chelsea asked. He got a shake of the head.

Chelsea felt his insides roiling and a sudden surge of adrenaline. Why was Harbin hesitating? Was it possible he was having trouble coping? He tapped Harbin's shoulder with a fingertip. "What now, Reuven?" he asked. "Let's not wait for another incident."

Harbin held up a finger, indicating he was thinking on it.

"Reuven . . ." Chelsea prodded impatiently. Meg watched them, then glanced at Ellie beside her. Aware of the men's strange manner, Ellie shook her head, the meaning clear: Don't interrupt them.

Harbin spoke almost in a whisper. He tossed a glance

to the zigzagging concrete stairway, approximately twenty yards below and fifty yards to their right. The foot traffic was busy with mostly teenagers and college students. Some elderly people rode the backs of the mule trains.

By this time Josh and the others were standing, aware something in their present itinerary was being changed. Josh held out his hands, palms up, questioning. Dave said nothing, but scanned the area with a brooding look. He took a deep draw on his soft drink and moved out from the table.

Harbin said, "We take the stone steps, the cable car is too far away. And . . ." he hesitated to make a strong point, "no mules. We walk it all the way down. Alongside the mules, if possible. They will make excellent cover." As all got ready to leave he delayed them. "I remind you that the steps can be very slippery from mule dung, so don't move too quickly."

Chelsea caught Josh. "Are you going to have trouble? You didn't bring your cane."

Josh made a face. "I didn't think it would be necessary. But don't worry, I won't hold up anybody."

Harbin touched his arm. "Yes, you will, in a way. You'll be setting the pace by leading us. Don't be embarrassed if you have to hang on to a mule strap. You might find it useful. Just don't get in back of them."

The cobblestone alleys constantly dipped and rose, making for tiring strolling. Since the walks were crowded, strolling was necessary. They finally reached the steps and hesitantly started down. Their noses twitched from the odors of the animals and their droppings. Harbin warned all to be careful of teenagers running wild on the steps. With that final instruction they were on their way.

Harbin excused himself to Meg saying he would be

taking up the rear. She placed a hand on the stone railing for support. Looking down, the steps seemed endless. Until the past few moments she felt relaxed, beginning to enjoy their travels once again. Now, the fear returned, as they constantly checked behind them to see if they were being trailed.

She returned to the thought she had shut from her conscious mind earlier: This was Reuven Harbin's life. And he would live it his own way, with or without anyone's permission.

"Are you okay?" Ellie, a step behind, now pulled alongside her. "Your shoulders are tensing. I can see it. Don't let the men's game-playing get to you. It's how they live . . . to enjoy . . ." She laughed between deep breaths. ". . . their retirement."

"And you can laugh it off so easily?"

"I've been on to them for decades. Why stop now?"

Meg appeared frustrated. "But, El, it's not a game!"

"I know, but I have to keep pretending. As you will have to, if you expect to . . ." She left it unfinished.

Meg didn't respond. Couldn't.

Suddenly something hit the stone wall beside them. "Shit!" Chelsea exploded. "A rifle with a silencer." He and Harbin both squatted at the side of a mule, hiding from the sniper.

"No," Harbin retorted. "A rifle would draw an audience. This man has to be using something special."

"Could he be copying our style? Following at the side of a mule?"

Harbin was searching for his men. If they were close he couldn't detect their presence.

"Are you carrying?" Chelsea asked, studying two different donkey trains a few yards behind them. They were in shooting range and could possibly be covering someone, but he couldn't pinpoint anyone who would draw suspicion. It was like a moving stairway with everyone in constant motion.

"No, but I have two men somewhere that are."

Chelsea peered down the steep stairway. Other than Dave two steps ahead of him no one was aware of what had happened—and it was just as well, he decided. He knew now for certain that he was the target.

About halfway down the staircase Dave fell back to join Chelsea. "You saw nothing, Joey? You should have been able to judge direction."

Chelsea blew out a deep breath. "No way. Too many people to single out."

"So! What then? We wait for the next shot? Jesus, Joey! It's still a long way down yet." He jerked his head toward Harbin, a mere five yards back. "What does he have to say?"

"Nothing. I never know what he's thinking—or planning until after the fact."

"Christ! I thought you and he were working together." Ward couldn't contain a groan.

"I trust him, Dave."

"Shit! I trust you. But where's it getting us right now? And, in particular, you? You're the target—for whatever the reason. Right now, I can't even tell the good guys from the bad guys."

Harbin hissed loud enough to catch Chelsea's attention. His finger pointed at a donkey three trains ahead of them, ascending. An old man pulled at a rope attached to a halter on the lead donkey. At the side of the third animal the denim-clad legs of a man were visible, his upper body bent so that he would be unseen by their party. Harbin hissed again, held up two fingers and pointed again. Another pair of jeans was evident behind a donkey ten yards beyond the first one.

Perspiration fell from Chelsea's forehead. He felt rather than saw Harbin's crouching figure leap across alley. Two people fell as he flew down the steps. Chelsea could wait no longer. To Dave's astonishment, the former captain ducked between two of the mules. The startled mules started braying loudly and the old man leading the train cried out in anger. Taking no heed Chelsea bulled his way past three bewildered people, his target the second pair of jeans.

A large dark-complexioned man lifted his head above the rump of the animal to check out the sudden disturbance, a 9mm Beretta with silencer hanging at his side. He didn't see Harbin until it was too late. A karate chop to the back of the neck dropped the big man to his knees. Shouts of confusion fell across the steps, stopping all progress on the stairway. Witnesses nearby shouted their indignation, but no one made any effort to stop the action. The short man Chelsea grabbed tore free from his grasp and burst through the circle of gawkers, racing up the steps, pushing aside anyone else in his path.

Chelsea joined Harbin in time to see him shove the Beretta under his shirt and into the back of his belt. While the curious onlookers stood by, Harbin slapped the man's face once, then again. Harbin spoke to him in Arabic. The man acted confused, with no comprehension whatsoever. The crowd surrounding them had multiplied, blocking all traffic. Shouts of derision and complaint came from both directions, wanting to know why the man had been knocked down. Harbin spoke hurriedly to the dark man who was now sneering at him. He pulled the man to his feet and shoved him away disgustedly. The man gaped for a second, but needed no added instruction. He erupted into movement and ran off instantly, taking the wide steps two at a time. Spying Chelsea and Ward, Harbin indicated he was finished and that they should continue their descent without further delay.

The women were stunned. The reflexes that the two men had displayed were extraordinary when one considered their ages. When Meg looked for comment from Ellie there was none forthcoming. Ellie knew her husband's limitations better than anyone. His back, if not out or going stiff, would need a massaging this evening. As for Harbin, it was his problem. But having observed much of his incredible accomplishment she doubted he needed consolation from anyone. In any case, she thought, somewhat angrily, Joe had no right to emulate their host regardless of the circumstances.

When Chelsea and Dave both confronted Harbin he waved them onward like a wagon master, as if expecting more trouble from behind. Harbin was concerned with the welfare of his two men. He felt an urge to retrace his steps; Dani and Egon were like family and he wanted to search for them. But he also recognized that he had a responsibility to return his guests to the ship safely.

Meg looked for him to return to her side, but Harbin still carried the rear. Joe and Dave accompanied him.

The *Sea Temple* had been moved to the end of the pier, saving its guests a long walk. Its engines were idling, and the yacht gave the appearance of being eager for departure.

Once on board Harbin quickly excused himself to

confer with Ari. Chelsea didn't mind his absence. He wished to privately discuss with Dave and Josh what proper procedure should be for them. "Do we offer him assistance in finding his missing men?" Chelsea asked. "He won't leave without making an effort . . ."

Josh answered, "Whatever for? Haven't you taken a good look at his crew?"

"Nevertheless . . ."

"What's with you guys?" Dave threw in. "What can we do that would improve on Reuven's methods?" He waved a hand emotionally. "Haven't you learned any-thing in the past few hours? I'll give odds those kami-kaze Arabs are still hanging around, just waiting for another opportunity."

"Kamikaze?" Josh blustered. "What the hell are you talking about!"

Chelsea waved a calming hand. "It's what Reuven believes. But I don't.

They took off at the first chance. If their lives were devoted to a cause why didn't they stay to finish the job?"

Dave waved his hands in disgust. "Joey, you're not thinking. You don't really believe they would return to their leader and confess failure, do you? If you do, then you don't know the terrorist mentality. Reuven is correct in his assumptions. He knows them a lot better than we do. We'd be fools not to trust his judgment in this matter."

"Are you suggesting we sit on our hands and do nothing unless asked?" Chelsea said, almost too quietly.

"Why not?" Josh exclaimed. "This is almost humili-ating. In no way can we compete with him or his younger crew."

Dave said, "Joey, when it's time for our expertise we'll

know how to jump in. What's your problem? Are you that eager for action?"

Chelsea gaped, then frowned. *Was he? Had he been seduced by the sudden action? Tired or not, he couldn't dismiss the exhilaration he had felt chasing that man.* He took a deep breath, then eased it out slowly. "Okay," he said finally. "Let's find out just what Reuven's planning."

"Yeah," Josh muttered. "And you better come up with something to satisfy Ellie. I don't think she's exactly applauding your performance today."

Dave smiled. "Did you see Meg? If Reuven's hoping to establish a close relationship with her, he's going to have a big problem."

Harbin was speaking to Ari. "If the Coast Guard station insists on knowing our next port of call, tell them Poros. Which was our original destination anyway."

"But we continue west, then north in the Ionian Sea. No tie-up until Corfu?"

Harbin shrugged. "We play it by ear. If the sea gets too rough for our guests we can decide on a closer port."

"Reuven, how long do we wait for Rebecca and Levi? We need a time limit."

"Everyone is safe while on board. Lunch will be set up on the afterdeck lounge, but dinner this evening will be served in the main dining room. Meanwhile I want the *Temple* idling about a thousand yards offshore. We depart at midnight unless either Levi or Rebecca calls in earlier."

Ari was about to add a thought, but changed his mind. Instead he spoke to his pilot who had remained silent at the helm. "Jakov, you heard the orders. Please follow through. Turn to port ten degrees, and no more than five knots speed." He got a nod from the tall, taciturn man but the look on his face was sour. The idea they might have to abandon part of the crew didn't sit well with him.

Rebecca's long blonde hair was tied back in a ponytail. A baseball cap sat on her head and dark sunglasses covered her bright blue eyes. She had recently passed her thirtieth birthday and looked younger in her short girlish skirt and multicolored blouse. Levi, about two years her junior and eight inches taller than her five-four, wore blue denims with Nike sneakers and a thin jacket covering a Michael Jordan T-shirt. A baseball cap worn backward completed his outfit. Attached to the shoulder of his jacket was an almost invisible walkie-talkie that could span a ten-mile area. After climbing the stone stairway, they scanned each alleyway suggested by Harbin. She shook her head at Levi, without expressing her thoughts. She was looking for signs of a possible scuffle, anything out of the ordinary. If either man had been assaulted a clue would have been left behind.

It was Levi who caught it. About fifteen feet from the intersection there was a flower stall full of colorful bouquets. On the ground near it lay a yellow daisy. At first glance it was just another flower broken loose from a bouquet, but the stem was too shiny to be real. It was the stem glinting on the metal that had caught his attention. He asked Rebecca to focus on it with her binoculars.

Rebecca nodded, her face grim, her lips a tight line. They walked slowly toward the flower stall.

A middle-aged woman was tending to the flower stall. She spoke broken English, holding up a bouquet. Rebecca shook her head and explained the colors weren't right; too many yellows. Perhaps she had more reds in the rear of the shop, something that could be added to one of the bouquets. When she moved farther inside the woman tried to stop her. "No! No go there. There is nothing but empty sacks."

So. The woman did speak some English—and she appeared frightened. While the woman tried to detain Rebecca, Levi slid past her and pushed behind a curtain.

Developing a sudden strength the older woman shoved Rebecca aside and darted past her. In seconds she was in the alley and lost amidst the busy strollers.

Rebecca followed Levi behind the curtain. In a corner, behind empty straw baskets, Dani and Egon sat on the ground, their legs and hands tied, their lips covered with tape. In seconds Levi had them untied. Both Dani and Egon started muttering epithets in Hebrew when freed. Levi remarked, "She must be a tough old woman to do this."

Dani sputtered, more embarrassed than angered, "We were drugged by flowered darts. Two men, Arabs I'd guess. I didn't get that good a look at them. The darts were pushed rather than shot into us."

Rebecca displayed the disguised dart. "This is it," she said, before wrapping it in a piece of burlap. "It's the only one I could find."

Levi spoke to the two men rubbing their faces. "Don't bother complaining. Just thank God we found you. Once dark you would have been taken who knows where."

Egon sniffed disdainfully. "Never mind thanking God. How do I explain this to Reuven? Like total amateurs we were caught. We don't even remember how they got us in here."

Levi tilted his head to speak into his walkie-talkie. His

code was understood in seconds. "Have the launch ready
for pickup. Everything A-OK. Will hold off explanation.
Signing off."

Once the others were all resting in their cabins, Chelsea
decided to search out Harbin. As he made his way toward
Reuven's office, he noticed that the door was ajar.
Chelsea thought it odd, but prepared to knock. A voice
from within made him hesitate.

It was Harbin talking to someone. Something in the
timbre of his voice caused Chelsea to step back and wait.
Harbin could be clearly heard. Though he felt guilty for
eavesdropping, Chelsea froze in position.

Inside, Harbin was plaintively addressing his late
wife's portrait. "Is my pursuit of Meg an injustice to
her?" he asked reverently. "Am I in search of her—or
you? I don't really know. When I look at her, I no longer
know who I want. Anya, do I want her for herself or
because she reminds me of you?"

There was a long silence; white noise surrounded
Chelsea and he feared making a sound. He took a deep
breath, but didn't dare release it. He then heard, "Anya,
you always accepted the personal hardships wrought by
my clandestine acts of patriotism. Yet, never once did I
know whether you condoned or condemned me for it.
And now, as then, you're not going to interfere or advise
me, are you? It is again for *me* to make the decision, *not
you*."

Chelsea, reminded of the portrait, could almost visualize the eyes of the late Anya following her husband as
he paced the floor.

Whatever else was to be said in the one-way conversation was halted by a fax machine in operation. Chelsea

finally released a deep breath and chanced walking away on tiptoes. The thick carpet helped. Increasing his stride he left the area, postponing the meeting he had sought with Harbin. He wondered whether he should tell any of this to anyone else.

Shortly before dinner the group assembled for a meeting at Harbin's request. A single glance told Harbin Meg was still annoyed with him. It provoked a mild ache in his chest that he couldn't get rid of. It had started when she had first rejected his behavior on the Santorini stairway. *She is not Anya!* Harbin's face remained impassive, no matter his thoughts. He started to address his audience. "Because of a particular problem—"

He halted abruptly, suddenly aware of the sounds of an approaching helicopter. He checked his watch while walking toward the starboard window. Three hours out of Santorini. A single glance and he guessed from the chopper's direction it had most likely come from Athens. He, along with the others, watched it circle the yacht twice before flying off in the direction from which it had come. In the semi-darkness identification was impossible.

Harbin went to the nearest phone and got Ari. "Did you try contacting the chopper?" Harbin asked. He learned the attempt was made, but all Ari had received was silence. "Keep trying, Ari . . . But this forces a necessary alteration in our plans once more." He watched the sky until the helicopter disappeared from sight. He then walked back to his previous position and waited for the others to return to their seats.

This time he noted Meg studying him. The look she wore said, "What is he up to now?" He almost smiled;

she was at least observing him again. Josh, glancing from one to the other, imperceptibly shook his head.

Harbin caught their attention. "Before the interruption I was about to offer you a new cruise plan, but . . . with the appearance of an unwanted audience, I'm about to make a request. As stated earlier I will allow you to make the final decision, providing I consider it safe."

Meg leaned forward from the sofa. "Which earlier plan? Flying out of Corfu—or continuing our cruise to Venice?"

Harbin deliberated for only a moment. "First off I must explain what you probably have already recognized. It is for Joe that we are going through these trials." Ellie bit her lip, was about to intervene, but Chelsea, chewing on a pipe stem, caught her eye and held a finger to his lips. Although perturbed, she settled back into the sofa.

Harbin continued. "Whoever is behind this—and why—has been open for speculation. But now it seems clear that it is Joe that is being targeted. In light of this, I would ask that you forgo the cruise after Corfu, and accept my offer of being my guests at Harbin's Haven."

The women started asking questions at once. "What exactly is Harbin's Haven?"

Harbin explained that it was a thirty-acre private island in the British Virgin Islands with its own desalinization plant and that all buildings there were outfitted with the latest modern conveniences. The mansion atop a two-hundred-foot rise consisted of twenty rooms and could accommodate all without any problems. "I would agree," Harbin said, "that Venice would be much more exciting than my private escape, but in no way as relaxing."

Ellie pushed herself to her feet. "Why would Joe be any safer there than anywhere else?"

Harbin rubbed the lobe of his ear and glanced at Chelsea. A message silently passed from one to the other. Chelsea nodded with full comprehension. It was something he himself had thought of and then dismissed. He nodded again, indicating that Harbin had his permission to continue.

"Ellie," Harbin began again, "I apologize to you—all of you—for not expressing myself more clearly. The invitation was confined to the women present, not the men."

This brought all the women to their feet. Meg took the forefront. "For what purpose? What do you expect to accomplish by this?"

Ellie jumped in. "No way am I leaving without Joe. We stay together."

Cindy and Mae just stared at their men without uttering a sound. Josh's lips tightened. *Where was Harbin going with this?*

Harbin glanced at Chelsea but addressed the women. "I'll have to have your final decision in the next few hours."

Meg stepped forward to confront him. "You didn't answer my question. Why do you want to do this? So you men can play macho games?"

"We must learn the source of Joe's dilemma. When and if we discover the source perhaps we can call for a truce and demand a meeting. Until then Joe will be constantly hounded. And it's better you ladies don't get involved. A lesson should have been learned from the Alliance affair. Without the responsibility of their wives'

presence the men can better cope with the danger lying in
wait for Joe."

Meg said, "Reuven, I don't want to leave . . . the
yacht . . . as yet."

Harbin sharpened his look. Was she about to say,
'leave you'? His eyes lifted to observe Ellie and the
others. Did they catch it—or was it simply wishful
thinking on his part? To Chelsea he said, "Joe, what
about it? It's your call. Do the women stay or leave? You
know my position. I promise to accept whatever all of
you decide."

Chelsea sighed and glanced questioningly at Josh and
Dave. In truth he was passing the buck. Surprisingly,
they said nothing. They would accept his decision,
guessing what it would be. He turned his gaze upon Ellie.
Would she? Cindy and Mae would go along with her.
Meg—by her last statement—wanted to stay aboard
indefinitely. Her reason was a real question mark.

Chelsea came forward. "Ellie, we're not in a position
to call the police. Although it's not been finally determined, we suspect a former member of the Alliance to
be the aggressor. For one last time, I ask you to play the
role of the policeman's wife and wait for me at home.
We're to work on an unfinished job and must do it in
the accustomed manner: alone, and knowing our families
are safe."

For at least ten seconds no one spoke. Mae finally
broke the oppressive silence. "Well, Joe . . . you've
done it again. When did I hear that speech before?"

"Now, Mae . . ." Dave admonished lightly. "You
know we must follow through. It will never end otherwise."

Her reply was a muttered, "Bloody fool!"

Harbin moved away, allowing them privacy. Meg made a gesture as if to follow him. He nodded at the door to the afterdeck.

Chelsea went to Ellie's side with the realization that she truly thought it too incredulous that her husband, here in Greece of all places, should be in dire trouble. It was all an excuse to her—to help Reuven Harbin, who was involved with some Arab.

Benefactor Alliance indeed! Ellie thought glumly. *The Alliance was a dead issue, it no longer existed. Why do they persist on playing it up? According to Dave's account, a strange woman had prevented someone from harming Joe. Really! And the commotion on that malodorous stairway? It was never fully explained by anyone. What's more, the attitudes of Cindy and Meg implied they believe as I do. The men are playing their security game for Reuven Harbin's benefit, to aid him in solving a problem with an old Arab.*

"Okay, Joe," she said, "I'll go along, as I always have. You're retired . . . but you're not retired. I only want to know for how long this time. How do I adapt to being on a vacation isle without you? And for how long? Four or five days—or longer?"

Chelsea looked for Harbin but he wasn't in the vicinity. Neither was Meg. "It's up to Reuven. We're playing on his field." He took her hand. "Nevertheless, Ellie, thanks for playing it cool. And on that note I'm about to ask a favor. Please talk Meg into leaving with you. She's showing intentions of staying."

Ellie looked askance. "Joe, Meg knows her own mind. Let her live her life as she wishes. You should ask Josh or Cindy for the favor, not me. More to the point, ask Meg herself."

Chelsea stepped back. "Are you kidding? Only family can interfere in this. Besides, affairs of the heart are not my specialty."

"Then why bother at all, Joe? Let her be. Both she and Reuven have been around long enough to be aware of their own problems—without help from either of us."

It was decided. They would continue to Corfu. Harbin would charter a plane to fly them to Milan, and from there they would return to the States and then on to the British Virgin Islands. Meg was staying with Harbin, no explanation offered.

Four of Harbin's crew, including Rebecca, would accompany the three women on the trip to Harbin's Haven. Ari would return the *Sea Temple III* to its home base in the British Virgin Islands. Harbin told the others that the still unsold *Sea Temple II*, a 127-foot yawl, was still based in the Caribbean for their pleasure. He said finally that they would most likely meet again in seven days.

13

In the airport on Corfu, the good-byes were emotional despite the assurance that it would be only a week until they were all together again. Meg insisted that they wait until the plane departed safely. The men gave her no argument.

Ellie had offered Meg a single piece of advice: "Step carefully. You never know what's underfoot."

Cindy merely said, "I hope you know what you're doing."

Mae, not to be left out, said, "Whatever you do, just don't get hurt." The platitudes seemed necessary.

The ride in the taxi back to the yacht was spent in silence. No one bothered watching the so-called scenery, most of which consisted only of commercial buildings and hotels. Corfu was an island designed for tourists and it had growing pains but, like everywhere else, it also had its good points.

Harbin, sitting beside Meg, gave her a glance. Her eyes gazed inwardly, engaged with personal thoughts. She had surprised him, asking permission to stay behind.

In recent years he had not had experience with the opposite sex. Wealth and good looks had made him an eligible bachelor, and therefore a target for single eager females. But he remained withdrawn. Faithful to his late wife's memory he managed to stay clear of entanglements. A commitment to anyone other than a business partner was the last thing he desired.

Although extremely attracted to Meg he still wasn't certain why. He had been out of circulation too long. He felt that he had to spend time with her to learn what his wants were.

"Are you going to be all right?" he finally asked her.

She nodded, avoiding his eyes. "Yes . . . I'll be fine—if you help me."

Harbin took her hand without saying anything, but wondered if anyone else had heard her. It was then that he realized she was suffering the same quandary he was. He sighed gently, wondering what the proper conduct for—

A loud booming sound erupted from the front end of the taxi as it exited a ramp that led onto a traffic-laden concrete pier. It seemed that the right front tire was blown. The driver cursed as he fought the steering wheel.

Harbin shouted for all to stay in their seats. Leaping to the side door he threw it open as the car slowed. Chelsea, unable to contain himself, jumped after him.

Harbin was examining the front tire as Chelsea looked over his shoulder.

Chelsea watched for only a moment, then looked back across the way, past the street from where they had entered the ramp. About a hundred yards from his position there was a line of two- and three-story nondescript white buildings facing the bay entrance. His eyes scanned rooftops from one end of the block to the other, but he spotted nothing out of the ordinary.

By this time a crowd of gawkers had gathered. Harbin pulled his phone out of his pocket and dialed Ari on board the *Temple*. "Are we prepared for immediate departure?" The *Temple*'s fuel and water tanks had been topped off and provisions were still plentiful, he was told.

During the hundred-yard walk back to the yacht Meg insisted on knowing what Harbin suspected. "It was no blowout. Someone used a high-powered rifle with a silencer attachment."

Although her face paled Meg made no comment.

Chelsea was answering Josh's and Dave's questions. "Yes, I'm sure. It was a rifle shot. That tire didn't blow out; it was shot out."

Back at the yacht, Harbin consulted Ari as Chelsea and Meg stood by. Josh and Dave had excused themselves immediately upon their return. The two men had appeared quite flustered. Chelsea, not wanting to interfere with Ari and Harbin's planning, began to observe Meg. In his former line of work, Chelsea had become extremely good at reading facial expressions. At the moment he read Meg's expression as a mixture of anxiety and something he could not quite fathom. Speculating, he decided she was torn between differing inclinations. He noted the way she would follow the shoreline landscape sliding by, then steal a glance at Harbin.

Chelsea touched her elbow gently. "Meg, if you're having a problem, I'm a good listener."

She was quiet for a moment, frowning, as if contemplating a momentous decision. "Thanks, Joe. Not necessary. If ever . . ."

Whatever she was about to say was cut short by Harbin. He was looking upon the two of them with deep concern. Clearly, he felt responsible for the group. "I'm trying to contact Shafik. I believe he's the key behind everything. Which way he leans—good or evil—is something we have yet to discover." Chelsea was aware that Harbin was searching Meg's face, searching for some kind of assurance.

"Are either of you hungry?" Harbin asked, abruptly switching subjects. "It's past noon."

"Okay, Chelsea said. "If there's nothing else of immediate urgency I can manage a sandwich and coffee. I'll be up on the top deck." He turned to leave but then stopped when he heard the fax machine start up.

It was a fax from Shafik. He was notifying Harbin that he was aboard his yacht heading east. He was planning to bypass southern Greece and round the tip of Italy's boot and then follow the coast north to Nice. If agreeable, he suggested that he could alter his course and meet with Harbin at Zakinthos, an island in the Ionian. Harbin gazed at Chelsea and nodded to Ari. "In twenty-four hours."

Meg, aware that Chelsea wished to speak with Harbin privately, said, "I'll wait on the top deck." She eyed Harbin for a second, then left.

Chelsea turned on Harbin. "What now? Do we get together on what questions we'll have ready for him? And while we're at it, why Zakinthos? He must have a good reason for the choice."

"Zakinthos? Since the 1953 earthquake, it has been a growing resort island. It's far from a deserted island."

Chelsea's look displayed doubts. "Do you have arma-
ments aboard, Reuven? I don't want to regret having this
meeting."

"Name your favorite weapon."

Chelsea's eyebrows lifted. "You're giving me a choice?"

Harbin caught Ari's attention. "Page Ward and Novick
and tell them to go straight to my private study."

"You have a .38 police special?" Chelsea asked. When
he got a nod he added, "How about a Beretta 9mm—or
a Glock 10mm that carries a fifteen-bullet cartridge?"
Naming the small-arms equipment was merely a jest; he
didn't really expect the information that was forthcoming.

"All that—and more. Let's go."

Chelsea, taken aback for a second, reached into his
shirt pocket for his tobacco pouch. Harbin waved a no-no
finger. "Not even I can smoke in my private study."

14

The *Sea Temple III* and the *Luxor Princess* were anchored in a cove not far from the lighthouse a few kilometers west of Keri, one of the southernmost towns on Zakinthos. The two boats were separated by a hundred yards of calm water. Shafik was invited aboard the *Temple*, a polite reciprocation for Chelsea and Harbin's visit to his yacht. Shafik and three of his men were escorted to the main lounge where Chelsea, Josh, and Dave waited. Dishes of fresh dates and figs were set out on low tables.

Harbin explained to Meg that Shafik had requested that no women attend their meeting. She decided to stay out of their way on the top deck of the yacht, from where she could view the thick vineyards and fields of olive trees. With the aid of binoculars she could clearly pick out farm workers shading their eyes from the sun as they studied the two large private vessels that rested in a cove that had no beaches to draw them there.

After introductions were made, Harbin offered Turkish coffee and sweet cakes. Shafik politely accepted, as did his entourage. Chelsea and his group found the honeyed refreshments too sweet.

After waiting out a polite few minutes, Harbin bluntly opened the discussion with, "Do you have a woman working for you?"

The old Arab winced. Whether from the query or the discomfort of his physical handicap, Harbin wasn't certain. Neither was Chelsea, who watched closely with a wary eye, wondering just how much credence Harbin would place in this man's reply.

The old Arab concentrated on discarding a pitted date into a porcelain dish before speaking. "Please explain. I have a number of women in my employ. In what respect do you mean 'employed'?"

"Shafik, I will be blunt and save a lot of time." He told him of the attempt on Chelsea's life when in Mykonos and the mystery woman's role in it.

Shafik nodded, his old eyes sparking beneath his sunglasses. He spoke slowly. "I wish I could understand what my old senses are feeling. I've finally accepted that you don't resemble Colonel Abu, yet . . ." He shrugged suddenly, as if ridding himself of an unwanted burden.

"The woman, Shafik . . . ?" Harbin prodded.

The Arab nodded. "Yes, she is temporarily in my employ. But, of this incident, I know nothing."

Chelsea asked, "If not you, then who gave orders for her to watch over me? And why?" He paused for a heartbeat. "Could it come from your nephew Spencer Medwal?"

The Arab eyed Chelsea. "You intimate that I cither want to save or eliminate you. Why would I do either? As for my nephew . . ." He shrugged. "You would have to ask him."

Harbin leaned back. Shafik was a cool one. Why wouldn't he admit that his own employees would never moonlight on the job?

"All right," Chelsea said, "leaving that for a moment, why would anyone attempt to kill our entire party?" Shafik removed his sunglasses; his dark eyes displayed a great curiosity.

"You must elaborate," he said almost too quietly, as if fearful of what he might learn.

Harbin told of the incident that took place on Corfu. Shafik, his old eyes suddenly glaring, turned to speak with a member of his crew. He spoke in Arabic.

Harbin smiled and waited for him to finish. "Shafik, you should be aware that I speak your language." The old man rubbed his cheek. Harbin continued. "There's no need for us to beat about the bush. You did have the woman watching us—or my friend Chelsea. At least on Mykonos. You appear now to be a friend. I must ask why."

The man was slow to reply. "Colonel Abu. That's why. I still don't understand my own reasons. She was to protect *you,* above all the others. For reasons, as I say, I simply can't comprehend. You state someone went after Mr. Chelsea. I can only assume that he has an enemy that stalked him there."

Harbin nodded, knowing he had to be extremely careful with his questioning. He assumed a look of compassion. "Shafik, you were close to Colonel Abu."

"Except for the three months after his return from imprisonment he and I were like blood brothers, not brothers-in-law."

"You have told me nothing," Harbin said solemnly. "Am I to fear someone from my past?"

The Arab's lips twisted in reflective thought. "Your past? No. Not any longer." He made an odd gesture, difficult to decipher. Harbin alone recognized it as his custom when he wished to conclude discussion. The tiredness was visible in the old man's lined face. Harbin almost smiled; he'd had his answer. The old man had displayed it in his mannerisms. Harbin's identity as Colonel Abu was an unfathomable puzzle to the Arab.

Shafik replaced his sunglasses before struggling to his feet. None of his followers dared offend him by offering assistance. "Now, if you will excuse me, I have to leave. My trip to Nice has been delayed too long. I bid you a safe voyage with your new ship. Salaam." He went through the motions of hand to heart and brow. Harbin reciprocated.

Seafood was being served at a table set up on the uppermost deck of the ship. A canvas windscreen had been erected to protect all from a fifteen-knot sea breeze.

Breaking apart a lobster claw Dave remarked, "Reuven, you do know how to live. I can almost forget that we are most likely in great danger. That cagey Arab gave you nothing but cryptic warnings despite his assertions that you have nothing to fear from your past. Do you truly believe him?"

"And what of the mystery woman?" Josh interjected. "Could we have missed something?"

Chelsea nodded at a small tape recorder at one end of the table. "Play it again. It's possible we overlooked something."

The tape machine, although no larger than a pack of cigarettes, could tape up to ninety minutes. It had been hidden beneath the coffee table and had caught the entire conversation with Shafik. Voice-activated, no one but Harbin and Chelsea had been aware of its presence.

Meg had listened carefully to all observations and instructions and added her own. "This time listen for possible innuendos in what he is saying."

She wondered why Harbin hadn't entered the discussion. Was it possible he didn't want to display an uncertainty? Was he waiting for Joe to make the final conclusions without him? She caught him looking landward. They were passing another one of those islands that appeared to be created from piles of white ash. Was his look one of concern for the group? Or was he simply looking back, regretting something in his past? A warm breeze tugged at his hair and he did nothing to push away a stray lock. She felt the impulse to stroke his cheek, but caught herself.

Minutes later Chelsea, sipping from a coffee mug, snapped off the tape machine with his free hand. To Harbin he said, "Why did Shafik take on the duty of . . . how should I put it? . . . befriending you now?"

"A sense of kinship. It's apparent that he and his brother-in-law were close. I suspect that when he first saw the yacht video he saw similarities between the Arab colonel and myself. Now, he has seen the impossibility of his suspicions."

"Then he's not an enemy," Josh exclaimed. "So where does that leave us? *Who* is the enemy?"

"More important, what do we do about it?" Meg asked. "Where are we going as of this moment?"

All looked to Harbin. Harbin leaned forward on his elbows and addressed no one in particular. "I've told you from the beginning that whatever I come up with, I will accept your decision as the final one."

"Let's hear it," Chelsea said, again thinking the man was impossible to read.

"My original plan was to wait out our mystery antagonist in the vicinity of Mykonos but, now knowing he is not Shafik, I've altered my thinking." He paused for effect. "I would suggest we join your families without delay."

"In the Caribbean?" Chelsea asked, more than a little disturbed. "Reuven, why there?"

"There is no safer place. There we can wait out a few days. If nothing occurs out of the ordinary we can forget the entire episode and return home."

Chelsea gave him a sidelong glance. "You're assuming a few days of quiet will end all danger."

"The man—whoever he may be—may not reach for my outpost."

"Outpost?"

Harbin smiled. "It has been called just that by my family. They mistakenly suspect the island is for keeping secret trysts with mysterious lady friends. In any case, the Caribbean would not be the bailiwick for an avenging Arab."

"You still think it has to be an Arab—and possibly Suliman?"

"It is impossible to think of any other. If I'm wrong, the island is still the safest place for all to be."

Harbin turned and leaned toward a low cabinet. Opening the small door he took out a phone. He got the captain's bridge. "Ari, call the airport in Zakinthos. I want passage for five—one-way—to Britain. From Britain, five first-class, one-way tickets to . . . Wait. Find out if there's a direct flight to St. Thomas. If not, try for a private charter to St. Thomas. Got all that? Okay, call me back." He put the phone away. "I suggest we all go and start packing."

As all stood up Dave remarked, "Reuven, I've said it before but I must repeat, you sure know how to live."

"Anyone can learn," he said. "You just have to know what you want."

And go after it, finished Meg silently.

Chelsea said, "Reuven, do you always get what you want?"

Harbin's smile was almost veiled. "Most of the time." Meg caught him looking at her.

15

The sprawling mansion stood at the highest point of the forty-acre island. A generator supplied electric power and a desalinization plant provided purified water at a rate of three thousand gallons daily. Although the women had been apprised of what to expect, they were overwhelmed by both the size and beauty of the island. The mansion was Spanish Mediterranean but its outer walls were of imported Jerusalem stone. The beige facade glowed in bright sunlight.

Ellie, Cindy, and Mae had spent hours exploring the vast estate and had still not seen all. It was the noon hour of their third day and they were having lunch served on the corner terrace overlooking a sloping lawn dotted with flowering acacia. A soft breeze did little to disturb the branches. A Jamaican butler, smiling broadly, served them with obvious pleasure. They were his first guests in almost four months.

Ellie looked at her wristwatch. "The boys should be here in about another three hours."

Cindy chewed on a piece of broiled lobster. "I'll be

only too happy to see them here," she said. "This place is simply too much to enjoy all by ourselves."

Mae seemed quite distracted by something and said suddenly, "I can't help wondering what they're hiding in the tower."

"Why would you think something's hidden there?"

Mae looked askance at her. "Why were we told it's off-limits?"

Ellie shrugged. "Look, whatever the reason, I couldn't care less. I'm not that curious."

"Speak for yourself," Cindy tossed in. "When Reuven gets here I'll ask. After Greece, I'm not happy with secrets."

"You know," Mae said, "there's always two men up there, but I've heard the voices of more than just two." She touched a finger to her lips. "It can't help but set one's imagination to working overtime."

"While it's working, do you have an opinion on the chief superintendent? Didn't you once work for the British government?"

Chief Superintendent Clyde Witteger, who was in charge of policing the British territorial islands, had paid them a visit two days earlier. "Routine," he had said, "just a passport check."

"I'd say he's typical," Mae said. "Thorough in everything he does. He already knew I once worked for MI5."

"A bit stiff-necked, wouldn't you say?" said Ellie.

"It goes with the position. I would guess he was military at one time in his career."

"Speak of the devil . . ." Cindy interrupted. "Isn't that the police boat coming toward our dock?"

All peered down the slope to the island's private pier, visible in the distance. Ellie said, "If it's the superinten-

dent he must have received word of our host's return. I
could be wrong, but I thought he seemed anxious to meet
with Reuven."

"I find that difficult to believe. The superintendents
I've met always executed their duties with aplomb,
concealing their inner thoughts, and rarely conveying
them to others." She glanced at Ellie. "Ellie, you're good
if you can see beyond the super's facade. A talent you've
learned from Joe?"

A coy smile appeared. "I suppose it's possible, having
lived so long with one man. Many things do rub off,
but . . ." The smile broadened. "But it doesn't tell me
how to greet a British superior at lunchtime. Do we invite
him to join us?"

"No. I can see Josif standing on the concrete pier,
waiting to greet him. Let's just wait and see what the
chief super really came for."

Clyde Witteger was of average height, a bit on the stocky
side. He had a sure stride and carried his weight well. His
gaze was direct and friendly when the occasion called for
it, but he could be stern when his position demanded it
His face was more weathered than his fifty-odd years
suggested.

Josif held his hand out. They had met a month earlier,
when Witteger had accepted the position left vacant
when the previous superintendent retired.

Witteger accepted the hand without expression. Josif
said, "Mr. Harbin is expected by fifteen-hundred."

"He'll be here within the hour," Witteger corrected.
"By helicopter. He picked one up at Beef Island." He
scanned the sky to the west. "I understand he will have
four guests with him."

"Yes. That is not unusual for Mr. Harbin. He rarely stays here alone."

"So I've heard." This was said reflectively. Something was on the chief's mind.

Witteger's aide, Sergeant Halliday, after instructing his crew of four how to tie up the sixty-foot power boat, joined his superior. Tall and lanky, and younger by twenty years, he appeared much more sprightly than the older man. His blond hair, bleached from the constant sun, appeared almost white. His oval face held a smile, but his eyes were invisible behind dark glasses. He leaned over to say something quietly in the chief's ear.

"Any minute, sir." His eyes scanned the area. "Where would he land?"

"The tennis courts, I presume." He looked for confirmation from Josif, who nodded.

"Would you like to come inside and wait, Superintendent?" Josif was never sure whether to address him as Chief or simply Superintendent. He remembered addressing the previous commander as Superintendent only.

Witteger held his gaze on Josif for a few moments, wondering whether this man in charge of such a vast estate always dressed in his present garb. Josif was dressed in blue denims, a short-sleeved white T-shirt, and sneakers. His dark hair was short and appeared to have been merely finger-combed. From his passport he knew the man held duel citizenship: in Israel and the United States. Judging from his stance and body movement, the superintendent decided that he was military-trained. But by which country was a mystery to him.

Witteger held up his hand to shield his eyes from the sun and looked northward. The sound of helicopter blades churning the air grew louder. The chopper was visible in seconds, frothing the usually calm waters of the cove before disappearing over the hilltop, beyond the mansion.

The mansion was built at the island's highest elevation, about two hundred feet above the shoreline. Witteger and his aide followed behind Josif as he led them to where the dock met a path that followed the perimeter of the island. They chose one of three golf carts that stood at the head of the pathway. As they neared the mansion and could see the ladies standing on the open terrace, Witteger adjusted his sunglasses and politely doffed his peaked cap. They arrived with the group from the helicopter.

The ladies were all smiles as the men came up the path. Ellie searched Meg's face as Harbin helped her up a short rise. She read nothing in Meg's expression that would suggest anything untoward had happened while they were away. "Stop nosing," Chelsca whispered in her ear after greeting her with a warm kiss.

Ellie leaned back and gazed at him. "You did miss me, didn't you?"

He grinned. "Don't I always when we're separated for more than a couple of hours?"

She returned his kiss, knowing it was true. Childless, they had had only each other for more than thirty-five years. She squeezed his hand and, for the moment, nothing more needed to be said. Glancing over at Harbin, she decided the men were two of a kind. She wondered if Meg would come to understand Reuven as well as she did Joe. No matter their ages, both men hadn't outgrown the fact that they were adventurers.

Harbin noted the remnants of the ladies' lunch. He

held a hand out for Witteger. "We finally meet, Chief Superintendent. Will you and your aide join us for lunch? I see the ladies have finished but we haven't yet started. It's an excellent occasion for us to get better acquainted."

Witteger accepted Harbin's invitation for himself and Halliday. Ian Wickers, the former superintendent, had warned him that Harbin's kindnesses were more than mere generosity.

Only five minutes into their luncheon Harbin was certain that the new superintendent hadn't been apprised of what had occurred on the private island a mere four months before. Witteger had been given only vague hints by Wickers and because of this Witteger's curiosity had been piqued.

Witteger said, "I understand this small isle had assumed the role of a fortress. For what purpose I was never told. Can you elaborate on what Ian Wickers seemed hesitant to tell me?"

"Fortress?" Harbin arched an eyebrow. "I suppose, in a way, it is a fortress. If you can picture the Caribbean as a moat."

"Mr. Harbin, I have only been at this station a few short weeks. In that time I have heard many rumors. I bring with me a solid reputation and I intend to keep it that way. Can you tell me why it was necessary I should be warned beforehand?"

"Warned of what, Chief? May I call you Chief, sir?"

He nodded affirmatively. "Quite all right. I would like a reply to the query."

So would I, thought Chelsea.

Harbin shrugged disarmingly, as though the subject were trivial. "Chief, I occasionally hold both business

and political sessions here with people of great importance worldwide. For that reason, while here as my
guests, they must be protected."

Witteger appeared to mull that over. "How do you go
about supplying protection? Your own private army? I
have heard rumors from among the older residents."

"I do have some men that have been trained, but
nothing out of the ordinary." He directed a glance to
Chelsea. "Mr. Chelsea was formerly with the New York
Police Department's homicide division. Mr. Novick is a
former police sergeant. Mr. Ward was a member of the
FBI. In case you've been wondering, all three are retired
and are here to enjoy some peace and quiet."

Witteger sat back. "I hope so, but I must confess quite
candidly that I know your help on this island are—or
were—members of Israel's Mossad. The so-called warnings I received—vague as they were—forced me to do
some checking. I tell you this because I desire no trouble
on my little space in the Caribbean."

After the chief departed with his aide, Chelsea asked
Harbin, "Do you go through this each time you visit your
own island?" When it drew a shrug, Chelsea threw
another question at him. "Why Mossad?"

"Who would I trust more?"

It was Chelsea's turn to shrug. "Why would you need
them in the first place?"

Dave intervened. "Can you trust us enough to tell us
what happened that Witteger hasn't discovered yet?"

Harbin sighed. "I was protecting three elderly sisters
from execution by a former member of a foreign government. Without going into complete detail, the body
count was four men, including one of mine. Wickers, the
retired super, along with Cyrus Desmond, an old friend

and retired member of Britain's Special Branch, were also involved. Needless to say it took some doing to keep it quiet. I couldn't have done it without their help."

Josh, impatient, said, "And what do we do now? Simply wait for another move by an unknown antagonist? No matter how inviting your place we can't stay here indefinitely."

"Just the remainder of this week and the weekend should do it. In the meantime be patient and enjoy your stay. For starters"—He signaled Josif who was waiting for his direction—"Josif will be your escort and acquaint you with our so-called defenses. You'll have to excuse me for a few minutes while I take care of some personal business." He touched Chelsea's shoulder. "My office, fully equipped with the latest electronic equipment, is also available to you at any time."

"How about now?" Chelsea said, eyeing Josh. "I must speak with Alex, our manager." Josh pulled at Dave's arm and then nodded to Josif. "Lead on, McDuff," he said, waving his cane.

Chelsea glanced at the ladies, who sat on cushioned wicker furniture located at the farther end of the terrace. He caught Ellie's eye and held up ten fingers, waving his hands twice, signifying twenty minutes. She nodded, although with a sigh. Mae and Cindy appeared mildly disturbed. They loved their surroundings but wished they were home.

Meg sat there, torn between her desire to stay and her need to go home. It was so unlike her, to be plagued by such indecisiveness. For a woman who presided over an office of five attorneys . . . She noticed Chelsea signaling Ellie and decided she would speak with Reuven upon his return.

From the terrace Josif ushered Josh and Dave to the house and through the marble-floored main entry hall, from where he led them to a caged elevator. Josif explained he was taking them to the domed tower.

The sprawling mansion consisted of two floors, but the tower was an additional two floors. The elevater stopped at the third floor from where they disembarked and then proceeded by foot to ascend a circular stairway. The stairway ended in the center of a thirty-foot circular room.

Josh and Dave gawked at the equipment in the room. Two men sat on stools that moved on tracks to face a number of computer and television monitors. Many of the screens were monitoring different spots on the island. They recognized the tennis courts and swimming pool and the rear of the house. The helicopter was gone. From the front of the mansion a camera lens zoomed down the path to an extended wooden dock where the *Sea Temple II* was tied up. A short distance away a concrete pier ran horizontal to the land. This larger docking area was reserved for the larger *Temple*.

Above the monitors glass walls surrounded the room. One could look in any direction and enjoy a panoramic view of the Caribbean Sea.

Dave fingered his beard and asked Josif, "Why do you find all this necessary?"

Josh could only remark, "Interesting."

Josif compressed his lips; his eyes took on a distracted look. "At times it's been extremely useful."

A thought coming to mind, Josh asked, "Lifesaving?"

It got a nod, but no explanation.

• • •

Reuven Harbin's office was immaculate. It spoke of a decorator's hand: an oak desk, a leather high-backed chair behind it, two upholstered chairs facing the desk, and a beige leather sofa against a wood-paneled wall. A cocktail table with a fresh flower centerpiece faced the sofa. Two other walls contained a variety of office equipment: fax with scanner and printer, a copier, a telex—nothing was omitted from what was a perfect office.

Chelsea took in all with a perfunctory glance while Harbin picked up papers from the desk, messages that Josif had left for study. Reading, Harbin's lips twisted in thought as though displeased with the contents. Nevertheless, to Chelsea he said, "Do you wish to use the equipment? Everything is at hand." He caught Chelsea's expression. "You find this interesting." It wasn't a question.

"Yes, extremely, Reuven, but you no longer surprise me. And, saying that, I nevertheless must ask one or two questions. He got a nod. "When on board ship you mentioned a choice of weapons was available—which we never used, or even saw. In truth I have a number of questions, but answers to a couple should suffice." He held up a finger. "With reservations for a third.

"Where was your alleged cache? And why was it necessary to have one?"

"In my office, behind a sliding secret panel. That's one. The answer to the second is protection against piracy. It's been a growing water hazard, although more so here in the Caribbean. The drug trade here has grown to proportions where it rivals that of arms dealers." He leveled his gaze with Chelsea's. "Your next question?"

"You're still a member of the Mossad." It wasn't a query.

"I thought I convinced you I wasn't. I told you the truth. I was—but am not now anything more than a consultant. And even then not very often."

Chelsea pulled out his tobacco pouch, but saw no ashtray. He stuffed it back into his shirt pocket. "Reuven, we've gone over this ground before. Your entire crew is obviously military-trained. For consulting? To protect against kidnapping?" He cocked his head. "Please, Reuven, don't try to kid an old policeman. Witteger was testing the ground here. What's making him antsy? He apparently doesn't know about the operation you mentioned earlier. What I don't comprehend is why the previous chief, although involved himself, didn't bother to apprise him of it."

When Chelsea paused Harbin decided to sit down behind his desk. "Please continue," he said quietly.

Chelsea fingered his shirt pocket. His crutch remained there. "It was, I suspect—or could have been—an international incident. So, despite this you still maintain you're not a member of the Mossad . . ." Chelsea halted and lifted his hands in a gesture of defeat. "Reuven, I give up. I must concede that you are still a man of surprises. It would be pointless for me to continue with wild conjecture." Chelsea decided to seat himself in the overstuffed chair facing the desk.

Harbin recognized that Chelsea was frustrated because he was used to being a controller, directing men on operations. Now he was again at a low ebb, no longer a leader of men in action. In truth they were two of a kind, neither able to sit still. Neither would accept that he was aging.

Harbin leaned back. "Joe, I want to show you something." He touched a button beneath his desk and in seconds the paneled wall behind the huge sofa slid behind the adjacent panel. A ten-by-ten-foot room was disclosed, its walls covered with rifles and handguns of a number of makes. Boxes of ammunition were piled floor to ceiling against the back wall. Harbin left his chair to feel behind the back wall. Machinery was heard and the wall with the handguns spun on a center axis. A dark tunnel was revealed. "It was built by pirates a couple of centuries back. It leads to a vast chamber where they kept their loot, and finally to a cave opening at the rear of the island."

Chelsea was flabbergasted. "You're not going to tell me you really have a use for this?"

"Unfortunately, the operation four months ago required its use."

"And you maintain this all occurred after your so-called retirement was in effect?"

"Absolutely!"

Chelsea released a sigh, then pulled out a handkerchief from the back pocket of his slacks. He dabbed at his face for a moment before saying, "I wish to select a weapon for myself. I've been feeling naked for too long a time." He held up a finger. "And Josh and Dave should also be allowed a choice."

"Granted. While it's open why not make a selection?"

Chelsea arose to study the arsenal: a Walther ppk, semi-automatic with Carswell silencer; a Glock 19, an ugly weapon but most effective; a Browning 9mm semi-automatic, and Berettas and S&Ws, also 9mms. There were also a number of uzis, some with silencers. He noticed a Colt .357 Magnum but chose the 9mm

Beretta, and then decided to keep it there until needed. He gazed with wonder at the collection of trip wires, photo-electric cells, and infrared lens equipment. Among the rifles were telescopic sights and laser beam attachments.

Chelsea shook his head then nodded toward crates piled up at a stone wall. "More of the same?" he asked. He laughed unexpectedly. "Christ! Reuven. You preparing for an invasion?" He pointed to a weapon high on the wall. A Sig Sauer P226 9mm. It held fifteen bullets in the magazine, one in the barrel. It could find a target in total darkness. "Amazing!" Chelsea exclaimed.

Harbin said nothing in reply, but picked up a sheet of paper from his desk. He waited for Chelsea to turn from the arsenal, then handed him the single sheet to read. While Chelsea read, the wall slowly returned to its normal position.

Chelsea looked up two minutes later. "Is this something that should concern me?"

The paper stated that one particular boat—a fortyfive-foot chartered bareboat—had anchored in a different cove each night for the past four days. Its occupants, three men, had been seen taking turns keeping watch on the island with binoculars.

Harbin, by way of answering, handed over another sheet. The three men on board the chartered yawl were employees of the Space Age International Agency. At first reading nothing registered for Chelsea. Then, "Christ Almighty! It's Nestor Hobbs's corporation!" He stared at Harbin. "You don't suppose this could be a coincidence?"

"I don't believe in coincidences."

Chelsea walked to the lone window in the study. It looked out upon a lawn that stretched down to a tangle of mangrove trees along the shoreline. No boats were in the vicinity. He checked the name of the bareboat again: *Spaced Out*. Coincidence? Like hell! *Nestor Hobbs!* Chelsea said evenly, "One of the directors of the Alliance. He's got to be . . . at least seventy-five years old. And a multimillionaire to boot. Why on earth should he feel threatened by me—or any of us?"

"Did you ever meet him?" Harbin asked.

"No, but we had him under investigation. Using our own small group, of course."

Harbin waved a finger. "On that note I think I could use Dave Ward. He's the computer expert here." He searched through the sheaf of papers until he found the right one. "This is a fax from my accountant. Someone's been buying up shares in my corporation in lots of five thousand. The fax here gives names of the individual purchasers, most coming from different countries. I'd like Dave to look into it, to seek a pattern in it."

"How many shares are you talking about?"

"So far, two hundred thousand."

Chelsea gave a silent whistle, but Harbin smiled. "I don't know why somebody is bothering. An outsider can never assume control."

"Maybe someone just likes your company. Has faith in it."

Harbin shook his head. "No. The buying is too sudden. There has to be an ulterior motive." He shrugged. "Let's get to the tower for consultation with . . ." He gave a little smile. ". . . with the Sunset Detectives."

•   •   •

"Why would Nestor Hobbs be taking over from Suliman? The guy's pretty old. Why bother himself with us?" Josh asked, astonished.

"Pride," Chelsea retorted. "And loss of power and prestige."

"Doesn't that border on overkill? The man has more money than God."

"His interest is in us, not money. We destroyed what to him must have been a plan for even greater power. For him personally it was a stultifying experience. He wants us to pay for it."

Josh sniffed. "How? By doing what? Killing us?"

Chelsea looked to Harbin, who had made no effort to intervene. "Reuven, what are your thoughts on this?"

"First, there's Suliman, with the mind and instincts of a terrorist. I have no doubt he was seeking revenge by killing. Death to the enemy is his solution for all problems. Hobbs—I place him in another category. I believe he'd use means other than elimination."

Chelsea asked, "What of Sheikh Shafik? You appear to trust him somewhat. Where do you figure he stands in this?"

Josh interrupted with, "And what of the mysterious woman? As long as you're working all subjects, I'd like to hear something more substantial on this one." He gave Chelsea a lingering stare. "Joe, if I didn't know you that well, I'd suspect . . ."

He didn't finish, sensing that Chelsea's eyes, although invisible behind sunglasses, bore into his. It was an egregious error to have insinuated something so ludicrous. "Sorry, Joe. It was stupid of me to . . ."

Chelsea waved it aside. "Let's get down to business." His eyes swept across the windows to note three boats of different lengths trailing convoylike as they entered the southern cove. "Your cove always this busy?" he asked Josif.

"It's not unusual for a weekend."

"The *Spaced Out* . . . it's been here how long?"

"Four days and nights."

"How long have you been listening to them?"

Josif thought a bit. "Two, two-and-a-half days."

"And what is their conversation about?"

"Fishing—and women also. They do a lot of boasting about their sexual escapades."

"No names ever? No friends or family?"

Josif took some time to search his memory. "It's odd, but I can't recall ever hearing them mention a name other than their own."

"They never mention their jobs or location of employment?"

Josif smiled. "Most people don't when on holiday."

Chelsea said, "Some people continually discuss their work. They live with it both away and at home, unable to walk away from it. They never retire."

Josh said, "I can't help wondering who you have in mind."

Chelsea grinned, then addressed Dave. "Your job is to dig into the backgrounds of the three men on the bareboat. Use whatever connections you still have. These men could be harmless—their presence a mere coincidence. Let's clarify their identities once and for all."

He looked at Josh. Josh appeared tired, his eyes bloodshot from too much sun and too little sleep. The way he was leaning on his ivory-headed cane made Chelsea think his leg was bothering him. It seemed it had been bothering him more with each passing month.

Chelsea knew his friend would be insulted if anyone
dared bring him a chair.

Chelsea turned to Harbin. "Are those golf carts available at any time?"

"Of course. They work on battery and are kept on full
charge. You need them for anything specific?"

"I'd like Josh and Dave to accompany me in an
inspection of your little hideaway. Just so we can get the
lay of the land."

Harbin nodded to Josif who immediately lifted a
phone from one of the desks fronting a monitor. Speaking into the mouthpiece he asked for a cart to be brought
to the front entrance.

As they made ready to leave the tower Josh asked
Harbin, "Is it possible for me to look over the *Temple II*
when we're finished with the island inspection?"

"Of course. Everything here is open, ready for both
your inspection and enjoyment. If you like, you can take
out the *Temple* for a morning sail."

Dave Ward, although in retirement from the Company
almost ten years, still had contacts; although, he had
warned Chelsea, only to a degree. Nevertheless, the bios
of the three men aboard *Spaced Out* were established
through diligent searching. All three had left the government before official retirement age, their ages ranging
from twenty-seven to thirty-five. They were in the
employ of Space Age International. Supposedly they
were taking a two-week vacation to enjoy some fishing
and sailing. Where better than the British Virgin Islands
to enjoy both?

Harbin checked his Rolex. "It will soon be dinnertime.
Dress will continue to be informal. The ladies were so

advised earlier. You're all to relax and simply enjoy the facilities of the island. I was told the ladies wish to visit Virgin Gorda tomorrow after breakfast. I see no reason at this time to forbid it. In fact, it should make for a pleasant day. Of course, three of my men will accompany them. Have I your okay on this?"

Chelsea chuckled. "Reuven, if you say it's okay, who am I to disagree?"

The room was dark, but the green dial displayed the time on the dresser clock: 1:30 A.M. Unable to sleep Chelsea moved the thin bedcover from his chest. The movement awakened Ellie. "What's up, Joe? Why aren't you asleep?"

A deep sigh escaped him. "When I was brushing my teeth tonight I saw myself in the mirror and thought I looked older than my father, as I remember him."

Ellie sat up. "You *are* older than your father was. He died at sixty-two." She was quiet a moment. "Why does that bother you?"

Chelsea placed his arms behind his head. "It's because of Reuven and Meg."

Ellie twisted to see his face in the dark but all she got was a shadowed impression. "What about them?"

"Reuven and I are about the same age. No longer an age where one would think of pursuing a woman."

"I don't understand. Why is this keeping you awake?"

He hesitated, finding it difficult to voice his fears. "Ellie, if anything happened to you—God forbid—I could never look at another woman, much less pursue one."

Ellie fell back into the pillow. "Oh, Joe, why couldn't you have taken up shuffleboard? It would be so simple just quietly living out the rest of our lives." Then, trying to make light of it she said, "Do you think anyone would give me a second look if I were a widow?"

"You? You're still an attractive woman, Ellie."

"In your eyes. And Meg's still attractive in Reuven's eyes. You and he see us as desirable, one hopes, despite our age."

"You mean like the AKs in our condo complex. Some of them are just dirty old men, whistling in the dark for their youth."

"If the feelings are reciprocated, why not simply enjoy it? For instance, the couple living together one floor beneath us each lost their partner of thirty-five years or more in the past year . . ."

"And now they're living together, their deceased mates forgotten. I don't . . . can't . . . understand it."

Ellie sighed. "What you don't understand is the need for companionship. There are some people that can't face life alone. No matter how good a past marriage had been."

Chelsea lay quiet, unable to respond to a philosophy he couldn't comprehend. How could Reuven and Meg have feelings for each other after such long and happy marriages?

Ellie put her arm across her husband's chest. "Joe, can we discuss this at another time?"

He nodded without speaking, but held her close.

The second floor roofed balcony ran the length of five bedroom suites at the rear of the mansion. Although it was close to 2 A.M. Harbin stood there, fully dressed, watching a star shoot across the blackness of the sky. In seconds it faded into oblivion, its weight displaced by space and other stars. *Should I have made a wish?* Harbin wondered.

In truth he couldn't know whether he needed or merely wanted her. And yet, in either case, he feared trying to perform as her—or anyone else's—lover. Guilt had made him remain celibate for too many years. But he knew he wouldn't want to become her lover unless he really cared for her.

He turned to gaze along the silent balcony. He had everything . . . Why did he feel a need for Meg? The answer was there, waiting only for the question to be asked. Reuven Harbin was a lonely man; he had no one with whom he could share his triumphs.

The acacia stirred in a sudden breeze, disturbing nesting creatures. He sighed, no less disturbed than the animals. More so, more from what he had just learned of himself. All the symptoms were present: He wanted Meg for herself, not for her resemblance to Anya. There was no mistaking the ache in his chest, the wanting to tell her.

He turned to the French doors leading into his suite. Opening them quietly he reentered the apartment. In the dark he settled into an overstuffed chair and simply sat there, trying to comprehend the latent emotions she had aroused in him.

He lost track of the time, gradually falling asleep. Something awakened him and for a moment he didn't know where he was. His warning senses immediately came alive, keeping him from stirring. Someone was at the French doors, turning the handle. A silhouette glided across the room.

Harbin tensed, preparing to leap at the figure . . . then recognized it.

Meg! It was Meg!

Frozen, he didn't wish to startle her, but . . .

He spoke in a soft whisper. "Meg, don't yell. I'm over here, to your right." He heard a stifled, pained, "Oh!"

He rose from the chair and walked the two steps to meet her.

Harbin took her in his arms and she immediately started sobbing. Her head on his shoulder she spoke haltingly. "Reuven, I've never done this before. I'm so ashamed, I can't begin to tell you . . ."

"You don't have to say anything." He stroked her hair, his heart threatening to leap from his chest. He pushed her gently from him. "Don't you dare apologize. I understand . . . I know exactly what's going through your mind. If I wasn't so stupid I . . ."

She placed a hand upon his lips. "It's the two of us. We've been sharing a like hunger. But with neither of us knowing how to handle it. And I am too old to learn the ways of the young and incorrigible."

"Incorrigible? You? Oh, Meg . . . " His voice trailed off. He kissed her gently, aware of the thin robe covering a lacy nightgown, then pulled back abruptly.

"Meg, I don't want it this way," he said. "Clandestine . . ." His voice was trembling, as he sought control.

"Reuven . . . I . . ."

A red light flashing on and off lit their faces eerily. A buzzing started in synch with the light. Harbin held her at arms' length. "It's an alert alarm," he said, hardly above a whisper. "Stay here." He moved quickly toward the desk phone.

Lifting the phone he hit a single button. "Yes," he said into the mouthpiece. Listening, he said, "Where?" He waited another ten seconds. "Okay, use deployment with extreme care. We'll join you in minutes."

He touched another button; the red light and the buzzing immediately ceased. But as he started back to Meg a shadow crossed the curtains draping his French doors. A rap on the door was followed by a husky voice asking if everything was okay inside.

Harbin opened the door to Chelsea, who was in pajamas. "Joe, it's an alert. We've got an intruder. Get dressed. If the others are asleep don't bother awakening them. The intruder is not in the house."

Chelsea looked to his right. Everyone was on the balcony, all shadows, all awake because of the buzzing sound. Chelsea shooed them back, telling them to get dressed, that explanations could wait.

Harbin delayed Meg, who had remained unseen in his room. Waiting for all to disappear, he then told her to return to her own room and get dressed. No one need know she was with him. Later . . . at the appropriate time . . .

In minutes Harbin met with Josif in the main entry hall. "So, where is he?" Harbin asked.

"It's a she."

Harbin looked askance, then said, "Where is she?"

"She's being brought through the cavern to your study. Blindfolded," he quickly added before an expected complaint should be forthcoming.

Harbin deliberated no more than a moment. "Rouse the cook, if she isn't already awake. Have her set up coffee, tea, and whatever in the terrace lounge. The ladies should be told to wait there until all is safe. Have Rebecca stay with them. I don't want them alone. Notify Chelsea, Novick, and Ward to join me in my private study."

Carrie Willis, minus her flippers, stood there in a wet suit. Once the blindfold was removed she adjusted her eyes to the room she had been brought into. Squinting, her eyes took in the area with open candor. It was more or less what she would have expected from a man like Harbin. His private office was equipped with electronic gear to accommodate any circumstance. She expected he would appear at any moment. Her elation was tempered only by her failure to penetrate his domain without being caught.

She stretched her arms behind her back, but handcuffs restricted her movement. She shook her head, her blonde tresses moving slightly. When Harbin entered, she spoke her first words. "Are these cuffs necessary?"

He studied her briefly. The blonde hair was natural this time, he decided. The accent was almost indistinguishable. It made him wonder.

To Egon he said, "Remove the cuffs." He waited, then told her to be seated. She chose the overstuffed leather armchair. Harbin went behind his desk to sit down and await the arrival of his partner-guests. In the meantime he observed her with sharp eyes. He said finally, "If you're properly dressed beneath your wet suit, you have my permission to remove it."

She smiled, but remained silent. Harbin sat back in contemplation. Maybe Chelsea could do better. It took two minutes of patient waiting.

When Chelsea, Josh, and Dave entered, Harbin said, "Joe, she's all yours."

The three men gazed at her more in wonder than puzzlement.

Chelsea pursed his lips, then finger-combed his unruly hair. "Name, please," he said.

She smiled. "You want my rank and serial number also?"

Dave harrumpfed. "If you have one," he said facetiously. "You're well-trained. I witnessed you in action."

Chelsea decided to be blunt. "Whose payroll you on?" She shrugged. "How about Spencer Medwal?" he asked. Her eyes flickered.

"Okay—how about Sheikh Shafik?"

A frown marred an otherwise smooth forehead. "Am I to be arrested?"

Harbin intervened. "If we don't get some answers soon, you may wish to be arrested."

The green eyes darkened. "I've been keeping both of you alive, whether you are aware of it or not."

Chelsea said, "We are very much aware of it. You were careless on two occasions: first at the country club, then at the Nassau marina. Now tell us why we're under observation."

How did they suspect she was in Medwal's employ?

Harbin leaned forward on his elbows. "I see no purpose in your effort to keep silent. As for protection, we don't require outside help."

"How about on Mykonos?" At this point Josh decided to seat himself on the sofa. He settled in, sighing, and shaking his head.

Carrie Willis appeared to be debating with herself. "What does it matter. Release me and let me go on my way. No harm's been done."

Harbin observed the well-fitted wet suit. "Where did you come ashore? And from what vessel?"

When she didn't respond Chelsea said, "You'd rather we call in the authorities to take over?"

Her silence continued. Harbin said, "Your name— your employer. Is that really so difficult? I remind you—if you need reminding—that though the island is under autonomous rule, the British governor is in charge of external affairs and local security."

Dave Ward confronted Chelsea angrily. "Joey, why are we bothering with this? She's a trained mercenary." He spun on Harbin. "No matter how well she manages English, Reuven, you of all people should recognize the tinge of Russian in her speech. Just turn her over to the authorities. Let Superintendent Witteger check with Interpol. If she has a record it won't take them long to discover it."

Josh rolled his eyes and groaned. *What have we gotten ourselves into now?*

Chelsea looked to Harbin; it was his island, his operation. He knew what he himself would have preferred, but . . .

"No, she stays. For a while, at least. We must know more." He gazed at her again. "Your so-called position as a protector . . . Who is it for? Me or Joe Chelsea?"

Willis thought it over. *Why not?* "You. Chelsea was a bonus I couldn't refuse when the opportunity presented itself."

Chelsea bowed slightly. "I thank you for that, but, now, whom else do I have to thank?"

Dave was ready to explode. "Joey, stop with the games. This woman came ashore on this island for a reason other than protecting anyone. She has to have a partner waiting in some boat offshore."

Harbin opened a drawer in his desk and pulled out a

cellular phone. He clicked a single button and waited no more than three seconds. "Well," he said, "anything?" He listened for about half a minute, all the time eyeing Carrie Willis. "You're certain?" He hung up and put the phone back in the drawer.

Harbin looked at his Rolex. "You have two minutes to start answering some questions. Otherwise I call the superintendent. The charge will not be just trespassing, but breaking and entering." He looked at his watch. "You now have one minute. Your name, please."

She shifted in her chair, uncomfortable in the scuba outfit. Her eyes displayed no fear. "Carrie Willis," she said. "I own a boutique on Fifth Avenue in New York."

"Name your sponsor for the mercenary training."

Willis sighed heavily, immersed in thought, knowing her undercover activities were finished. "Spencer Medwal is my present sponsor. The KGB trained me for many years before my arrival in America. I was meant to be a sleeper, but was never called upon to act. Since the breakup of the USSR I've been on my own." She spoke easily, without hesitation, her eyes shifting between Harbin and Chelsea. When no queries or comments immediately followed her confession she said, "I was born in Russia."

Harbin merely nodded, not surprised by anything she said. "Who issued the orders to protect me? And why?"

She shrugged as if it was of no importance. "Spencer Medwal."

Chelsea asked, "Who gave him orders?"

"It could have been the old Arab, Shafik. The man's his uncle. As to why those specific orders—I have no idea. I received them only after arriving in Mykonos."

"Before Mykonos, what was your mission?"

Willis concentrated her gaze on Harbin. "To look into your background."

Dave faced Harbin across his desk, his disapproval of the proceedings obvious. "Reuven, how long do we keep this up? Turn her over to the authorities and be done with it."

Chelsea wondered what there was about Carrie Willis that bothered his friend. Was he scared of her? He looked to Harbin who seemed to be pondering a decision.

Harbin said, "She stays, Dave. Temporarily. Her alleged partner has taken off—deserted her." Willis showed no change in expression. Harbin asked, "Was that the alternate plan? If you're caught or delayed, you're on your own?" He didn't wait for confirmation. "Where's he headed? You must have a meeting place."

Willis smiled. Medwal had said Harbin was smart. "My clothes and equipment are on Virgin Gorda, but he could be headed for either Tortola or any of the other islands. For him Virgin Gorda was out if I was detained in any way."

Josh joined Dave in the looks of disgust, but Chelsea didn't display disapproval of Harbin's orders. It was Josh who made the initial complaint. He spoke to no one in particular. "What do we gain by inviting the fox into the hen house? Did I lose something in the translation?"

Carrie Willis listened intently, knowing that Harbin and Chelsea ran whatever operation was in progress. But what the operation was . . . She shrugged, unable to fret about it, confident that she could handle anything they threw at her. She was trained for all emergencies. At the same time, she couldn't help wondering what Reuven Harbin had in store for her. For a number of reasons she thought it mildly entertaining. Reuven Harbin, alleged to be a billionaire, was a man with many secrets. He was a man who had a finger in countless industries and yet had a life of unknown qualities. The man truly intrigued her. She didn't know whether to admire or fear him. *Who was he really?*

She caught Harbin watching her. She felt certain that her thoughts were well concealed. Had she not been the pupil in highest standing? But she did note an almost imperceptible smile on his dark face. A forbidden doubt crept in. Should it worry her? She avoided his eyes and caught Chelsea observing her, also with an imperceptible smile. *What did they have in store for her?*

Harbin asked for the name of her hotel, then said her bags would be picked up later in the morning by a member of his crew. In the meantime, Rebecca or Yetta would find something for her to wear in place of the scuba outfit.

"This is some paradise," Dave said disdainfully. "On the other hand, paradise had a snake living there, lying in wait."

Chelsea laughed, rubbed his face, and started to check his watch, which he wasn't wearing. "It must be late—or early, whichever. It's time to change and get ready for breakfast."

Dave detained Chelsea by touching his elbow. He looked serious. "Joey, all told, we were involved in three different incidents on this so-called holiday. When are you going to decide we're getting too old for this crap?"

"Dave, my mind and body rule my decisions, not the calendar."

"How about your body calendar?" Josh interjected. "I think mine has been ready to call it quits for quite a time."

Chelsea, as always, had a ready answer. "This vacation will last another four days at most. Let's not think about anything else. As for me, after breakfast while you're sailing, I intend to sit around the pool and relax, possibly take a nap."

16

Harbin and Chelsea sat on lounge chairs by the pool. They were alone, sipping and enjoying pre-lunch drinks. All of Harbin's guests except Chelsea and Carrie Willis had left aboard the *Temple II* for Virgin Gorda. Josif, Levi, Sandor, and Rebecca accompanied them. Josif took the opportunity to teach Josh and Dave the art of sailing a 127-foot yawl.

Harbin, rarely a hard drinker, took a sip of his gin and tonic. He admitted to Chelsea that he had overheard the latter part of Chelsea's earlier conversation with Josh and Dave about retirement. Harbin said, "Joe, you can't believe you will never retire."

"Until I am physically unable, I will never sit still."

"You know it will happen eventually. You may slow down the aging process, Joe, but it is not in our power to stop it."

Chelsea nodded, but reluctantly. "Reuven, I'm fully aware that there will come a time when I will be forced to eat my own platitudes." He lifted his drink, as if offering a toast. "Until then . . ." He finished his vodka tonic.

Harbin appeared thoughtful. "On that note, Joe, since we have only a prescribed number of years allotted us, let me ask you this: Do you believe the world will ever know we were here? What have we accomplished that makes the world a better place?"

"Hmm. All I can do is be the good guy fighting the bad guy. Beyond that . . . the world's problems become too heavy." He was silent a moment. "I haven't even left any progeny to remember what little—if any—accomplishment is attributed to me." Chelsea sighed heavily, a bit morose. "Sorry, Reuven, this is becoming maudlin. Is there anything new in the works?"

Harbin apologized for creating the somber mood then told him that he had faxed Ari a message aboard the *Temple III* docked in Piraeus. Ari had been instructed to leave two men in charge of the yacht while he and the remaining crew returned to the Caribbean. "We'll have a full crew here by this time tomorrow," he added.

Chelsea gave him a sidelong glance. "You expecting something?"

"No. Just keeping a step ahead of the game."

"What about Willis? Where will you fit her in? Or are you baiting Spencer Medwal?"

Harbin gave Chelsea a small smile. "Have you noticed, Joe, how often we're beginning to think alike?"

"Is that good or bad?"

"I'm not certain. There may come a time when it might be wiser for one of us to assume the role of devil's advocate."

After a brief silence Chelsea pushed back the peak of his Greek Fisherman cap and said, "I prefer it to be you.

I admit you are more experienced in this field. I, as a former city cop, don't have your background."

"Don't belittle yourself." Harbin stopped suddenly to look up. A flock of birds, rousted from the trees by a sharp gust of wind, flew by. Windswept white clouds cluttered an otherwise blue sky. The clouds resembled balls of cotton that had been stretched into thin lengths. "A change in weather?" Chelsea asked.

"Not predicted," Harbin said, scanning the landscape until it merged with the watery horizon. To his right the north cove was protected by a spit of land. Only two boats—neither one the *Spaced Out*—occupied the safe water. It was early yet for boats to anchor. Eventually there would be about a dozen more. It was an excellent anchorage, but not that good for anyone wanting to come ashore. Mangrove roots grew profusely along the shore-line, discouraging trespassers.

Harbin pushed up his sunglasses to better scan the horizon, then sniffed the air. Chelsea asked, "What are you checking?"

"Nothing," he answered hastily. "I'm smelling the weather. I can sometimes sense change."

Chelsea had the feeling that Harbin had a sixth sense there might be trouble.

"Should we be armed?" Chelsea asked.

Harbin waved a hand. "Not necessary. At least, not yet."

A portable phone on the table at his side rang. He lifted it and listened. It was Josif calling from the marina just north of Spanish Town on Virgin Gorda. "We've been tailed ever since we docked," Josif said. He described a man and asked if the description rang any bells. Harbin told him to repeat the description to Chelsea. He handed the phone to Joe.

Chelsea nodded halfway through the conversation. To Harbin he said, "It has to be Spencer Medwal." He returned the phone to Harbin and added, "Tell Josif to accost the man and ask if he wishes to see Willis. If so, invite him to return with his own boat at seven and stay for dinner." He looked to Harbin for confirmation and got the expected nod.

Harbin smiled after hanging up the phone. "You do like to grab the bull by the horns, Joe."

"Saves a lot of time and sometimes flusters the opposition. He *is* supposed to be 'friendly.' He also might know something of the men on *Spaced Out*."

"Why do you think he will accept the invitation?"

"Something in the way Willis spoke about Medwal led me to believe there might be something going on between them. You didn't catch it?"

"I had a suspicion, but couldn't be as certain as you are." Chelsea nodded, but waited for Harbin to continue. "What will you be seeking from Medwal?"

Chelsea's eyebrows lifted. "I thought I'd leave that to you. He is, after all, the sheikh's nephew. The sheikh is the one most likely issuing orders for your protection. Why? Tonight will be the time to find out."

"You feel certain he will show?"

"I'll bet on it."

"And how will you make him talk?"

"Again, I will leave that to you. Somehow I believe you're more gifted at this than I."

Harbin lifted the portable phone and punched in a number. "Yetta? How's our guest doing?" He listened for a few seconds. "Okay, please bring her here. To the pool area. I wish to speak with her."

When brought to the pool patio, Willis was wearing a borrowed jumpsuit. Harbin asked if she was comfortable in her stay, to which she replied, "I'll know better when I find out what you're expecting from me."

Harbin said, "I'm expecting Medwal to show for dinner tonight."

Willis's astonishment was apparent. "By invitation? And he agreed?"

Chelsea said, "Why does this surprise you? Did you believe he would abandon you totally?"

The question caught her off balance. "Well, I have no way of really knowing what to expect from him. Yes, it does surprise—no—shock me. I wouldn't under any circumstance expect him to come after me. It goes against his own rules." She glanced from Chelsea to Harbin. "If I may ask: What did either of you offer to induce him?"

Harbin smiled. "I wanted to know if he wished to see you." Her lips compressed in what could have been a silent whistle.

"What do you hope to gain by this?"

"Information," Harbin said. "Do you think it will be possible?"

Willis pondered his question. "I don't really know. I've worked *for* him, but never with him."

She was standing, having refused a seat earlier. Harbin asked her again to seat herself. Vinyl lounges were plentiful on the patio. This time she accepted. He asked her if she wished a drink of any kind, which she declined. She finally asked the question lingering in her mind. "Mr. Harbin, I was hired to protect you, but was never told why. Can you tell me this much?"

Harbin said, "I'm hoping Medwal will divulge this information. You have no idea?"

"I did overhear something about a young boy, but the subject was never discussed with me."

Harbin was taken aback for a moment. *So—the boy—Shafik doesn't give up. He still believes* . . . He hesitated in his thinking, not desiring to dwell upon it. But, of course, it couldn't be dismissed. *Was it possible?*

Chelsea observed both parties in silence. Harbin, in spite of former denial, was concerned with this particular boy. Before Chelsea could ask Harbin anything, a house servant arrived to announce luncheon.

Spencer Medwal was a little shook up by his encounter with one of Harbin's men. He could only reprimand himself silently. To Josif he had said, "When did you suspect me?"

"Leaving the docks, then going through the enclosed mall."

"I was that obvious?"

"Not really. I lost you a couple of times."

"Then you didn't see the man who was shadowing me?"

It was Josif's turn to appear surprised. "No, was there another working for you?"

"Certainly not for me. I thought he might be one of yours. That's probably where I got careless, watching my back rather than you."

"When did you notice him?"

"In the hotel lobby. I was waiting and hoping for Willis to return."

Josif's gaze was level with Medwal's. "You know anything about a bareboat named *Spaced Out*?"

"Never heard of it." He spoke easily, without doubts, now that he knew Carrie Willis was safe. As for why his presence was wanted, he hadn't a clue. Willis must have talked, he decided. He suspected Harbin of being a more complex man than he had thought. His uncle might have been guessing the situation correctly. Although a bit far out—the kid didn't even resemble Harbin in the slightest—his uncle Shafik insisted there was something peculiar about the entire incident at the time. It was because of the boy Medwal was to buy up common shares in Harbin's investment corporation. He intended for the boy to own them eventually. His uncle believed it was owed the boy.

Josif glanced at his watch. "It's best you leave now. I'll be on the lookout to see if I'm being followed by anyone else." He left Medwal and joined his own group. Rebecca wanted to know if Medwal was agreeable, to which Josif replied, "Reuven apparently has the situation well in hand. The man agreed." He then said, "Don't be obvious, but check carefully every once in a while to see if we are being tailed, possibly by one of the men from the bareboat."

Rebecca sighed. "Josif, I hope we're not getting involved in something resembling our last mission on the island."

Josif rolled his eyes. "Trust Reuven. He's not looking for it either."

They were interrupted by Meg who reminded them that they had better hurry if they wanted to get in a swim at the Baths. The Baths lay at the southern end of Virgin Gorda—a haphazard formation of huge boulders created by a cataclysmic event eons ago. Sea waters had worn them smooth over the centuries. In some areas the house-high boulders leaned on one another, forming pools in dark caves.

Spencer Medwal, back at the hotel, was still trying to comprehend Harbin's invitation. Harbin's man had inferred that Carrie was unharmed and was a guest rather than a captive despite her unlawful entry onto the estate. From his wardrobe he selected a white jacket and dark trousers and laid them out on the bed along with a white shirt. He might as well be dressed for whatever the occasion demanded. He found himself humming as he took a shower and it took a while before he realized it. It was the fact that Carrie Willis was unharmed. He decided then and there that he would not use her again in these operations. He then wondered whether he himself had had it with undercover work.

"So, Josh, what's your decision on the *Temple*? Will Cindy go along with a purchase—if that's what you want?" asked Dave.

"She's already in love with it, and you can't beat the price. The short cruise to the Virgin Gorda Yacht Harbor was enough to sell her. She's taken to sails like an old sailor."

Josif said, "You wish to pilot the return trip? If so, I suggest you leave the marina under power. Once offshore we can set whatever sails you'd like."

"Agreed," Josh exclaimed eagerly.

The women joined them. Dave asked Mae how they had enjoyed the afternoon ashore. The ladies were all smiles. Even Meg seemed more relaxed than when going ashore. She said to Josh, "By your face I gather you might be purchasing this yacht, Josh."

"Under sail a boat could be slower, but it's definitely more exciting. Just listening to the water slapping against the hull as it moves soundlessly otherwise makes me feel like an adventurous seafarer."

As they prepared for departure any danger of unexpected encounters was forgotten. All were eager to participate in the untying of lines. Everyone was aware Cindy needed no persuasion and all were happy for her and Josh, knowing full well that Harbin's asking price was more than fair.

Ellie was just finishing her cosmetic touch-up when she addressed Chelsea. "I hope you don't intend sailing the new yacht back to Boca with Josh should he ask you."

"The thought never entered my mind. Harbin's saving Josh the trouble. Part of the deal will include a crew to deliver it to Boca."

Ellie looked away from the makeup mirror. "Joe, can I ask you a serious question?"

"Shoot. Have I ever stopped you?"

"Are we in real trouble here? You know what I mean. You never did explain what happened on the Santorini steps."

Chelsea made a face. He was not in the habit of hiding things from her. "It wasn't important. Reuven and I were mistaken for somebody else."

Ellie rolled her eyes. "Joe, don't be obvious. We *are* in trouble. Reuven wouldn't have shunted us from Greece otherwise. He admitted just so much to us. Don't try to make it a trifling matter. Give us girls some credit. On Virgin Gorda Josif and his crew watched over us like bodyguards protecting VIPs. Let's have it, Joe. Confession time. We never kept anything from each other before. Why now?"

Chelsea was fiddling with a tie until Ellie took it from him. "You don't need it. Stop stalling, Joe."

Chelsea repressed a sigh, then plunged in. "At first we believed Sheikh Shafik was after Reuven. Because of something in his past."

He hesitated just a bit too long for Ellie. She said, "Okay, then what? That was an 'at first.'"

"The Sheikh's brother-in-law then entered the picture." Chelsea watched for her reaction when adding, "His brother-in-law is Suliman, a former member of the board of directors of the Benefactor Alliance."

Her eyebrows arched. "Not again, Joe. We're not going to have a repeat performance of last fall. When will it end?" Her eyes displayed fear. "What is he after this time? You said the organization was finished."

"It is. The Alliance itself doesn't exist any longer. Suliman, and perhaps one other, Nestor Hobbs, are the lone culprits today."

"Bluntly put, then you're the target—not Reuven." When he didn't add anything more, Ellie said, "So, what are we doing about it, besides waiting for the shoe to drop?"

"We can't make the first move." It was said simply, without resorting to worry.

Ellie's expression was grave, a tinge of anger applied. "Joe, it doesn't bother you one bit. You're really thriving on it. Another adventure for the man in retirement. Do Josh and Dave go along with whatever you're attempting? I can tell you now we girls won't accept this latest news lightly." As if just reminded, she added, "And can I assume you now have Reuven involved in this latest episode of the Sunset Detectives?" The last was stated harshly.

Chelsea was at a loss as to how to diminish her fears. "This is Reuven's territory. He knows best how to protect his guests. It's the reason we're here. There will be no repetition of the peril we suffered last time."

Ellie tilted her head defiantly. "I wonder how Meg will accept this. I know this is far from what she's been expecting from Reuven."

"Since we're on the subject, just what was she expecting from him?"

"Please, Joe, don't be obtuse. The two of them are obvious. Whatever Meg's searching for she's in a position of being greatly disappointed or terribly hurt. They need our troubles like a hole in the head. And to be quite candid, Joe, I believe Meg knows far more about Reuven than any of us."

Chelsea had suspected as much. Reuven was making a move toward a closer relationship with Meg and had confided more of himself to her than anyone else. This had been gleaned from conversations with him. He wanted her to understand his past commitments, and that he was no longer associated with them. Should he be called upon for any reserve duty, it would be only as a consultant. Harbin said she agreed to accept him on those terms.

He faced his wife, his manner sober. "Ellie, I'm curious. Would you venture a guess and say they've slept together?"

She made a face, as if tasting something sour. "Joe, it's none of our business. Why do you ask?"

"Josh has wondered out loud in my presence."

Ellie straightened her back. "He has no right to say

anything. Meg knows her own mind—and she's very capable of handling her own private affairs."

He patted his hair down with an open palm. "Okay, okay, I won't mention it again. Now, are we ready to join the others?"

She turned to face him. "Should we be expecting any excitement tonight?"

"Not to my knowledge." His fingers were crossed behind his back. "In any case, we won't start it." Ellie shook her head. Past experience said Murphy's Law was still in effect.

The blond man wiped his fingers with a wet cloth after finishing his fifth buffalo wing. Red was sipping a mug of hot coffee. Bubba, a giant of a man, six-foot-three and 230 pounds, was chewing on a toothpick. Bubba was the man who issued the orders. A former CIA and Special Forces man in Vietnam, he was accustomed to leading. Although his manner indicated his intelligence was superior to that of his cohorts, he was under strict orders to do nothing until instructed by Nestor Hobbs, with whom he didn't always agree. Hobbs was too much of a pussyfooter. Bubba believed in going for the throat when the opportunity arrived. Hobbs didn't want to start a war on Reuven Harbin's home ground. He said that Harbin was too much of a VIP to mess with and, besides, he had no quarrel with him. Chelsea had to be taken care of with finesse. How to accomplish that Hobbs left to Bubba's ingenuity.

Bubba stood on the rear deck of the *Spaced Out* holding a star scope to his eyes. A dinner party was taking place at the Harbin mansion. And strangely enough there was Spencer Medwal and his lady partner.

Had they involuntarily joined forces with Chelsea? If so, what was their game? He scratched his chin, feeling the stubble of a full day's growth. Unusual for him; most times his appearance was impeccable, his face cleanly shaved and his attire proper for whatever the occasion demanded. The trouble was that they were acting the roles of sport fishermen. This meant that they wear only the cutoff shorts and colorful print shirts of men on a lazy vacation. Watching the *Sea Temple* tied up in dock he became aware the crew had been enlarged. Could it be possible they suspected something was in the works? It meant he had to get in touch with Hobbs. Bubba was no fool. The job had taken on a new twist. There simply were too many men guarding the island. The odds had turned against the crew of *Spaced Out*.

As the group finished with dinner Harbin announced that since the weather was so mild dessert would be served on the outdoor terrace. A light breeze stirred the upper fronds of stately palms nearby. Medwal was having trouble comprehending Harbin's invitation and the friendly atmosphere since his arrival. Shortly before being seated for dinner Harbin had quietly told him that there would be no discussion of "business" until after the meal.

At first Willis seemed subdued, but it didn't require much observation to see she was really at ease here, that she was even enjoying herself. At the table he had learned that she had revealed the secret of her Russian background and upbringing. This he couldn't understand. What had changed her? A softening of attitude—outlook? It was almost as if she had allowed herself to be adopted by the women here. Was it a craving for family ties? He could only wonder what use she would be to him now. The thought left him distraught. Then it struck him that perhaps she was playing a role of acceptance. If she was, she was fooling him as much as anyone else.

Chelsea accompanied Medwal to the terrace. He had had little chance to pump him at the dinner table. Josh and Dave didn't trust Medwal despite Harbin's relaxed attitude about his presence. In the open air Chelsea went right to the core of Medwal's business and asked him whether Willis was ever required to do wet work for him. He had been told Willis had been fully trained in martial arts in Russia but had never become operational in the States. Medwal insisted that he had never required her for such an operation.

"How about others? How deep were your mercenaries extended in their duties?"

Medwal eyed Chelsea carefully. "I sent men to South America and occasionally to Africa. Once there they took orders from the local powers."

"They accepted employment anywhere you sent them?"

Medwal smiled abstemiously. "I'm not their conscience. They have the right to refuse any mission."

"Except in Willis's case. There your conscience ruled."

Medwal's lips tightened. He said finally, "Am I that obvious?"

"I think so, but I don't look upon it as a weakness."

Medwal reached into his jacket for his wallet. He withdrew a business card. The card read SOUTHERN CABLE COMPANY, PRESIDENT SPENCER MEDWAL. "This is my front business, started by my father, but it does well enough should I wish to retire from my sideline business."

Chelsea gave him a knowing look. "I saw some of your trucks. Are they all equipped with satellite dishes?"

Medwal smiled. "Who was the first to recognize its purpose? You or Harbin?"

"Does it matter?"

"Not really. Just making conversation."

Medwal had lost the edge—if he had ever had one—with Chelsea and Harbin. He was no longer in charge of affairs. It was a new experience for him. But whose direction was he now following? He recognized that the two men shared an equal leadership. And that both were qualified to handle any situation that arose. As a former captain of New York's homicide division Chelsea had the experience of command. Harbin, as far as he had learned, was a former colonel in Israel's Air Force, and Medwal suspected the man also had the experience of command. Based on this he was forced to ask himself why it was necessary for his uncle to request protection for either man.

Nothing he had seen so far lent credence to his uncle's suspicions. Reuven Harbin's island fortress was impenetrable, guarded as it was by his personal force. Willis had been discovered so easily—and she had been sent only to reconnoiter.

To Chelsea he said, "Can I ask you a personal question regarding Carrie Willis?"

"You can try."

"Is she a prisoner here?"

Chelsea debated a proper reply. "Let's say she's on a temporary stay."

"For how long—and for what purpose?"

"The time frame is indefinite. As to purpose it depends on what we still have to learn from her." He gave Medwal a sidelong glance. "Perhaps you can do better with supplying us the information we want."

"Pertaining to what?"

"We need something more tangible. Yes, we know about the sheikh's nephew and what he wants to believe, but why does this become a catalyst for the murderous attempts on our lives?"

Medwal seemed puzzled. "I assumed you knew about Sheikh Suliman, Shafik's brother-in-law."

Chelsea registered no surprise. "Yes, we know about him, but it doesn't explain the extra tail on us, the one that doesn't work for you. Speculating, rather than assuming, a good guess says they work for Nestor Hobbs, a former associate of Suliman."

"You said 'they.'"

Chelsea smiled appreciatively. Medwal was on the ball. "We believe there are three men keeping us under observation. Most likely they're aware of your arrival."

"If they are who you say they are, then you know more about them than I do."

"What can you tell me about Suliman?"

"He's a hothead—always has been. He used to help finance the PLO. He may still. I met him only once— many years ago—and was warned to never antagonize him. What did you do to make an enemy of him?"

Chelsea waved a hand. "It's a long story. But I must ask you: If you're looking out for our welfare aren't you antagonizing him?"

Medwal smiled tentatively. "Not if he doesn't know it."

"Doesn't know what?" Dave Ward asked, walking up and jumping into the conversation.

"We're discussing Suliman," Chelsea said. "We still don't know whether he's working together with Hobbs."

"What's the difference? It doesn't change anything.

Right now I'm more interested in whether you . . ." he pointed to Medwal ". . . know the guys who are supposedly former CIA members."

"You have names? Can't tell the players without a scorecard."

"Very funny," Josh said, joining in.

Chelsea said, "We'll know the names in the morning."

"Then what?" Medwal asked with little enthusiasm, aware he wasn't being taken fully into the fold. "And by the way, will I be allowed to leave later tonight? Or will I be in the same category as Ms. Willis? On temporary hold?"

Chelsea said, "As host it's Harbin's privilege to negotiate with you."

"He may ask for your services," Josh offered. "In any case, I think it wise that you listen to him."

Medwal continued to be puzzled. Their attitudes were always altering. At times he felt as though he was their enemy, then, suddenly, their partner-in-arms. Why would they seek his services? He didn't know what to make of it. Did they need him? Or was it an original form of confrontation? Although it was not his custom to relinquish being in charge, he recognized he was in the company of commanders. In spite of himself, he was being persuaded that he listen—or as they said so nonchalantly, "negotiate." *And besides,* he convinced himself, *it had become an interesting diversion. There was always room to learn more about the business when dealing with experts.*

He looked for Carrie and wondered what she had picked up during her stay. They hadn't had the chance to speak with each other in private—or perhaps hadn't been allowed the opportunity to do so. He shook his head. There were too many questions still unanswered. "Let patience be your guide" was what Harbin had said to him earlier.

He sighed deeply. So be it.

Bubba read the fax message he had just received.

ABORT THE MISSION AT THIS TIME. USE THE TIME TO BETTER PREPARE YOURSELVES FOR YOUR MEETING WITH THE SUBJECTS IN FLORIDA.

There was no signature; none was necessary. Bubba read the message to his cohorts, which brought snickers from both men. Red said, "It sounds like he's not satisfied with our work."

"With what he's paying us, we shouldn't complain," Bubba said scornfully. "It's the man's privilege."

"So, now what?" the blond Adonis said. "We continue to sit around with the glasses? What good does it do?"

Bubba deliberated only briefly. "We go ashore with the proper electronic gear. It's a waste of time using it here from the boat. There's simply too much interference."

Red said, "How do we do that? The house is too well guarded. Not only with men, but with sophisticated equipment."

"We use the infrared glasses to circumvent the laser beams. It can be done."

"Okay. When?"

Bubba scratched at his knee. Wearing denim cutoffs, his legs resembled those of an NFL lineman. As a matter of fact, all three were built like they were primed for the

Super Bowl. Bubba straightened and said, "No better time than tonight. Everyone who matters is there."

Red said, "Yeah, maybe we can get a make on the guy who was tailing them on Virgin Gorda."

The blond Adonis said, "How do you figure him now showing up as a guest? My original thought was that Hobbs might have hired him as backup for us. But you say Hobbs denies all knowledge of him. Now I don't know what to think."

Bubba shook his head; his cohorts didn't have too much in the brain department. The man had to be working for a third party and then had to have been turned by Harbin's men when he was caught by them.

"Who stays aboard and who goes ashore?" Red asked.

"You're to come with me," he answered. "We all keep in touch with hand mikes, but use earphones to prevent anyone picking up voices."

"Where we going in?" Red asked.

"On the mangrove side. It would be the least expected and therefore the least protected area."

The Adonis looked disappointed. He had expected that they would go into Roadtown on Tortola and pick up some female companionship. With two cruise liners in port there was bound to be some available. Bubba regarded him with disgust. "We don't play when we're working" was a warning oft repeated.

The *Spaced Out* dropped anchor thirty minutes later, in the area Bubba had marked out on the map. There were no other boats in the vicinity, at least none closer than fifty yards from the shoreline. No one wanted to chance having an anchor entangled with mangrove roots—they were sharp enough to punch holes in any craft. Within a half-hour Bubba and Red were in black scuba outfits with spear guns in hand. Slipping into the water they barely disrupted the surface of the calm lagoon. The night was warm and there was no breeze to carry the sounds they were making.

Once they had maneuvered across the mangrove growth they stood on the shore. Red took a pair of night goggles for each of them from his waterproof backpack. The goggles had the ability to detect the laser beams that crossed the perimeter trail. Bubba signaled Red to follow him as instructed. Both men crawled on their stomachs to stay clear of the beams. Bubba's target was the top of a knoll about fifty yards from the path.

It took twenty minutes to establish the base. From the pack Bubba withdrew a saucerlike dish and then attached a cone to its center. It resembled an old-fashioned room heater. Wires protruding from the rear of the dish were connected to earphones that they plugged into their ears. Bubba then turned the dish, adjusting it for direction until he heard voices come through clearly.

All were on the screened-in terrace patio. A table had been set with carafes of iced tea and plates loaded with delicate pastries. Their conversation was interrupted by Sandor, who had come down from the tower with an important message. He leaned into Harbin's ear. "The *Spaced Out* has dropped anchor in the north cove, about fifty yards off shore."

"How long has it been there?"

"About ten minutes."

"No movement on board?"

"None caught." He waited a beat. "Any instructions?"

Harbin waved a dismissing hand. "Not at the moment.

I may take a walk with my guests. You can keep an eye
on the monitors, but do nothing until you hear my
orders."

Chelsea, listening in, glanced at Harbin questioningly.
Harbin whispered, "Get Josh and Dave. We're going for
a walk."

Chelsea lifted a finger, signaling Dave and Josh to join
him. To Harbin he said, "How about Medwal?" Harbin
nodded. "Bring him also."

Harbin turned to Medwal. "Do you have other opera-
tives working this area?"

"Absolutely none. Why ask now?"

"I believe we're about to have intruders." And thinking of the ten-minute interval after dropping anchor,
added, "They might be on the island already."

Chelsea said, "I thought your security couldn't be
bridged."

"Pros can always find shortcuts, Joe."

Red scratched at his face, the bugs feasting on him.
"Christ! I hope there's no snakes here. That's all we'd
need. If it weren't for these rubber suits we'd be eaten
alive."

"Quiet. Something's wrong. They're either speaking in
whispers or have stopped talking altogether." He put on
the infrared glasses to reacquaint himself with the land
before them. In an instant he became aware there were no
longer laser beams crossing the path below them. Then
he noticed that there were five men walking down the
grassy hillside, seemingly without a worry in the world.
He felt Red stiffen at his side. Turning he saw a wild
rabbit staring at them. "Don't you dare frighten him,"
Bubba warned. The whisper caused the rabbit to take off

amidst a flurry of loose leaves and disappear into the wild growth. Bubba turned up the volume of the electronic ear.

"What was that?" asked Josh nervously.

"An animal," Harbin said. "Most likely a rabbit."

Dave said, "Something disturbed that animal."

"Why are we strolling like this? Could be we're walking into an ambush," Chelsea said.

"I don't think so. One or two men are not about to take us on."

"So what's the purpose of our walk?" Josh asked.

Medwal listened but kept silent. He knew Harbin was trying to spook whoever had come ashore. He could almost visualize them hiding amidst the dense brush bordering the hillside. He scanned the area where they had heard the disturbance, but nothing could be seen in the darkness.

Harbin halted abruptly. "Let's return to the women."

Chelsea nodded, understanding Reuven's tactic. He was giving the intruders a chance to get back to their boat safely. Josif, in the tower, probably had the boat under surveillance using sophisticated equipment Chelsea hadn't even seen in operation yet.

Chelsea felt a sense of letdown. He had hoped for something to open up. The strange excitement bubbling a moment ago had now abated. He hated sitting back, waiting for the shoe to drop. He was different from Dave and Josh in that he needed the excitement. He never wanted retirement and couldn't accept it as they had. But although his two friends would never admit it, their blood stirred when the action did arrive. Their griping was all a put-on. Chelsea glanced from one friend to the

other, watching their faces, and as always they both gave
him looks that asked how the hell he got them involved
in these ventures. Josh was leaning on his cane, struggling with it as it sank into the grass, but there was no
complaint forthcoming. As for Dave, he was puffing hard
on a cigarette as his eyes scanned the area. If asked he
probably would have admitted his worst hardship at the
moment was wearing slacks in place of cutoff shorts.

After they had taken a few steps back in the direction
from which they had come Medwal asked Harbin, "What
do you have in mind for a followup? Our trespassers get
back on their boat, then what?"

Harbin smiled. "We wait for the chief super's visit
tomorrow. He'll have some news for us that I am sure
will be valuable."

17

Chief Superintendent Clyde Witteger's cruiser arrived at Harbin's dock shortly before noon. He and his aide, Sergeant Halliday, declined the use of a golf cart to take them to the mansion. The chief said he preferred to walk. The day was warm, the sky blue and cloudless; there was no hint of the showers predicted for later in the day. Blooming red hibiscus bordered the path most of the way, but neither man seemed to notice it. The chief's face remained impassive. The sergeant, younger by twenty years, found himself hard put to keep pace with his superior. Both men wore khaki Bermuda shorts, matching knee socks, short-sleeved shirts, and caps. When they arrived at the front door, neither man seemed to be perspiring in the slightest.

The chief studied the facade of the building before hitting a button beside the massive door. He noted the Jerusalem stone. "The man does have a flair for Palestine architecture." He frowned, thinking, *I must remember to say Israel, not Palestine, should the subject arise.*

A Jamaican servant ushered them through a large

foyer to the rear terrace. The two men greeted the guests. Harbin announced that after lunch they would take a tour of the grounds.

To this the chief responded, "There's no need. I've seen it all from the air on a previous occasion."

The conversation over the entree of poached salmon was restricted to local goings-on of no real import. Chelsea would have preferred discussing police methods on the islands but, instead, followed Harbin's lead. After lunch would be more appropriate he had said. "Yes, when the stomach is full," Chelsea had added to himself.

Finishing a cup of tea, Witteger asked Harbin if smoking was permitted on the premises. He was told that as long as it remained out-of-doors he had no objection, whereupon the chief stepped off the terrace and retrieved a Dunhill tobacco pouch from his jacket. As he filled the briar bowl, all of the men with the exception of Medwal stepped down to join him. Shortly, the chief asked, "About that information you requested? You still interested?" Harbin nodded, holding a gold lighter to a cigar.

When the chief noted Chelsea lighting his own pipe he asked, "Your tobacco—an American brand?"

"Yes. A cherry blend. Not so intriguing as your own."

Witteger sniffed the aroma. "Yes, I suspected as much. But it's too much on the mild side for me."

Meanwhile, Sergeant Halliday answered the ladies' questions about the history of the British Virgin Islands. The women understood the men's need for privacy.

Harbin invited the men to grab chairs and sit around a table beneath an umbrella. He asked if anyone wanted drinks, which all declined. "Now," he said, "Chief, what can you tell us of the *Spaced Out* crew?"

Witteger faced him with a sharp eye. "Why do I have

the feeling I won't be telling you anything you don't already know? Sir, your reputation precedes you."

Harbin's eyebrows lifted. "I wasn't aware I had a reputation."

"Sir, I met Cyrus Desmond in London before I left the main office. He warned me to be prepared for anything when you're here in the islands."

"Why would he do that?" Harbin asked, keeping his tone gentle.

"Unfortunately, for whatever the reasons, Cyrus offered no additional advice." He eyed Harbin with some suspicion. "I gather the subject was something of an international nature, very hush-hush. Are you at liberty to elaborate on it?"

"I will admit to 'something of an international nature.'"

"Occasionally you have world figures as your guests and because of this you have taken precautions against untoward action here. I must assume this is true, since I've studied the background of the members of your crew who are in attendance here." He stopped to study Harbin with a penetrating stare. "No matter your denial of this we know it as fact."

Harbin smiled appreciatively. It was time to speak more openly. "Chief, you are obviously a busy man. And I do confirm these facts. As I told you earlier, my present guests are semi-retired men from law enforcement."

Witteger nodded. "I know much of the details of their backgrounds, although not everything. What I don't have knowledge of is their present involvement. How does this Spencer Medwal fit into the overall picture? I'm aware he's former CIA, as are the three men on their chartered bareboat." Again he studied Harbin warily. "Is there another international incident about to occur?"

Harbin realized he had to give the chief something, to do otherwise would be to slight an important man in the islands. The previous superintendent became involved only when the circumstances began to get out of hand. Harbin wished no repeat performance. He said, "Chief, I can give you a much better picture after hearing what you've learned of the three men."

Halliday, who had only moments before joined them, glanced at his superior, as if wondering how his chief would accept the request. The chief liked to run things in his own way and at his own pace. After all, Reuven Harbin, no matter his wealth, was merely a citizen of the islands. He had no official capacity to make requests in these territorial waters. Halliday was surprised when Witteger nodded that he would grant Harbin's request. Witteger was playing it cool, he decided, for whatever his reason.

Witteger checked his briar, which had gone out. He placed it in an ashtray on the table, seeming to measure what he was about to say. "I interviewed the men early this morning." Noting Harbin's eyebrows lift he said hastily, "I repeat, 'interviewed,' not interrogated. The apparent head of the trio is Bubba Pruett, thirty-five years old, a former member of the CIA, now an employee of Hobbs Aeronautics, the security division of Space Age International. The other two, namely Harold "Red" Tryon and Bart Colt, have the same profiles. They're here in the islands supposedly enjoying a fishing holiday. I personally see no cause for alarm at their presence." He levelled his eyes with Harbin's. "Do you see differently?"

Chelsea noted the man's eyes. He had seen the challenging look too often in the past. Smiling, he watched Harbin to see how he would weather it.

Harbin concentrated on a proper reply; it was important he didn't antagonize the official. One never knew when one was needed. "My apologies," he said, "if I appear to have an imperious manner. Unfortunately, this bad habit was instilled in me at an early age by a patriarchal parent. Now I admit I don't recognize strong signs to suggest these men are a cause for alarm."

"But the possibility is there," Witteger prompted.

"There's always a possibility."

"Again, I ask: Why do you have hired help who have had military training?"

Anyone else might have been taken aback by the relentless questioning, but not Harbin. He was quick to reply. "I thought I had answered that earlier. On occasion I have important guests staying here. You must admit, as of late the Caribbean has been inundated with pirates."

"Yes, drug pirates—not political pirates."

"Perhaps so, Chief, but I still must play it safe."

Witteger tapped his ashes into the ashtray. He appeared to be considering his next question. "Why are you interested in the *Spaced Out* crew?" He smiled tentatively. "You can't believe they're pirates. I think it's time you told me what I want to know."

"Very well. Those men could be a threat. We have just returned from Greece where Joe Chelsea's life was threatened. Twice, as a matter of fact. We believe these men have been hired to make an additional strike against him."

Witteger appeared to accept the information passively— almost as if he didn't believe it to be the truth. His attitude bothered Chelsea. He couldn't contain himself. "Everything you've heard is the God's honest truth. The only reason we're here as guests on this island is for protection."

Witteger's back straightened. "Why don't you tell me the reason for these acts against you?"

Chelsea looked at Harbin, but spoke to the chief. "Can you recall ever hearing of an organization called the Benefactor Alliance?"

"No. Never."

"Do you remember reading anything about the destruction of an island off Nassau last fall?"

Witteger frowned as something stirred in his memory. "What about it?"

Josh decided to jump in. "We were the ones to break up the Alliance cartel."

Dave followed up with, "It seems that there are certain former members of this cartel that would still like to do us harm."

Witteger held up his hand. "Just tell me the whole story from the beginning."

Chelsea took over the reins, confiding the story of the Benefactor Alliance. Trying to maintain a modest tone, he wound up by explaining that their small group had been successful in toppling the entire structure of the organization.

Witteger turned to Harbin. "And what, if any, was your involvement in all of this?"

Chelsea stated that it had never been any concern of Harbin's. "But now it is."

Witteger sat back in his chair. "You've been a wonderful host, and I am very appreciative."

Harbin stood up. "Chief, I have an open door policy here. Your presence is always welcome."

"I ask only that you notify my office should any difficulty arise. Can I have your word on that? This territory is my responsibility."

Harbin held a hand to his chest. "You have my word."

Just as Witteger was preparing to leave, a house servant arrived with a letter. "There's a special delivery, sir, for Captain Joseph Chelsea."

Harbin looked at Chelsea, who appeared to be quite surprised. "Who knows you are here?"

"No one but those at Novick Security. Let me see the sender . . . Alex? Why would he send anything other than a fax? I spoke to him yesterday. He said nothing about a letter being on its way."

Dave stepped forward. "Joe, don't dare open it. It needs to be checked out."

Dave took the beige envelope and studied the postmark. "Out of West Palm," he said, holding the envelope daintily by its edges as if fearful of catching a disease merely by touching it. He took it over to the swimming pool, placed it in the water and stood there watching it float for a moment. "Let it soak until the flap opens by itself."

Nothing happened for five minutes and then the flap began to separate from the envelope. Suddenly, a great geyser shot up twenty feet into the air and a loud boom sounded. Waves of pool water rushed over the sides of the pool.

"Well, well," Witteger commented. "It appears someone doesn't find your presence too welcome, Captain Chelsea." He turned to Harbin. "I would like to have whatever scrap is left of that letter if you please."

Harbin nodded. He was pleased to see that the new chief was now displaying the same stoic sort of calm as his predecessor. He also liked that the chief seemed faintly excited by the whole thing as well.

The ladies and Medwal joined them. Medwal and Carrie nodded to each other once they saw the damage. "A letter bomb," Medwal said quietly.

Suddenly Mae Warren erupted. "Mr. Harbin, you've been a wonderful host but I have to say that the entertainment has sometimes been lacking. I say it's time we took leave of this place." She looked to the other women for backup.

Harbin shook his head. "I don't think it wise, ladies. Regardless of what just happened, it's safer for you here than at home."

Chelsea then turned to Harbin. "Reuven, I think it's time we stop waiting around for others to make their move. The chief said this is his bailiwick. Well, Palm Beach County is mine. Simply put, I work better in home territory."

Harbin attempted to curb his disappointment. "Joe, whatever you wish I will go along with. But let me just say that I'm still not clear that you are the only target here. Perhaps it's time that Medwal told us everything he knows about why he was asked by his uncle to protect me and why his brother-in-law Suliman might wish Joe or myself harm. There must be some logic here."

Medwal looked down at the ground for a moment before speaking. "I truly wish that I could answer your questions but I am afraid I am only a hired hand in all of this."

A few moments passed as everyone stood together wondering who or what was behind the danger they were confronted with. Harbin, ever the host, said finally, "Well, I am afraid there is no answer ready at hand. Perhaps we should all take a siesta and join together on the terrace for cocktails at 5:00?"

All travel plans were completed before dinner was served. The party would depart by motor launch from Harbin's island after breakfast the following day. They would then all board a flight out of St. Thomas. Harbin promised Josh that the *Sea Temple II* would be docked in the Boca Raton marina of his choice within two weeks. It seemed that the new boat was approximately ten feet too long for Josh's private dock. With the exception of Meg and Harbin everyone seemed content that this was the right course of action.

Medwal and Carrie Willis sat together on lounge chairs on a discrete terrace on the south side of the mansion. Willis again began the conversation they had started when they first sat down together.

"You can't really believe that our services have been of any real value to these men at this point. Harbin's got a trained army here. No, they are well equipped for any emergency."

Medwal was silent for a few seconds. "Haven't you been curious to see how the situation plays out here? Do you realize you're observing two masters of the trade at work?"

"So what! I've already had my training. And, since you have brought up the subject, I think I've had my fill of this line of work."

He gave her an odd look. "You know there never was a pension plan attached to your employment?"

She smiled. "My boutique does very well and my

overall financial situation is in good order. I don't really
need to be moonlighting as a secret agent. It's time for
me to settle down and find a hobby more to my liking, a
little less dark and sinister."

Medwal appeared to be embarrassed, caught off guard.
"Do I surprise you that much?" she asked.

"So when do you plan to tell our host that you are no
longer engaged in this business and would like to leave
his little paradise?"

"I don't imagine he'll have any problem with us
leaving now."

Medwal became flustered. Us. She said *us*. "Okay,
we'll speak to him about it this evening."

"Good. By the way, my plan is to return to New York,
not West Palm. I hope this isn't an inconvenience to
you."

He nodded. "It'll be okay." Under his breath he added,
"We'll see."

Meg stood in the doorway of her bedroom observing the
cloudless sky that was crowded with stars. They lent a
vague light to her surroundings. The hour was two a.m.
A slight breeze tugged at her robe. She was unable to
sleep.

Suddenly, she found herself moving toward Harbin's
door and pulling it open. The carpet in his room was
thick, drowning her footsteps. She heard no sound until
she got closer to the bed and then she heard him stirring.

Her heart pounding, she advanced to the bed's edge.
This wasn't her, an inner voice shouted. *What am I
doing?* She almost cried out as a hand reached out to take
her own. She heard him say, "Meg, I've been waiting for
a long time."

She let her robe fall to the floor and slipped into his bed. His arms slid around her gently. Her heart was pounding. When was the last time she'd been held like this?

His voice tremulous, Harbin spoke quietly, "Meg, as much as I've wanted you, it's been many years since I shared . . . I don't know if I am capable . . ."

She placed a finger over his lips. "Don't talk," she said. "Just act."

The rest followed naturally.

In the early morning hours of the last night the retirees would spend on Harbin's Haven, two men sat in the living room of a posh Palm Beach mansion engaged in a heated discussion. The 40,000-square-foot early Florida home belonged to one of the men, Nestor Hobbs. Despite the hour, Hobbs's mane of white hair was immaculately combed. His face was dark and heavily lined. It was the face of a seventy-five-year-old man who was now more concerned with his drink, a bourbon and water, than he was with what his partner in crime had to say.

His guest was Suliman ben-Hussad, a heavy-jowled man who weighed almost 150 more pounds than Hobbs. Clad in a Mideast caftan, his figure appeared quite huge.

Hobbs checked his gold Paget: 2:30 A.M. "As we sit here, my dear Sheikh, the main attack is about to begin. There is no one better than Rodgers to command this—for want of a better word—expedition. No one would suspect him as he is supposed to be living another life in the witness protection program. It is the sole reason he no longer works for Wellington Security. For safety's sake even I don't have Wellington backing my security. Yes, indeed, no one is better suited to handle

these so-called Sunset Detectives. He has his own score
to settle with them. And as for this Reuven Harbin, have
you confirmed that he is a former Israeli spy? If so,
we will make your brother-in-law happy as well. Kill two
birds with one stone, as they say."

"And if this is not a successful attack?"

Hobbs made a face. "It has to finish in the Caribbean.
I can't continue to do battle here in the U.S. I have to
protect my image."

Suliman glanced upward. "If only Allah could hear my
prayers."

Hobbs snorted derisively. "Rely on yourself, not on an
invisible deity. You are your own creator."

Suliman appeared shocked. "If you believe so, we can
only fail once again." His eyes glinted angrily as he
gestured around the opulent room. "You believe you
created this without Allah's help?"

Hobbs waved a deprecating hand. "I don't wish to
debate religion with you. If it makes you feel better say
a prayer for Rodgers. He has no simple job on this night."

18

The women stood just outside the front entrance of the mansion watching the flaming dock. Fifteen minutes earlier—at 3:00 A.M. on the dot—all were awakened by a loud explosion.

Mae said, "I hate to say it but I think this was just the lead-in to a much bigger performance."

"That is quite possible," Willis replied softly.

Ellie said only, "I thought after the Alliance breakup it would all be over; the games would be finished." She groaned. "If this is retirement, what comes next?"

Willis started to speak, then thought better of it. "Please," she said, trying to herd them back into the building. "Let's all get dressed. I'll try to get someone on the staff to make coffee."

Chelsea boarded the *Temple* and confronted Harbin and Josif. "Reuven, the bomb was most likely only a diversion. I suggest doubling the perimeter patrol immediately."

"It's been done already, Joe."

"So, what's your next move?" Josh asked, leaning on his cane. "What do you expect will occur at this point?"

Harbin tilted his head, seeking the tower above the mansion. "If there's movement of any kind they'll let us know. Now, if you will please follow me back to my study, I will allow you the choice of small arms equipment."

They were no more than a few yards from the entrance to the house when Harbin's cellular phone beeped. It was Sandor from the tower.

"There's a Mosquito boat without lights sneaking into the north cove and another one at the south cove. No hint yet of what they're up to. Any specific orders, Reuven?"

"Get two men armed and into wet suits. The north cove. They should be prepared for anything." Chelsea watched Harbin closely. The man spoke without hesitation. Dave, seated beside Chelsea, leaned over and said, "Mosquito boats can do 75 knots. They're mostly used for racing or by drug runners. I've never seen one outside of Miami waters.

"So, what would they be doing here?"

"I think we'll know soon enough," Chelsea murmured.

They followed behind Harbin as he led them to his study in the east wing of the house. Once inside he strode across the room to a shelf of books. He removed three books from one of the built-in shelves and a button console appeared. He punched in four numbers and the entire wall of shelves moved forward, then sideways. A long dark tunnel confronted them. Harbin pulled a switch; lamps illuminated an arsenal of handguns. Automatics, semi-automatics, including rifles of all makes, were staked to the wall.

"Pick whatever you're comfortable with," Harbin said

calmly. "Each one comes with a silencer, but I don't think you'll need it." Chelsea selected a Glock 9mm and added an extra clip. Josh lifted a police special .38, Dave a Beretta 9mm. From past experience they were all familiar with the weapons Harbin had available. Harbin took down an uzi and two magazines. And then, as an afterthought, added an M16 assault rifle with a magazine attached.

He waved his hand, indicating they follow him through the tunnel. "This was built by pirates almost two centuries ago," Harbin explained as they followed him through the damp tunnel.

After a fifty-yard walk Chelsea broke the silence. "Reuven, where does this take us?"

"We go through an armory with more supplies just ahead, then continue to the original cave opening. Which just happens to be close to the north cove. There we watch for further development."

When they reached the so-called armory the three guests scanned the area with curious eyes. Crates of food supplies, including bottles of drinking water, lined the walls. There was even a restroom. Open cases of grenade launchers and bazookas were in evidence in one corner of the room.

Chelsea muttered, "My God! Reuven. You expecting a war to break out!"

"I've been threatened by terrorists previously. I can't afford not being prepared for any emergency. What's more—"

Whatever he was going to say was stopped mid-sentence. A booming sound reverberated through the tunnel; dust shimmered off the dirt walls.

"Damn!" Josh shouted. "The ground shook."

Harbin leaped toward the restroom to a phone attached opposite the door. He punched in a single number. From the tower an angry voice almost shouted into the phone, "The north cove Mosquito boat just shot a rocket at the mansion. The west wing was the target."

"Get Josif and Rebecca and have them bring the ladies into the tunnel from my study. You have the men in wet suits?"

"They're awaiting your instructions."

"They need plastique for the Mosquito boat."

Harbin turned to Chelsea. "Joe, my hands are full. Can you carry that bazooka? And Josh, take the cart by the back wall and load it with shells." He noted Josh's cane. "Dave, give him a hand. And hurry. We're taking it out of the cave opening. It's only a few feet ahead."

In less than a minute they pushed aside tree branches and were outside. Looking back toward the mansion they could see smoke rising. The odor of cordite drifted in from the sea. Harbin led them to a small knoll and said to Chelsea, "Joe, can you handle the bazooka?"

"It's been years, but I'll manage. Where's the target?"

Harbin cursed, he had forgotten binoculars. "Look to the south cove. Can you spot the Mosquito there?"

"Just barely." He twisted around. "I can see the north boat. Why don't I try for it?"

"No, I have divers going after that target."

As he spoke a spurt of flame shot from the boat mentioned and whooshed toward the house. The explosion came seconds later; the ground around them shook.

"Jesus! Reuven," Chelsea cried out. "If anything's happened to the women . . ." The smell of burning debris drifted across the island.

Harbin spoke confidently. "It only takes a couple of

minutes to get into the tunnel. They should be safe by now." Chelsea prayed he was right.

Dave shook his head. "I think they're using Russian SAM rockets. You better be right about our ladies being in the tunnel." He scrunched his shoulders, feeling cold suddenly.

Harbin withdrew a miniature cellular phone from his shirt pocket. It wouldn't have worked in the tunnel. He got someone on the *Temple*. He asked for damage control and was told there were two huge holes in the west wing wall of the mansion, and that there were four men on fire detail hosing it down. The dock was left to burn itself out. When asked if he should send his final four men in the powerboat to the north cove, Harbin ordered him to stay put, that the Mosquito boat would blow them out of the water using Russian SAM missiles.

Harbin's personnel would be shorthanded until later in the day—which would be too late—when Ari would arrive with the *Temple III*'s crew. He instructed his man to notify Witteger and have him call in the U.S. Coast Guard, the authority patrolling these waters.

After hanging up Harbin asked the tower to connect him with perimeter control. He learned that two of the wet-suited men were in the water, heading for the Mosquito boat. With that Harbin turned on Chelsea. "Can you sight on the boat in the south cove?"

Chelsea nodded. "Will this missile carry that far? It's at least two hundred yards."

"Target over its position, to prevent its falling short."

Chelsea held the bazooka on his right shoulder and asked Josh to feed the missile. Josh was only too eager to assist. He lifted the long shell from the cart and dropped it into the launcher.

Chelsea's first shot exploded in the mangroves, twenty yards short of the Mosquito boat. It took him seconds to re-aim and order Josh to refill the tube.

The smell of cordite filled their nostrils. When the boat flashed into a fireball all shouted gleefully. Chelsea breathed heavily and spun around. "What about the one opposite? It should be easier."

Harbin shook his head. "No. My men should be attaching plastique to the keel right now. We wait."

Chelsea glanced at him. The man was so confident. He had men putting their lives on the line for him and he was accepting it as a way of life. Harbin twisted around as if reading Chelsea's mind. "Ordinarily, I would never ask anyone to do this job for me, but my men insist I maintain rank and command."

Harbin snapped the cellular phone open again, this time for the tower. He got Sandor. "Get Witteger again. Tell him we've been attacked by terrorists and the body count warrants a coroner and whatever assistance he has ready to handle the situation.

"And Sandor, what's happening in the cove? Were any yachts in the bay hit?"

"No one was hit—most have already sailed for the safety of Tortola.

"Reuven, the *Hatteras* is ready, if needed." The *Hatteras* was their powerboat; it could do better than fifty knots.

"Hold the line open for a few seconds."

Josh whispered to Dave. "How many men do you think were on that boat?"

He got a shrug. "What's the difference now? Besides, we still have another to contend with."

As if directed, the north cove Mosquito boat suddenly

revved its engines and started taking off. Whatever raid was originally planned had been definitively aborted.

"Now!" Harbin shouted into the phone. "Order three men armed with uzis to trail the Mosquito. It's just a precaution. The *Hatteras* won't be able to catch the faster boat. I just want their destination tracked. Right now they're heading in the direction of Jost Van Dyke, but it could change.

"Also let me know whether the divers completed their mission."

Harbin put the miniature phone back into his shirt pocket. "It's over," he said. "Let's return through the tunnel and see that everyone is faring well."

Chelsea stayed him a moment. "Reuven, doesn't it bother you that your divers haven't returned?"

Harbin stared at him. "I have full confidence that they've accomplished their mission. If you wish to wait for confirmation we can do so." He turned to walk down to the perimeter path. He delayed a second and indicated all to follow him. "Leave the bazooka, Joe. It will be taken care of."

Three of Harbin's men were waiting at the waterline. In five minutes two other men walked out of the sea to join them. Their wet suits gleamed even in the darkness. The two divers saw Harbin and scrambled through marshy reeds to meet him. The lead one said, "We have two explosives attached to the keel, fore and aft. They're timed for fifteen minutes." The man checked his waterproof watch. "Starting five minutes ago."

Harbin nodded, but Chelsea grimaced. *How nice it would be if you could convince your brain that the men you were killing were evil.* And then wondered whether any of the others shared a like thought. In appearance they all accepted the information casually. The diver might have been confirming a shopping list. Chelsea noted their faces. But for Josh and Dave, no distress was displayed. Josh and Dave wore tired expressions, but whether from physical exhaustion or discomfitted principles he couldn't determine. He wondered about the body count—and how Harbin would handle it. Two boats—at least three men in each—and that's if they can be found. In any case the superintendent certainly wouldn't be a happy man. How would he handle it? If the chief were to believe Harbin, he would have to bring in an anti-terrorist group to at least investigate.

Chelsea sighed heavily. "How will we know the result of the plastique?"

"In the blackness of night, even miles away the explosion should light up the horizon."

In the tunnel Medwal winced, thinking of the two explosions. A cloud of dust from the shock wave still hovered in the damp air. Curiously, the wives of Harbin's guests didn't appear to be extremely affected. Were they all as callous as their husbands? They took everything in stride as if it were a duty. He glanced at Willis and said, "I'm going out. I have to know what's happening out there."

"What for? You don't work for Harbin."

He glared at her. "What's happened to you? Why are you so disinterested?"

Meg sidled toward them. "Is there some sort of problem?" she asked. She also was becoming antsy. "Can I help?"

Medwal answered her. "No, thanks. Not necessary.

We're just becoming restless hanging around. It's time I ventured a look outside."

Ellie moved in. "I don't think it's a good idea. You may go if you wish but I think everyone else should stay put until someone tells us it's all clear."

Rebecca joined them. "I brought you here to keep you safe. Should anyone leave, you would only disrupt the order of things. I can't detain you," she said to Medwal, "but I'd be very careful out there. You don't know the grounds."

Medwal stared in disbelief. "Are you warning me the property is booby-trapped?"

"In some areas, yes. You can see why it's necessary. This isn't the first time something like this has happened. There are warnings posted in the dock area."

Medwal was stunned. *This island was like a military base! Who the hell was Reuven Harbin?* A similar attack had happened before, his soldier-woman had said. Medwal shook his head. The more he learned, the more curious he became. He had to go outside. To Rebecca he said, "I've been trained to catch the signs."

Willis started to lift a restraining hand, then changed her mind. All watched him depart without saying anything.

Within five minutes Medwal was outside the cave entrance. He had no flashlight, but he could see his way by starlight. He leaned over to better study the ground, looking for footprints. There were many; he followed them carefully. It had been many years since 'Nam. Suddenly he heard voices. He moved stealthily, careful not to be mistaken for an invader. He saw the bazooka on the ground and it felt warm. It had been fired. What did it signify? From his position on the knoll he saw the knot of men at the shoreline. All were armed and looking out across the dark waters; seemingly in expectation. On the opposite side of the island a boat was on fire in the water. As yet unseen by them Medwal raised his arms above his head, the movement catching their attention. He cried out hastily, "Don't shoot. It's only me. Medwal."

Harbin shouted back, "Descend straight down from your location."

"Are the others okay?" Chelsea asked.

A small smile appeared. "Not only okay, but accepting everything calmly." The smile turned into a grin. "Your women are well trained."

"Don't kid yourself," Josh retorted. "We'll hear all about this later."

Dave paid them no attention; his eyes were locked on the horizon. Harbin's Hatteras hadn't called in and the expected explosion of the Mosquito was overdue. He asked one of the wet suits, "What kind of timer—?"

The explosion hit the night sky with a bright light, although it had to be at least ten miles distant. "Jesus!" Dave cried out. "It looks like you hit an ammo dump."

In the next moment Harbin's cellular beeped. It was the tower calling. "I just received word from the Hatteras. A davit from a cargo ship was hauling up the Mosquito when it exploded. The ship's deck is afire. You want the Coast Guard notified?"

"Right away!" Harbin barked into the phone. "You get the name of the ship?"

"Only that it's Greek-sounding."

Chelsea was muttering a curse under his breath. "Dammit! Reuven! There's no way you can clean this up. The chief super is going to have a fit."

Josh was trying to lean on his cane, which kept sinking

into the soft ground. He kept shaking his head and muttering, "This is going to hit world headlines. I can see it now: TERRORISTS ATTACK PRIVATE CARIBBEAN ISLAND." He spun on Chelsea. "Joe, where the hell are we going with this?"

"Yes. O great leader, I also would like to know where we're headed," Dave added smugly.

Chelsea appeared to be mulling it over. Josh prodded his elbow. "Joe, I asked, how are we going to end it?"

Chelsea wore an odd expression. "We fax a message to Hobbs and call for a meeting."

"Just like that," Josh remarked dryly.

"And then what?" Harbin tossed at him.

Chelsea half-shrugged. "Except for your property damage all the losses are on his side. This has cost him a lot of manpower. I have a hunch he'll be ready to call for a truce."

"And why would the loss of manpower have any meaning for him? He most likely believes that human lives are merely part of the cost of building or saving an empire."

"You've hit the nail on the head. It's the publicity he can't stand. As it is he needs a very large rug to sweep his activities under."

Harbin nodded, unable to fault his reasoning. He tilted his head toward the perimeter path. "Let's go check our damage."

Chelsea held back, delaying him. "As to manpower being an added cost in building an empire, Reuven, I have as yet to hear you inquire into the health of your personnel here."

Harbin took time to measure a reply. "Joe, when my men report damage control they automatically include

personal injury. If none is mentioned, it doesn't exist."
He gazed at Chelsea.

"Okay, I'll accept that. But you go ahead, I want to
check on the ladies in the tunnel. I'll meet you in your
study by the fax machine in about twenty minutes."

Nestor Hobbs was rereading the first of the two faxes he
had received within the past twenty minutes. It was from
Bubba Pruett.

WHAT YOU PLANNED HAS TURNED INTO A FIASCO. WHAT'S NEXT?

Hobbs gritted his teeth and dropped the message on
the coffee table. He reread the second message:

IT'S TIME TO DISCUSS STOPPING THE NON-SENSE. NAME THE PLACE.

Harbin's fax number was given, but Chelsea's name
was on it.

Nestor Hobbs was livid. He yelled at Sheikh Suliman,
who stood his ground with a serene expression. Suliman
said, "It's an excellent idea. I would like to meet with this
Chelsea person. I would like to see the man who, at all
turns, has thwarted our way."

The veins in Hobbs's neck bulged as if trying to break
through. "See him? You can't be present when he arrives.
I must convince him that it's over, that I will accept a
truce. With you here that will not be possible. I have to
make my own deal. I can't afford taking blame for the
fiasco. Any hint of duplicity on my part will cause the
cancellation of all government contracts with the space
program. Not to mention that I could also go to prison.

The blame will have to fall upon unknown terrorists. The former Alliance no longer exists to help us."

Suliman burped and held his chest. "This Harbin is an infidel—as is this former police captain and his allies. How is it they can best us so often? And what about this Calvin Rodgers—you were so certain of his skills—you trusted hin to take care of the entire situation. How could you have been so wrong?" The Arab's eyes were dark and angry. His blubbery cheeks shook as if they had a life of their own.

Hobbs stood his ground. "I have said my piece. I'm calling a halt before everything blows up in my face. As for you, you're on your own if you persist in pursuing them. For me, it's a dead issue. I repeat, I will offer them a deal. I don't believe they will refuse."

Suliman started for the door but then hesitated. "You're a fool. Once you start a mission, it must continue until consummated. Nothing can alter the course that Allah commands."

Hobbs's eyes were about to pop out. "Again with Allah! You are a fool not to believe in yourself above all else. It's *your* desire, not Allah's, that requires confirmation. There is no superpower but yourself to guide you. But at the moment, as a friend, I'm offering you guidance. Take it. Retire to your gold tent in the desert. You are fighting a lost cause here. It is apparent we are not—and never have been—in the right. To continue to be greedy is foolhardy. Be grateful that we are still in command of our own industry despite the fall of the Alliance."

"And Calvin Rodgers—where is the promise you had with him? You've heard nothing from him. If he was unsuccessful with Wellington Security, why did you enlist his services?"

Hobbs snickered, looking down on the Arab. "He pleaded ignorance of the Benefactor Alliance directorship other than Seltzmann—our deceased leader and his son. The information he offered was the sole reason for Rodgers having been placed in the witness program. Except with us, he uses a fictitious name. Which, incidentally, I have difficulty keeping in mind."

"For obvious reasons he couldn't return as a Wellington employee."

Suliman delayed at the door. "If and when you should hear from him, I want to rehire him for my own personal use. Is that understood?"

Hobbs gave him a harsh glare, he hated verbal fencing with anyone. Then he nodded. "You're a fool, but you can have him." He was happy to see the Arab finally depart.

He walked across the immense library to the fax machine in one corner. Still no word from Rodgers. *Had he been eliminated?* Bubba had not mentioned any details as of yet. How had he so misjudged his opposition? The merging of Reuven Harbin and Joe Chelsea had made them an invincible combination. The two had brought him to the verge of total disaster. It was ironic that Chelsea himself was offering him a face-saving exit by calling for a meeting.

The immense house was quiet, all servants at their stations, ready to service the master's needs when required. Security patrolled the grounds of the huge estate, which dated back to the twenties. Hobbs sat down at the Queen Anne desk to work out a fax reply. At first he deliberated calling his attorney, then decided against it. This had to be private. He winced suddenly and opened a drawer to retrieve antacid tablets lying there. He had been told by his physician that he suspected that Hobbs might have an ulcer, but his obstinate vanity denied further examination. He was in his middle seventies and had never been seriously ill in his life. He swallowed three pills, then pulled out a pad from the desk drawer. Changing his mind again he turned to the IBM computer and started to compose a message for E-mail delivery.

All the men were in Harbin's private study when the E-mail showed up on the screen. Hobbs was proposing they meet at his home in Palm Beach. He proposed that the meeting would be a truce. He named a date and time forty-eight hours away and asked if it met with their approval.

"He doesn't mention any security," Josh said. "You believe he can be trusted?"

Harbin said, "We won't go unprepared, but I do believe he's had it."

"What of the damage to your estate? How will you handle it?"

The west wing had to be reconstructed and all furnishings replaced. Harbin smiled as if enjoying a thought. "I'm handing him a bill for $300,000 in damages. And no ifs, ands, or buts, I will expect him to take care of it."

"What of the manpower it cost him?" Dave asked.

"That's his problem, not ours." He answered another question before it presented itself. "Witteger has requested a cleanup crew from MI5. The government will use any means to prevent unwanted publicity for their territory."

Josh shook his head. "I wouldn't want their job. How will they explain the cargo ship fire?"

"Careless packaging of combustibles."

Medwal asked suddenly, "Harbin, you've been through this before, yet little is known about you. Who are you truthfully? How does a billionaire get involved in this type of exercise?"

"I've been known to help out a friend in need. The publicity is always held to a minimum."

Medwal gave him a sidelong glance. "And that warrants the arsenal you have?"

"I once had a vice president here as my guest. I can't rely entirely on outside security. I'm prepared for any emergency."

Josh, getting restless, interjected, "What about the meeting? It's two days away. Do we accept his invitation as stated?"

Chelsea's stomach growled: He checked his watch: 4:30 A.M. "I suggest we have breakfast, then get ready to depart for St. Thomas. We'll catch up on sleep aboard the plane. To Dave, he said, "Send Hobbs a reply: We accept his invitation."

Dave's smile expanded into a grin. "Then I take it our vacation is definitely over. We're going home. Right?"

Harbin looked unhappy. "I'm sorry it turned out as it did. Maybe another time we can try it again."

"Reuven, put it on hold for a while," Josh commented. With that, he turned to the door while Dave sat at the computer. "Let's get our girls together for our final island breakfast."

All seemed relieved, but Harbin. He had hoped for more time with Meg. Sighing, he stood over Dave as he fingered the keyboard. Chelsea gave Harbin a quick

study without voicing his thoughts. The man's mind was
stewing with something. He wondered whether it dealt
with the damaged property or his affair with Meg.
Chelsea had seen Meg returning hurriedly from Harbin's
room shortly after the blast had occurred.

19

It was late afternoon when two waiting limos picked them up at Miami International. All were delivered to their proper residences. In private Harbin arranged to see Meg at her Palm Beach residence later in the evening.

After Chelsea and Ellie arrived at their oceanfront condo, Chelsea pleaded he had to check out his mail at Novick Security. "It should be no more than an hour—two at the most," he promised. "You want me to pick up supper on the way back or would you rather eat out?"

Ellie plopped into a lounge chair and kicked off her shoes. "I've had enough dining out for a while. Bring back Chinese for a change. Make your own selections. I'm not moving until you get back."

Chelsea was checking messages on his answering machine: A funeral home offering prepaid plans; a hearing service for deafness; a nursing home invitation. Chelsea erased the messages. So what else is new in Florida? Nothing had changed since they'd left.

He put in a call to Alex and told him he was coming in. Alex seemed overjoyed to hear from him, but didn't offer any reason. He merely said he was glad Chelsea was back. Chelsea suspected a reluctance to speak on the phone. *Now what!* he muttered to himself. Before hanging up he told Alex to call Josh. Briefly he wondered whether he should notify Harbin, but quickly decided to hold off until learning more.

A twenty-car asphalt parking lot fronted the cinderblock, white painted building that housed Novick Security in Boca. The single-story structure was located off the Dixie Highway, not far from the railroad tracks. Chelsea scanned the area for a few seconds. Nothing had changed. It would be a month before Harbin's wrecking crew would start tearing down all the buildings on the block.

Alex was waiting for Chelsea when he entered the building. A Vietnam veteran and former Green Beret, Alex had come highly recommended and had put himself in good standing. His experience in the service had put him in good stead when both Chelsea and Josh needed him in the struggle with the Benefactor Alliance. An inch short of six feet, he carried his 160 pounds well. His hazel eyes had seen much in his lifetime and the job had given him a better outlook for the future. It was rumored a widow of a former army buddy was living with him.

Chelsea put an avuncular arm around his shoulder. Alex was like an adopted son. Searching, he noted worry in the younger man's eyes. "Okay, Alex, let's get right down to the bones. What's bothering you?"

While Alex led him to his office Chelsea greeted other employees on the way. Everyone appeared happy to see him back. He waited for Alex to seat himself at his desk before taking a seat opposite. Alex pointed to the Compaq computer. "I've been exchanging E-mail messages daily with someone who hasn't identified himself yet." He reached into a drawer for some printouts and pushed them across the desk. "I printed them after the first day."

Chelsea gave the sheets a peremptory study then put them aside. "I'll look it over later. Give me the guts of what it contains."

"Josh is on his way. Should we wait?"

"No. I'll fill him in with what he's missed. Please continue. Start with the first day."

The message was meant for Alex specifically. The party knew Chelsea and Josh were away on a trip to the Greek Islands. Omitting superfluous details, Alex said he was offered a new job at double his present wage.

"For doing what?"

"Working undercover here in the office."

Chelsea looked astonished. "He wants you to play a mole? What did you tell him?"

"First of all, Joe, I should explain that the man knew everything about me, including my service record in 'Nam, which is supposed to be top secret. A lot of stuff I'd have thought would never even have been filed."

"All right, so he knew your background totally. What did you tell him?"

"Using E-mail I told him to take, pardon the expression, a hot crap."

Chelsea smiled. Alex rarely lost his temper. "Okay, Alex, did you get any of his background?"

"Nothing, but an educated guess would be that he's former CIA."

"What exactly did he want?"

"He wanted to know what you, Josh, and Dave have been up to."

Chelsea was quiet for a moment. "How about Reuven Harbin? His name never came up?"

"He was mentioned later. I think you were singled out as his principal interest. Read the sheets; see for yourself."

"And you can't venture a guess as to his identity? How do you contact him?"

"He found me on the first day. He gave me his access code, but I never used it. He instituted all calls. I would turn on the machine to check the mailbox for messages, and there he was, every day without fail, recorded any time between noon and five. When I didn't reply to any of them, he would try again on the hour."

"He never clued you with a true purpose?"

At this point Josh walked in. He greeted Alex and shook hands and asked, "What's up?" Chelsea slid the printed sheets toward him.

In silence Josh scanned the sheets for about two minutes. "What's this? A new game for us? Who's the player?"

"Take a guess," Chelsea said. "And make it good. I have an idea as farfetched as it may be."

A frown appeared. "Rodgers?"

"Why not? Who else could orchestrate the setup we encountered at Reuven's island? Hobbs and Suliman both have the finances, but not the ken." Chelsea shrugged. "I'll concede maybe the Arab, but the area is too far from his home court. He'd be lost here."

Chelsea addressed Alex. "Your mystery caller never left a hint? Rodgers liked to lord it a bit." He waited a beat, then said, "Try to contact him now. It's still early. Tell him you're sincerely thinking it over. That you had

more than enough of officers running your life since
'Nam."

Josh appeared stunned. "Joe, tell me you're kidding.
Haven't we had enough of the guy? We're seeing Hobbs
soon. Why can't that hold you?"

"Let's see if it does anything to affect Hobbs's
decision for a truce. If he's serious about it, it means that
Rodgers is on his own—a new player."

Josh shook his head in disbelief. "You can't be trusting
the bastard, Joe. No matter what he says. Haven't we
learned a lesson yet?

"And what of Dave? Shouldn't he be in on it?"

Chelsea held up a finger. Alex was typing the access
code for Rodgers's mailbox. He said to Josh, "Give Dave
a call when we're finished with this and bring him up to
date."

Alex typed a message as Chelsea instructed. In minutes it was answered.

"Surprise! Surprise! This is too sudden. I require a better explanation."

"Is the job still open? Do we meet for instructions? E-mail is not that private."

"Not yet. You still have to prove yourself."

"Okay, as long as it's not of a terminal nature.
I've had my fill of wet work."

The screen remained blank for twenty seconds. Then:

"Why do I sense an outside influence in your
change of attitude? Could it be there's someone
coaching you at your elbow? Captain Chelsea
perhaps?"

"Is your offer open or not? Why bother me with
your suspicions?"

"Forget it! I'll handle the situation by myself. If the captain's there, tell him I'm coming for him."

Chelsea could sense Rodgers's anger in the typed words. Chelsea wrote something on a pad for Alex. Alex typed it in.

"Rodgers, this Chelsea. What are you after?"
"What do you think? You made a fool of me a few months back. At the time I warned you I would be back. As a starter, here is my welcoming."

The screen remained clear. He had signed off, his final message unclear until a few seconds later.

Chelsea was almost shaken from his feet by the blast. It had come from his own office, two rooms beyond Alex's. He pushed through a cloud of spreading dust, Josh and Alex at his heels.

The outer wall of the building in Chelsea's office had disappeared entirely, leaving cinder block rubble. The carnage left no doubt to its intent. It was meant to kill anyone occupying his office. Chelsea's desk was smashed by the weight of the flying debris.

"Dammit! Joe!" Josh cried out, exercising frustration and anger. "How are we going to end this stupidity?"

"Before we work on that, let's have a story prepared for the fire and police investigation. And because of the bombing we can expect an FBI appearance."

"Is this a follow-up on what happened to you in the Caribbean?" Alex asked. Chelsea nodded but delayed explanation for later.

"Shouldn't we call Reuven?" Josh asaked.

"Yes, he has a partner's right to know."

"But Calvin Rodgers . . ." Alex persisted, ". . . wasn't a terrorist. He worked for the Alliance, which now should be a dead issue."

Chelsea answered patiently, "The Alliance *per se* does not exist, but certain avenging members do."

Alex's lips compressed. Not in fear but resignation. "Well, here we go again." He scanned the destruction. One third of the outer wall was spread across the room and its furnishings. "I suppose we have to wait for the authorities before starting cleanup?"

"We can look around but nothing here is to be touched."

Chelsea stepped gingerly over the demolished cinder blocks to return to Alex's office. No one else was now in the building, all employees having left for the day. He used a phone to call Reuven at his Palm Beach condo. In short minutes he had Harbin filled in. Harbin said he would call Meg and advised that Dave should be notified of all probabilities, that Rodgers could be running amok.

"Good. Now I'm going to hang up, Joe. I want to call Meg. Because of Rodgers's unconventional behaviour, we have to check in every direction."

Meg answered the phone on the first ring. "Reuven, I've been waiting for you to call. Would it be terribly inconvenient for you to come over. I know you must have important messages waiting, but I . . ."

"Meg, listen to me. I want you to speak with your houseman and ask if anyone went through your home for any reason at all while you were away. If any packages were delivered do not open them. I repeat, Meg, do not open them. An unexpected problem has arisen and we have to be very careful. I can be with you in ten minutes but, in the meantime, check with your houseman."

"Very well, Reuven, I'll comply with all instructions, but do bring a bag with you for an overnight stay."

"Meg, are you certain this is the way you want things to stand?"

"For now, yes. Later—I don't know . . . I can't make that decision at this moment. Not until I'm certain of knowing what I'm seeking. Bear with me, Reuven. An affair, illicit or otherwise, is difficult enough for me as it is."

"Meg, I'm not of the younger generation. I don't know what your expectations are. I've been out of the field for a long time."

"Reuven, age is not a problem for either of us. That was proven last night. The truth—do you want out? Last evening meant nothing to you?"

Harbin sighed heavily. Until the previous evening he had thought loving someone again was not meant to be. The awakening of the wanting and the urges was like the dawn of a new age. He hadn't realized how much loving and being loved had been missing from his life. Meg had become the missing chemical in his physical makeup and now fearing for her safety caused a terrible ache in his chest.

"Meg, ten minutes—I'll be there to tell you how important you have become for me. I love you, Meg." They were words he hadn't uttered to a woman for what seemed like decades. He smiled suddenly, hanging up the phone. There was a release within him.

He turned to the pile of mail left on his desk by his valet. He lifted each envelope gingerly, feeling the thickness and seeking any clues of hidden springs.

• • •

The silence was overbearing until Harbin arrived. He left his BMW convertible in the driveway. A ten-minute summer storm had dwindled to a drizzle. In the foyer the houseman took his rain jacket and the overnight bag he had dropped. He was directed to the study where Meg greeted him with a warm hug and kiss. "Thank God you've come."

"Have you eaten?" he asked. "We can go out. There are many good restaurants in the area."

"Oh, no. I have something prepared. Cold turkey and roast beef, salad, and I can have hot soup ready in minutes. The freezer is always well stocked."

Harbin took her hands in his own. "Meg, it can wait. We have to talk."

"What is there to say? We've taken the plunge. I certainly am not sorry." She noted his frown and wondered what it meant. She waited for his comment, beginning to fret.

" 'The plunge,' " he repeated. "Is that an aphorism for falling in love? Meg, I want more. We're both at an age when a commitment should be required. And by commitment I don't mean sneaking in love trysts whenever it's covenient."

Meg's eyes widened. "Reuven, are you proposing marriage?"

"Yes. I'm too old for a backstreet affair." He held her by the shoulders, at arm's length. "Meg, what do you say? I hope you're not going to insist I get down on my knees."

The tears came. "Reuven, we don't even know each other."

Harbin kissed her gently. "What better way to learn

than on the job? You certainly can't feel we're too old to learn." He caught her eyes. "I have only one request tonight."

"You don't have to ask; we can use the guest room."

The pressure in Harbin's chest eased somewhat, now that the die was cast. He felt Meg breathing easier also. He wondered what thoughts were going through her mind. As for himself, he said a silent prayer, hoping Anya would understand.

Meg wiped a teardrop from her cheek. She had agreed to marry a man no less a stranger than her first husband had been when he had proposed. Such a sheltered life, no other men had ever touched her. But the two men in her life were totally different. Her husband's life was an open book, without secrets. Reuven's existence consisted of playing other lives. And at times, she realized, he was still adopting other roles. Yes, she thought, there had to be a learning period for them. There were questions she had to ask.

It was obvious her mood had altered. "Meg, have I assumed too much? Too quickly? If I appear hasty, it's because I wish to take advantage of whatever years are left us. The calendar keeps advancing. I can see it in my mirror and feel it in my bones. Perhaps in a love-filled, caring marriage we can resurrect a semblance of our youth."

Meg looked somewhat distraught. "Why must you feel we have to concentrate on resurrecting our youth? Why is it necessary? I don't see you as an old man, or myself as an old woman. Reuven, I do believe you've become vulnerable to Chelsea's grumbling complaints about his forced retirement."

He was taken aback. "Is that how you read me? I

would have thought of myself as more self-assured." He appeared reflective. "You could be right." He took her in his arms. "Perhaps I should be more assertive. I don't really believe I'm too old to start a new life with you."

Chelsea, in keeping to his policy of telling Ellie everything, told her of the bombing at the security firm. "Joe, when is this going to stop? Our friends are beginning to think we're Jonahs."

Chelsea scanned the table. He had brought home Chinese food and it was only half-eaten. Their nerves were too stretched to enjoy eating.

He stood up from the table. "Ellie, I never asked for this excitement. It's unfinished business. Hopefully, tomorrow we might bring it to conclusion."

Ellie rolled her eyes. "Hopefully! When have I heard that before?" Her eyes sparked. "Put it in writing, Joe."

"Shall I get it notarized also?"

She stared at him, then burst into laughter. Laughter being contagious it took all of five minutes for it to conclude. As it happens so often it takes very little to launch a laughing jag. Finally, holding her side, she managed, "Joe, I'm serious. There's no humor in this."

Still smiling he said, "I know there isn't." He walked to the sliding glass door that opened onto the balcony of their eighth-floor apartment. He peered through the glass without attempting to open it. South Florida was well-noted for its summer humidity. The swimming pool below was lit a pale blue and from his location it very much resembled a huge ice cube. Surrounding palm trees, also lit up, stirred silently in a slight breeze. Floral bushes were accented by spotlights, causing the beach and ocean water beyond to appear dark and mysterious.

Chelsea enjoyed the serene nightly scene; it made him wonder why it did not offset the evil lurking in the land.

Ellie took a forkful of fried rice. "The food's cold," she said. She got to her feet and lifted a platter of mixed vegetables. "I'll warm it up in the microwave."

Chelsea watched her leave. His mind in a turmoil he asked himself, *What can I do about this need I have for adventure?* The meeting with Hobbs was set for tomorrow evening at his Palm Beach estate. How could he force an issue before then?

And then it came to him. Farfetched, perhaps, but an idea. He lifted the phone from the side table and called the office, knowing Alex was waiting for the night crew.

"Contact Rodgers by E-mail and tell him Hobbs has called for a truce at his Palm Beach residence. Invite him to attend the session for tomorrow evening, around eight."

Alex wanted to know if he should alert Harbin. Chelsea said he would take care of it.

He tried phoning Harbin at his penthouse condo, but got the answering machine. He left a message to call back. By the time he hung up Ellie was returning with the hot platter. He then wondered whether he should phone Meg, on the chance that Harbin might be with her. He asked Ellie what she thought of the idea that the two of them might be together.

Upon learning Harbin wasn't at home at this hour she thought it very likely. He told her what he had seen on the night of the explosion.

She didn't appear shocked, or even surprised. "You knew?" he asked.

"Not really, but the signs were there to be recognized."

"So, what do you think about it?"

"What I think is not important. They certainly don't need anyone's permission."

Chelsea shrugged impatiently. "I mean the bedroom tryst. I find it hard to believe that Meg took the initiative."

Ellie smiled. "Apparently she was ready for it. Good for her. I think Reuven's a good choice."

"But do you think Harbin's serious about her?"

Her eyes sparkled with humor. "You mean she might be a rich man's whim? I know nothing of Reuven's private life. But from what I've observed I would say it's serious between them." She looked up. "What does Josh say?"

"He doesn't know what I've told you. I don't think I should tell him."

"Suit yourself. He's not blind, he can draw his own conclusions."

The dawn was breaking. The sun was coming up over the hillside. Shafik stood at the rear deck of the *Luxor Princess* watching the dawn approach with tired eyes. The dark waters of the bay churned with choppy wakes caused by fishing boats departing to check their nets. He had scarcely slept. He had just been on the phone chartering a plane to Athens and then a jet flight to America. It was possible he would be in Palm Beach within fourteen hours. Ten minutes earlier he had spoken with his nephew Spencer Medwal. Dissatisfied and unhappy with the turn in events described by him, Shafik had ordered him to reserve a suite at the Breakers.

A sound from behind startled him for a moment. A servant told him the shuttle plane was waiting at Mykonos airport. Shafik nodded and walked inside to the dining room table. He lifted an urn to pour a last cup of the sweet, thick Turkish coffee. He nodded in appreciation of both the liquid and his preparations. He had warned his nephew that Reuven Harbin was in great danger and that he should continue to keep him under protective surveillance.

Harbin, after calling his answering service, phoned Chelsea from Meg's home. After discussing the bombing, he said, "I think we should hire Medwal for protective services. I believe him to be an excellent operative. I'll assume the cost. And ask him to scout Hobbs's residence beforehand. We could be walking into a trap."

"What about Willis? Medwal's talked her into staying in Palm Beach until further notice."

"If he thinks she can be of use she should be hired also. Right now we're shorthanded. My crew is on its way here with Josh's *Temple* and it's too late for them to alter plans. Chelsea, take care. I'll see you tomorrow, before the meeting."

20

Hobbs's beachfront residence was over 40,000 square feet, its architecture Mizneresque with Moorish Mediterranean arches in every doorway. Built in the 1920s it was a prime example of the foremost style of the period. Its flamingo-tinted facade was a mirror image of its neighbors. An eight-foot-high stucco cinder block wall offered privacy and added security. The wall surrounded the estate on three sides, leaving an open end on the beach side.

Promptly at eight Harbin's hired limo faced the front gate. Speaking into a box at one side Harbin announced their presence. They were told to wait. A man would arrive to direct them to the house.

As the gates opened a man waved the limo through. They then followed a driveway that was bordered with hibiscus hedges. It curved to the front of the mansion, which was set back about a hundred feet from the street. Harbin, Chelsea, Josh, and Dave were to attend the meeting. Medwal and Willis were in one of his cable company's vans parked on the street about fifty yards short of the estate gate. Obeying Harbin's instructions Medwal had a small radio tuned in to channel three for further instructions when and if needed.

Medwal left the van to reconnoiter at the property borderline. He climbed up an Australian pine tree overlooking the wall from the adjacent property and surveyed the property with the use of a star scope. A green figure showed up shortly—security patrol. He would have to wait to learn the routine. He had told Willis he needed thirty minutes on his own. It took twenty minutes for another security man to appear.

He slid down the tree, grateful for the chinos he had chosen to wear. The pine tree was wet from an earlier rainfall and the humidity lingered tenaciously. He returned to the van and told her he had found a way in other than the gate. She nodded and felt her purse for reassurance. Inside it was a Glock 9mm pistol.

A servant ushered the men into the vast private residence. Chelsea had learned beforehand that Nestor Hobbs, a widower of ten years, lived alone. His three children and grandchildren lived elsewhere on their own estates. The four men were led through an immense marble foyer to what looked to be a music room. At the far end of the forty-foot-long room a Steinway grand piano stood on a raised one-foot-high platform. There was space for at least a quintet of musicians if need be. There were a number of overstuffed armchairs and sofas to accommodate many guests. Tapestries displaying Seminole Indians in old Florida hung on the walls, muting sound.

The visitors took in their surroundings without speaking. The servant, a middle-aged, gray-haired, slender man asked if they wished something to drink while

waiting. All declined. Chelsea took out his pipe and
wondered whether it would be proper to smoke it. He
held off, then felt for the 9mm Beretta, borrowed from
Harbin, tucked into his belt. In fact, all four were armed.
Both Chelsea and Harbin had found it curious that no one
had patted them down upon entry to the estate.

After five minutes of waiting Nestor Hobbs walked
into the room. Heavy bags under his eyes indicated that
he was exhausted. His jaw worked, seeking an unprepared opening statement. His visage was a mixture of
embarrassment and shame. Chelsea decided the man was
finding it difficult to admit defeat. He looked to Harbin,
silently asking if he should be the one to open negotia-
tions. He got a comprehending nod and Harbin addressed
Hobbs. "We're here to end all hostilities. Do you wish to
make an opening statement before we present our demands?"

Hobbs moved to seat himself in an upholstered armchair. "Do you mind? Arthritis unfortunately." Josh followed his action without saying anything. He put his
cane aside and took a similar chair; the others remained
standing.

Hobbs rubbed a leathery cheek, as if reminding
himself to perform. "I must tell you at the outset that the
entire venture was instigated by Sheikh Suliman. While
this does not make me blameless, I truly insist I never
condoned the taking of any lives."

Unable to accept the statement, Josh interrupted with,
"Then what was the purpose behind all this?"

Hobbs's features screwed up as if in pain. "Suliman
was very persuasive. Perhaps it was age and he caught
me in a weak moment. He made everything sound so
practical, so logical. Upon hearing of the fiasco in the

Caribbean and the lives it cost . . ." He waved his hands in a useless gesture. "I'm willing to pay the expense for all damages incurred by the stupidity of this vengeful old Arab."

Chelsea shook his head. He found the statements preposterous. "Are you telling us that you took no umbrage from the breakup of the Benefactor Alliance?"

"In the beginning, yes. Later I came to feel that it was foolish to crave more power. We each controlled our own industry. According to our late leader, Jon Seltzmann, we were going to seek other planets to conquer. Looking back, we must have been mad to follow him." He again gestured dismissively. "Just give me the dollar amount. I'll make out a check for the total amount, plus a ten-percent addition."

Harbin said, "How do you pay for the lives lost?"

Hobbs shrugged. "You come up with an idea. I'll accept it. For the record, they were under Rodgers's command."

Chelsea said, "Yes, what of Calvin Rodgers? I don't see him here. Does he go along with you?"

Dave volunteered a question. "And what of Suliman? Do we still have to contend with him?"

Before Hobbs could reply, the front chimes rang. Someone else had arrived.

Medwal couldn't believe his eyes. *What is he doing here?* He eyed the limo at the gate, but easily recognized his uncle as the passenger. "This could be trouble," he said to Willis, who appeared unconcerned. She was still wondering what she should expect by having allowed Medwal into talking her into staying over in Palm Beach with him.

To be sure, it certainly wasn't the excitement of continuing the undercover work. She'd had her fill. The desire to retire from that lifestyle had been growing stronger ever since spending time with the wives of the men she and Medwal were to protect. She was still young enough to have a child, if she so desired. The thought made her glance at him. They had spent their first intimate night together. And yet he had offered no clue, no words of endearment. Was he that cold that her lovemaking couldn't affect him? Curiously her eyes misted. She couldn't remember a single occasion of it ever happening before. Tossing her head she dismissed these thoughts. Finish this final job. That's all that mattered at this moment.

Sheikh Shafik walked in, leaning heavily on his cane. His face lit up, dispelling the pain that overtook him with each step. As if he had been expected he said, "Ah, I see you're all still in conference. Thank Allah peace remains with us."

"What are you doing here?" Hobbs sputtered indignantly, never having had any business with him.

Shafik's eyes darkened. "To oversee the truce. I knew of the meeting from Suliman. Why is he not present?" His eyes searched the room in vain.

Harbin said, "Was he expected?"

Shafik shook his head sadly. "Regrettably, there can be no peace without him."

Dave nudged Josh and whispered, "I've got a growing feeling there's trouble brewing."

"Yeah, I smell it, too."

Harbin put his hand in his jacket and snapped on the switch of the pocket radio. He hoped Medwal remembered to leave his own tuned in. The sound would be muffled somewhat because of its enclosed location, but he might get something from it nevertheless.

Spencer Medwal and Carrie Willis both heard Chelsea, muffled but understandable. Medwal pulled out a set of earphones from the dashboard compartment and plugged it into the radio and then reset the volume. It couldn't be heard outside the van. He held up his hand for Willis, his finger spread indicating a five-minute wait. She lifted her purse from the floor and removed the Glock 9mm. She then stuck it into a pocket of the jumpsuit she was wearing.

After two or three minutes had passed, he replaced the earphones with an earplug. "We go," he murmured. "We follow the wall at the property's edge."

"I thought you intended to drop in from the pine tree," she said.

"Changed my mind. I remembered a city ordinance. A private wall can't extend into the ocean. We go in from the oceanfront."

She hesitated briefly. "What should we expect?"

Medwal frowned. "I'm not sure. First Chelsea's, then Harbin's voice didn't sound right. It's as if they're expecting a confrontation from outside the room they're in. Turning on the radio was a signal."

Each got out, Medwal leading. She trailed him through dense hedges; heavy humidity dripped off her waterproof outfit. Spongy grass muffled their footsteps as they advanced past the neighboring building. The wall ended above the shoreline. The beach was open property, but not deserted.

There were four men in all. They had made it to shore

by using a dinghy. In all probability it had come from the sixty-foot cruiser bobbing in small swells fifty yards off the shoreline. Using the star scope Medwal could see the men were armed and heading for the Hobbs mansion. Their faces were blackened. He assumed the leader was Calvin Rodgers, whom he had never seen. Medwal fingered his radio, but there was no way he could contact Harbin without alerting others.

Willis touched his shoulder, awaiting instructions. "We tail them," he whispered. "For now." He gave her a brief glance. Though she was breathing heavier she displayed no fear. He touched her cheek. "Follow my instructions. Don't do anything on your own."

Chelsea, disregarding Hobbs, spoke to Harbin. "I don't like this. Watch the doorways." He faced Josh and Dave. "Be ready for anything."

"Terrific," Josh grunted, muttering to himself. "We've been ready for anything since you retired. It's become our way of life."

Shafik faced Hobbs. "Suliman is or has been here. The odor of his Turkish tobacco reeks of his presence." He rubbed his nose gingerly.

"He was, but not at my bidding," insisted Hobbs. "Before everyone arrived." His eyes had widened, now afraid that Suliman might be hiding somewhere on the premises.

Chelsea was quick to note his manner—the suspicion. He pulled out his Beretta; the others followed suit. They weren't about to be surprised. Chelsea waved Dave to an arched doorway leading to the rear. Dave instantly strode into the open area. Other arches led to a maze of hallways. All he could do was stand quiet and listen for any unusual sounds.

The sounds came. A sliding footstep from far down the long corridor. The bloated form of Suliman slipped into view, as if he was paged.

"Gentlemen," he said, "I believe I'm expected." His head turned to study each face separately, then lingered on Chelsea's. "Ah, the captain, the nemesis of the Alliance." He shook his head, as if about to reprimand a child. "You have no idea what your interference cost us."

No more than five feet separated the Arab from Dave, whose weapon was aimed at his chest. "Put it away," Suliman ordered officiously. "You're not going to shoot me."

Shafik stirred restlessly. "Suliman, you are a fool. What are you attempting to do here? We have come to make peace, to end this farce. What are you avenging? The loss of money you don't need?"

Suliman's face was a massive sneer. His chins shook with uncontrolled rage. "*You* are the fool, not I! Harbin was your personal enemy. You have said as much. Why do you desire to protect him? Because of the boy? Why protect him for that personal insult? An Israeli, no less! An infidel!"

Shafik's face clouded mournfully. "Should I slay my adopted son's sire?" His eyes bore into his brother-in-law. "Is that what Allah asks of me?"

Harbin listened without any intention of interrupting. He could only wonder where it was all leading. The utmost thought was that Shafik truly believed him to be the father of the boy, a boy whose name he couldn't remember. He himself didn't know whether he had fathered the boy. His own feelings were unclear.

A sharp sound came from Dave's direction. All stiffened, most recognizing it. A silencer. "Can you see anything, Dave?" Chelsea asked.

"Nothing. It's beyond the doorway at the end of the corridor. Could be outside the house."

"It was a single shot," Harbin said, wondering whether Medwal and Willis were in trouble. Chelsea gave orders for Dave to escort Suliman to the sofa. When the sheikh sulked, Chelsea said, "Please, we do not wish to use force. Do as you're directed."

The Arab shuffled slowly across the deep carpet, muttering to himself. It was not his custom to take orders. Harbin stared at him. "Sheikh Suliman, who is working for you? Rodgers?" He looked at Hobbs.

"I gave you my word." Hobbs pleaded innocence. "I have no one out there but ground security."

"How many?"

He reflected a moment. "Four—all told. They work the grounds and don't enter the residence except to answer alarms."

Harbin removed the shortwave radio from his pocket. He kept his voice to a whisper. "Spencer, what's happening?" He clicked to receive.

A whisper came back. "Four men came in from the ocean. One has taken out a security man patrolling the beachfront."

"What's their location right now?"

"They're about to enter the building. I think I recognize one of the men from *Spaced Out*. We can guess the other three. As of right now, I'm no more than twenty feet behind them, but out of sight. What's your play on this?"

"Just tail them without interfering. You're backup

when they try to confront us here in what appears to be a large music roo—"

The sound was sharper this time. Harbin held his voice to a tight whisper. "Are you okay?"

"Yes. We're okay, but they knocked out another guard." There was a slight pause. "This is crazy. I may be wrong, but I think they're using dart guns, not live ammunition. There's no flashes. Could be air pistols."

"Any movement from the victims? Darts could be poison-tipped."

"Nothing. They're still as death."

"Okay. Watch your step and keep tuned to me."

Willis moved in front of Medwal. She'd heard nothing of Harbin's instructions: Medwal was wearing his ear-plugs. "Why don't we make a move on them? They don't even know they're being shadowed."

Medwal controlled an angry retort. "This is Chelsea and Harbin's operation. We obey orders. And what are you doing in front of me? Get back where you were." He wondered why he had insisted she accompany him on this assignment. He wanted her to stay in Florida with him but not to share any missions.

Willis stared at him, her eyes inches from his. "You're protecting me, aren't you? Why?" She was torn between being angered and elated. "Damn!" she mustered in a whisper. "Last evening you treated me like an evening rental. Now, suddenly, you've decided to be my knight in shining armor. What goes with you? Is this something new in your character?"

"Stop with the damn questions! We have a job on our hands. Keep your mind on it. Just follow orders."

Despite his attitude she smiled. The man did have

feelings, but he was too macho to express them. A true
chauvinist to the bitter end.

"They passed the swimming pool and are going into
the house," Medwal said. "Let's go. And stay *behind*
me."

Chelsea directed Josh and Dave to keep watch over the
Arabs and Hobbs while he and Harbin advanced to the
corridor. With guns drawn they moved stealthily toward
the far doorway. They had made it no more than halfway
when a gas-spewing cannister suddenly slid across the
parquet flooring. A cloud was forming rapidly. Both
Chelsea and Harbin, pinching their noses, dropped to the
floor. The white cloud hovered above their heads, the
room too large to be covered by a single cannister.

Chelsea tilted his head, sneaking a look. He caught
Harbin pointing to one of the few wooden doors in the
area. The door was suddenly shoved open. Four men,
armed and wearing gas masks, strode in confidently.
They aimed at Chelsea and Harbin, one shouting, "Push
your weapons aside." The position they were caught in
offered no alternative but to comply without complaint.

Chelsea thought he recognized Rodgers's voice although
it had been months since they had last met. At that time
Rodgers had been under arrest. He noticed that the gas
was dissipating, being drawn into the air conditioning
system.

Harbin was looking for some sign of Medwal and
Willis, aware that one man kept looking over his shoulder as if expecting someone. He whispered to a partner.
The partner pointed in the direction from where they had
come, ordering him to investigate whatever his com-

plaint was. His partner retraced his steps and went through the door.

A dull sound, as if someone had fallen, followed a moment later from the other side of the door. The lead invader cursed. He spoke to the man beside him, calling him by name. "Bubba, see what the hell's going on. We've got unfinished business here. We still have to get everyone aboard the yacht."

Chelsea glanced at Harbin to see if he had heard right. It was apparent they were to be taken prisoners; they wanted no bloodshed here. *Was it Hobbs's idea or Suliman's?* He guessed the Arab, believing Hobbs was sincere about the truce.

Shafik addressed Suliman angrily. "Have you gone mad? This is your doing. Is it not?" When all he got was a sneer Shafik said, "I don't want the Israeli harmed. Do you understand?"

"Understand! I understand you are an old fool! Allah is showing me the way to rid myself of old enemies. Do not turn on me, Shafik, because of foolish sentimental values."

Rodgers, losing patience, ordered Chelsea and Harbin to stand, then directed all to follow him out to the beach. Whatever else he wanted to do was stalled by Bubba's return alone. "We've got trouble. Red's disappeared. I don't know where he's gone or what's happened to him."

At that moment Willis's voice shouted across the corridor from another entrance. "You're all covered. Drop your weapons." In the next second she appeared with Medwal at her side.

Rodgers growled and, using an air pistol, fired in her direction. The shot broke off a piece of stucco from the wall behind her. Medwal returned the fire, hitting Rodg-

ers in the shoulder, spinning him around. Rodgers's
cohorts dropped their weapons, surrendering immediately.

Harbin and Chelsea retrieved their own guns and
turned to confront the two sheikhs. Suliman was enraged
by the turn of events. He reached inside his caftan and
yanked out a curved dagger from a hidden scabbard. It
flashed through the air, catching all but Shafik off guard.
Despite his handicap, Shafik leaped toward Harbin. A
groan escaped when the dagger dug into the old man's
back. Harbin got off a shot that caught Suliman in the
arm. Suliman, thrown off balance, dropped to one knee.
Chelsea burst toward him and hit him with his fist,
knocking him to the floor. Josh and Dave joined Harbin
at Shafik's side. Hobbs plopped into a chair, unable to
comprehend all of the sudden action.

Shafik had blood coming from his mouth, his voice
rasped hoarsely as he tried to speak. Harbin held his
head, knowing the Arab had saved his life. "Reuven
Harbin, only you alone must know the entire truth of the
boy's birthright. Abu couldn't father children—he was
impotent. Promise me—you will help guide his future.
At present, he owns more than 200,000 shares of Harbin
Enterprises."

Harbin nodded assent. It was the least he could do for
the dying man. The Arab had lain down his life for him.
"As you wish, it will be done, Shafik."

Shafik smiled and closed his eyes. His head fell back
and his chest allowed a final breath of air. At the same
moment a cry escaped from Suliman. An anguished sob
followed. He had slain his brother-in-law. Allah would
surely make him atone for his evil transgression. On his
knees he bowed his head to the floor.

Harbin turned away and sought Medwal. "You and Willis leave now. You can't be found here. Let me have your Beretta. I'll assume blame for the ballistic report."

Josh turned to Chelsea. "Joe, what happens now? How are we going to clean up this affair?"

Chelsea responded instantly. "Try to get Carbolo." Rudy Carbolo, a lieutenant with the Palm Beach County Sheriff's office, had worked with them on the Benefactor Alliance case. "Tell him that Rodgers broke his witness protection cover. And give him the damage account: one dead." He looked to Medwal for confirmation. "Two injured?"

"There's two more dead at the rear of the property, both poisoned by dart guns." He and Willis turned to go.

Chelsea turned to Harbin. "Okay. How do you want to play this?" He indicated the Arab kneeling and pleading for absolution from Allah.

Harbin spoke without hesitation. "Let your friend Carbolo handle it. I wash my hands of the sheikh. Suliman has plenty of attorneys to plead his case. Most likely they will claim diplomatic immunity."

Dave said, "Which means it will be swept under the rug by the federals. They don't want a Middle East situation on their hands."

Josh waved the two remaining captives to a sofa. Bubba turned on Hobbs. "Aren't you getting us out of this?"

Hobbs's face flushed with anger. "I dismissed you. You worked under Rodgers for Suliman. Don't plead help from me!"

Harbin was holding the knife in his hand with the protection of a handkerchief. He laid it down alongside Shafik's body.

Chelsea put a hand upon his shoulder. "Reuven, I think it's finally finished. When Suliman is taken away it will signify the hunt is over. No one will be taking Suliman's place."

Josh rubbed his hands as if he were drying them. "Amen to that. Now, Joe, just put it in writing."

When the lieutenant walked into the music room, he took a moment to glance around the room before addressing Chelsea. "Well, you retirees have done it again."

"In here," he shouted behind him. Two other detectives entered along with the medical examiner and his two assistants.

"There's two more in the back," Chelsea said, "by the pool."

Carbolo was wearing a three-piece beige suit. His jet-black hair was slicked back. Gold chains, including a crucifix, hung from his neck. His manner of dress made Chelsea smile. Carbolo hadn't changed since he had last seen him. He still thought he looked like a gigolo in an old movie.

Carbolo knelt to study the victim and then the kneeling Arab. He allowed a deep sigh and stood up to face Chelsea. "Am I going to need an embassy man here? Shee—it! Looks like I'll also need the feds." He then faced Harbin. "And you're . . ."

Harbim introduced himself.

"Nobody warned you about joining Chelsea's group?" Carbolo said. Reuven shook his head.

"Haven't you heard that Chelsea always leaves bodies lying around . . . ? Wait a minute. Harbin . . . aren't you the financial genius? What's your involvement in this?"

Harbin shrugged, gave Chelsea a you-or-me look and said, "Lieutenant, I'll give you the rundown." It took a half hour before everything had been explained.

"So you're telling me that this was all unfinished business with the Benefactor Alliance?"

"That's right," said Joe. "As incredible as it sounds."

"Okay then. I'll need all of you to sign statements."

Leaving the room for the front entrance Harbin looked uneasy. Chelsea asked, "What's up? You don't look happy."

"This was too easy. It doesn't feel right." Passing through the library he noticed a phone on a side table. He quickly went to it and dialed Meg's number.

Five rings and no answer.

"Let's go," Harbin said excitedly. "Something's wrong. I told Meg to stay home and wait for my call."

Meg had let the man in when he had stated that he was in Harbin's employ and had been sent as her personal bodyguard. When he had started locking all the doors, she had become suspicious and asked what he was doing. The man, dark-skinned and about six feet tall, held a revolver to her back and told her to walk into the living room. There, using wire from a ripped out phone, he tied her into an armchair and said only, "We wait."

"For what?" she asked, her voice hoarse and her heart pounding.

He gave a slight smile. "We are what American agents call 'a contingency plan.' If my master does not call in twenty minutes we wait for your friend."

Forty-five minutes passed, and no call. He kept checking his watch. Perspiring and uncomfortable, her hands numb, Meg fought a sense of despair. *What is he waiting for? And why doesn't Reuven call?*

The phone rang, but the Arab did not pick up. It rang five times before stopping. "We wait," he said imperiously. He then opened his jacket. Meg was horrified. Earlier she had thought his jacket the wrong size. Now she understood why. Four sticks of dynamite were attached to his belt. *God! A suicide bomber! And he's waiting for Reuven to show before setting it off!*

She heard the front door jiggling.

"I don't have a key," Harbin said.

"Let me at it," Chelsea said. He pulled out a small kit from his jacket. He worked on the lock and had it open in seconds.

Josh and Dave held back as Harbin stared at the open doorway with distrust. "Reuven," Chelsea said, "you go in. We'll go around the back to the beach side." All had handguns drawn as they departed.

Harbin moved in slowly, silently. No one in the foyer. No one in the library. As he approached the living room he detected a sound—heavy breathing. He peered around an open doorway and saw Meg sitting in a chair adjacent to the bridge table. He correctly guessed the dark man, holding the pistol to her side, to be an Arab. What froze him was the Arab's hand on his belt, his finger on a trigger of sorts, attached to dynamite. Whether it was a detonator or a battery-operated switch would be pure speculation.

The man waved him in. "Please, we've been expecting you. First, I insist you drop your weapon on the floor, then kick it away." He jammed his own pistol into Meg's ear threateningly.

Harbin was offered no options. He could have shot the man in the head, but the action could have forced his finger to automatically set off the dynamite. He laid his Beretta on the floor, kicked it away, then held his hands up midway to his shoulders.

The Arab said, "That's better. Now I must ask about my master, Sheikh Suliman. Have you detained him in any way?"

"I'm afraid so. I don't believe you should expect him."

The man's features hardened. "Then you leave me no alternative." His hand trembled, holding the dynamite switch.

"Hold it!" Harbin shouted. "There is no need for you to die for someone else's cause. You have a wife? Children? You want to leave them for a lost cause?"

"My master has provided for my family's future. My only fear is to not obey my master's wishes. Now please join us. Bring a chair to sit beside you—how shall I put it?—your beloved. It is only proper that you depart this world together. I will allow you that much."

Meg's eyes were pleading. *Do something to overcome this madman!*

Harbin was helpless.

The beach was dark, the rising wind forming whitecaps on a dark ocean. Reflected light from the waters of the swimming pool rippled across the concrete patio. The trio of men crossed the patio and Chelsea had to use his lock kit again to gain entry past the sliding doors.

As soon as they entered they could hear voices. They came from a room beyond the dining room. The kitchen to their left was empty. They moved to the far end as one voice became louder. It had a Middle East cant. Chelsea ventured a look beyond open pocket doors and took in the situation at a glance.

Suddenly, Chelsea had an idea. He pulled a cell phone out of his pocket and dialed the house number. Startled at first, the Arab then ordered Harbin to answer. The Arab was thinking that Harbin had lied, that perhaps his master was calling. Harbin lifted the phone. "The Tolan residence."

Chelsea murmured into the phone, "I'm in the next room. Tell the Arab Suliman wishes to speak to the Syrian. If he removes his finger from his belt I'll get him. Go to it."

Harbin held the phone away from him. "The sheikh asked for the Syrian." He held the phone out for him.

At first disbelieving, the Arab cocked his head and told Harbin to put down the phone and move away. He then stepped toward the phone, his left hand holding the pistol aimed at Harbin, his right on the detonator. He then released his hand from the explosives to lift the instrument to his ear.

Chelsea took careful aim. The Arab's neck. A whispering sound shot across the room. The Arab dropped the phone and abruptly reached for the back of his neck. It was his last conscious effort. A single sigh escaped from the Arab as his body folded and dropped to the floor. Harbin was instantly at his side to prevent his hands from accidentally tripping the bomb. He took a few moments to check the connection of wires and knowledgeably pulled them apart.

Chelsea entered the living room slowly. He looked at the gun in his trembling hand and set it down on the dining room table.

"I'm indebted to you, Joe, to all of you," Harbin said as he held Meg close. "For many, many reasons, Joe."

Josh glanced at his sister. "Should I be expecting some sort of announcement?"

"Later, Josh. At the moment I need a drink. Does anyone wish to join me?" All followed her into the library where there was a bar. Dave got on the phone with Carbolo to discuss the latest body. They all heard him say, "Rudy, you're right, I'm not arguing. I don't know why we don't retire either." He held the phone away from his ear.

Suddenly Harbin spoke with a quiet earnestness, "Josh, I would like to ask your permission to marry your sister."

"How old are you anyway?" asked Josh

"Josh," Chelsea interceded, "I've seen Reuven work out. He might not be a spring chicken but I think he's up to it. He will make Meg an excellent husband. You can't deny they look great together."

"Jesus Christ, wait until Mae hears about this," said Dave with dismay.

"Dave! When are you two going to get hitched?" Chelsea exclaimed.

"Probably as soon as she hears about Meg and Reuven. First there'll be an ultimatum, then tears . . . or maybe I should just take her out to dinner tonight and pop the question. That would be a good way to avoid a messy conversation!"

EPILOGUE

Chelsea, Josh, and Dave stood watching a wrecking ball prepare to crash through an outer wall of an old building on Harbin's real estate development. He, of course, gave his friends the best offices available. Two weeks had passed since all of the excitement and the work of transporting all of the office equipment to the new quarters had taken its place.

Harbin and Meg had made arrangements for their families to meet. A wedding date was set for four months later. The guests would number no more than fifty, including family and close friends.

Chelsea sighed and said, "One episode of our lives ends and another begins."

Dave gave him an odd look. "Joey, don't start me worrying. Are you just being philosophical?"

Chelsea grinned. "Stop reading into what I say. I am excited that we are expanding our business. This will be a great adventure."

Josh shook his head dolefully. "Joe, I wish I could believe you."

HERMAN WEISS

SUNSET DETECTIVES

Two retired cops are learning to enjoy the easy life—the hard way...

The sun...the sand...the shuffleboard. Florida is not what Joe Chelsea pictured when he thought of retiring. But then again, Chelsea never thought of retiring from the NYPD until he was forced to. Now, he owns a condo on the beach and a security firm with his old partner, Josh Novick. The two former detectives are trying to put the past behind them. The problem is, no one told them retirement would be so boring...

But the sun never sets on crime, even in Florida. When a local sheriff consults them on a murder case, Chelsea and Novick find the temptation to investigate on their own too hard to resist. And before they know what hits them, they're in over their heads. A serial killer is on the loose. And he's targeting Holocaust survivors...

___0-425-15514-5/$5.99